From the Desk of...

Silas Duran

Well, it looks like I'm stuck on this godforsaken island until someone can get me the part I need for my plane. And it's a good thing I brought a lot of paperwork with me, because there's nothing to do here—nothing, that is, except look at the lovely proprietress of the area's only hotel.

Her name is...Hester something, I think. And though she's not my type at all—I can tell she doesn't have a business-oriented bone in her body—she is not without charms. She's kind of easy on the eye. So for a temporary diversion, she might do fine. I just need to remember that even here, summer can't last forever.

Or *can* it?

Dear Reader,

Destinations South is such a special book for me, not just because it was my first novel, but because of the personal significance attached to it—I began my married life in the Caribbean (my husband was stationed in Puerto Rico with the U.S. Coast Guard). In fact, I began writing it during a severe bout of homesickness for that part of the world after we were transferred to New Jersey. Virtually overnight, I went from being an unemployed beach bum lounging on a tranquil, sun-drenched beach, to waiting for the bus in the freezing rain. A good part of *Destinations South* was conceived and developed as I rode the M Bus to work.

Work—*my* work (at least my *ride* to work)—figured prominently in the writing of the novel and just like my hero, Silas Duran, I needed a break from my job. Luckily he and I both found one on a mythical Caribbean island generated in my imagination. I hope you enjoy your visit there as much as I did. Have a piña colada on me.

Bon voyage,

Elizabeth Bevarly

ELIZABETH BEVARLY

Destinations South

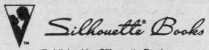
Silhouette Books

Published by Silhouette Books

America's Publisher of Contemporary Romance

ISBN-13: 978-0-373-47073-0
ISBN-10:   0-373-47073-8

DESTINATIONS SOUTH

Visit Silhouette Books at www.eHarlequin.com

Printed in U.S.A.

For my husband, David,
without whose support and indulgence,
not to mention culinary skills,
this book would not be possible.
I love you.

Prologue

H. M. Somerset stared dolefully at her reflection in the bathroom mirror. She looked like hell. Her normally fair complexion had become sallow, and purple crescents had formed below her reddened, spiritless eyes. Not yet 6:00 a.m., already a cigarette dangled from her lips, and she desperately craved a cup of strong black coffee.

She stumbled into her ultramodern kitchen, blinking and mumbling irritably at the bright fluorescent light that bounced garishly off the white walls and silver appliances. After she had shoveled several scoopfuls of gourmet coffee into her high-tech brewer, she wiped her hands on her silk pajamas and pressed her forehead against the cool glass of the kitchen window. It was raining in New York City. Seemed to be doing a lot of that lately. The November weather reflected her mood—gray, dreary, hopeless.

After the coffee maker gasped its last breath, H.M. lit a second cigarette with the still-glowing butt of her first and filled an oversize mug with the pungent brew. The way she made coffee it looked like mud and tasted worse, but it managed to jump start her on mornings like these when she just wasn't sure she could go on another day. Clutching the mug like a lifeline and munching an antacid, she wandered automatically into the living room to collect her morning paper from the hallway outside her front door. She slumped into her sleekly sophisticated leather conversation pit that her decorator had chosen and she'd never much noticed, and discarded every useless section of the paper but the one that mattered. Staring blindly at the business and financial section, H. M. Somerset took a moment to wonder morosely at what she had become.

Originally from the rough and dangerous streets of a particularly notorious Bronx neighborhood, by the age of fourteen, Hester Somerset had become what was politely known as a "troubled teenager." She was in fact a juvenile delinquent. Dumped on her reluctant grandmother as a toddler by her single mother who "just got tired of looking at her," Hester never got much of a shot at a normal childhood. She rarely bothered to attend school, and instead achieved the bulk of her education in back alleys and basements, on playgrounds and door stoops. Her grandmother, Lydia, frequently and colorfully voiced her displeasure at Hester's wild behavior, but between collecting her welfare checks and bouts with the bottle, had to admit it was a hopeless situation, and it was best just to ignore the child altogether.

So Hester rushed at breakneck speed toward early disaster. She joined a gang that specialized in petty crimes and general mischief, and had the time of her life, as long as she could dodge her grandmother and keep up with her friends. Eluding the police posed no problem.

Then one hot July evening in her fourteenth year, something happened to Hester. Something terrible that even now she chose to push to the back of her mind. It was something that made Hester think, and think hard. She was forced to look dead-on at her future, and the prospects were none too bright. So Hester changed. She started going to school. She even got above-average grades, especially in math. Her teachers were stunned by the turnaround in her behavior, but their surprise became awe when Hester tested for college entrance. Not only did she score high in every area, but in mathematics was near perfect. Her IQ, it was eventually discovered, was in the genius range.

By the time Hester graduated from high school, she was well behaved and making excellent grades. She got a job, moved out of Lydia's tenement in the ghetto, and with an academic scholarship attended the City University of New York. Five years later she had not only a bachelor's degree in mathematics and finance, but an MBA as well. Hester had been what was known in academic circles as a "whiz kid."

Job offers came quickly and in abundance. At the age of twenty-three, Hester became H. M. Somerset, stockbroker and investment adviser in the firm of Thompson, Michaels, Tobias and Leech and Associates, more commonly referred to as Thompson-Michaels, with all due respect to Mr. Tobias and Mr. Leech. She added an initial to her name, calling herself H.M. because it sounded serious and responsible, and symbolically, it obliterated her past identity as a common street punk. She was a real person now, with a real job. A career. She would do everything she had to in order to keep it that way.

H.M. worked hard to be a success. And worked. And worked. And she succeeded quite impressively. Now at the age of twenty-seven, she owned a swank condominium overlooking Central Park, a late-model Porsche, numerous pieces of artwork, frivolous small appliances and a wardrobe suitable for big business or serious socializing, even though she didn't have time for much of the latter. She assumed these were the things she should own, being the high-powered executive she was. She'd never really given much consideration to the things she bought. They just seemed like things a woman in her position should have.

A ferocious clap of thunder startled H.M. back to reality and she jumped and splashed coffee onto the Dow-Jones averages. She gasped, then the gasp became a cough and the cough became a ceaseless hacking that made her eyes water. Her lungs finally cleared just as she convinced herself that she was having a major coronary arrest. She took a final deep breath and wanted to cry, but she just didn't think she had the strength to manage it.

After heaving herself up from the couch, she began her morning preparations without much enthusiasm. Today would be spent just as yesterday had been and tomorrow would be. She'd stare at a computer screen until her vision blurred, trying to decide which way the market would move, and she'd attend meetings with amoral business parasites and overly ambitious executives. They'd all demand one thing from her: make me richer and more important and do it now. She'd afforded herself a reputation among the stock exchange as a moneymaker. Her knack for numbers was making her famous and sending her salary right through the roof. And the more her reputation grew, the more in demand she became. If she was overworked and over-stressed now, what would her life be like in ten years, ten months even? As it was, it took a double Scotch to calm her down after work and another to help her sleep at night.

It occurred to H.M. on that particular rainy morning that she'd never in her life set foot outside the city of New York. She had no interests other than her job, no hobbies, no close friends, no family. She'd never really even been involved with a man, unless she included that short-lived, less than fulfilling affair with Leo Sternmacher. During her childhood on the streets, she'd been too poor and preoccupied with day-to-day survival to find any hobbies or set any goals. At college, she'd been too busy with classes and homework. Now her career consumed all her time. How had she come to such a point in her life without having planned any of it? She had no idea what kind of person she really was. She'd never had a chance to explore. She wasn't sure what type of music or books she liked, or if she had any talents. Her condominium had been designed by the most ''in'' decorator, her wardrobe arranged by a personal-style consultant recommended by the public relations department at Thompson-Michaels. Nothing about her reflected who she was.

H.M. was getting a migraine. She'd been getting them a lot lately. Along with stomachaches, backaches, chest pains and any number of other stress-related maladies. Her life-style was slowly killing her.

Looking at her clock, she realized she'd have to rush. She dressed hurriedly in an expensive raw-silk suit and silk blouse. She owned quite a lot of silk. After leaving a note for her housekeeper, she picked up her alligator briefcase and headed for the parking garage to begin the long, nerve-racking drive to work. Despite the grueling driving conditions in New York, H.M. felt the need somehow to participate in the morning and evening traffic crunches. Often it was her only chance to associate with others on a social, as opposed to business level.

She lit a cigarette, turned the car radio dial from the jazz station she normally tuned in to a progressive rock station and pulled away from her apartment building. H.M. didn't really pay much attention to where she was going until she realized vaguely that somewhere along the way to her office she'd managed to get turned around and was speeding away from Manhattan instead of toward it. Oddly, though, the realization didn't alarm her.

When she pulled into the long-term parking lot at JFK International, she still wasn't sure of her plans. The rain kept falling in icy torrents as she splashed through cold puddles, clutching an umbrella in one hand and her purse and briefcase in the other. Once inside the main terminal, she checked the contents of her wallet. Forty-eight dollars in cash and three major credit cards with fully paid balances. Someone entered through the automatic doors behind her, bringing with them a chill wind that swept through her. Warm. She wanted to be warm.

H.M. approached the first airline counter she came to and took her place at the end of the line, her mind empty and her mood a little lighter. When it was her turn, she looked levelly at the young, fresh-faced woman behind the desk and thought, She's probably the same age as me; why does she look and seem so much younger?

"What's the next flight you have going south?" H.M. asked her matter-of-factly.

"Where south?" the ticketing agent responded blankly.

"Anywhere."

"Well, how far south?"

"Um, someplace with a beach, I think," H.M. said after a moment's thought. "I've never really seen the ocean before, outside New York harbor."

The ticketing agent stared at H.M. for a moment, then deciding she was serious, punched some buttons on the terminal before her.

"We have a flight leaving for St. Croix in a little over an hour," she said. "There are still several seats available."

"St. Croix," H.M. repeated the name as a child might. "Sounds lovely. And there's a beach there?"

"There are several. It's an island, ma'am."

H.M. realized she must sound terribly stupid. St. Croix was probably a major resort, but how was she supposed to know that? Her training was in mathematics and finance, not geography, and she'd never had the need or inclination to plan a vacation.

"I'd like to go to St. Croix, please," she said with as much dignity as she could muster.

"Will that be coach or first class?"

"First class," H.M. replied without hesitation.

"Round-trip?"

"One-way."

"Smoking or nonsmoking?"

H.M. thought for a moment before reluctantly responding, "Nonsmoking."

"Bags to check?" the agent concluded her inquisition.

"None," H.M. told her.

After she had paid for her ticket, H.M. placed a call to her apartment. Her housekeeper would be there by now, and H.M. would need to make arrangements for the woman to take care of the place until further notice. That done, she called her boss, Pete Larsen, to explain why she wouldn't be in today—or ever again for that matter. He was really going to be mad about the Baytop contract, H.M. realized suddenly. She'd forgotten she was supposed to meet with the president of the corporation this morning. She chewed absently on an antacid tablet while she waited for the phone to ring, wanting more than anything to smoke just one last cigarette.

On the plane her grandmother's rusty voice came back one final time to haunt her. "You're gonna have to make some changes in your life, little girlie, if you ever hope to be more than the stupid, worthless little troublemaker you are now, you hear me? Some changes!"

H.M. crumpled the half-full pack of cigarettes in her jacket pocket into a tiny ball of broken tobacco. "Some changes *will* be made."

Chapter One

"**Y**ou're going to do what?"

"I said I'll fly down to Rio and take care of this myself."

Ethan MacKenzie glared at his brother-in-law and sighed in exasperation. Silas Duran could be an indomitable force whenever his stubbornness set in, which was nearly every day.

"Silas, you're going to Nantucket on vacation this week, remember?" Ethan reminded him. "Everything's been arranged, all the bases here have been covered, and you need some time off. *I'll* go down to Rio and handle this. It's just a minor problem."

"Minor?" Silas thundered. "You call it minor when the head of our entire South American division decided to run off to the Falkland Islands with a samba dancer to study the mating habits of penguins?"

"I think he minored in marine biology in college,"

Ethan stated thoughtfully, as if that would explain everything.

Silas glowered at him.

"At any rate," Ethan began again hurriedly, "I can go down there until things are settled. You go ahead to Nantucket. Amanda and I have been trying for months to get you to take some time off. You've earned this vacation. And with the pressures you've been under lately, if you don't take it, you're going to drop dead of a heart attack."

The two men stood face to face in Silas's office at Duran Industries. Silas muttered something unintelligible and turned his back on his sister's husband. His was a corner office on the twenty-fourth floor of the new, and much publicized, Duran Building. Two massive picture windows offered a magnificent panorama of New York City, but Silas had never taken much notice of it. Outside the bright sun and brilliant blue sky effectively disguised the fact that it was a brutally cold January afternoon. Silas rubbed his temples. His head hurt. He paced the length of his elegant office, the plush dove-gray carpet muffling his steps, and opened the top left drawer of his mahogany desk. Inside, he readily ignored a variety of prescriptions, and reached instead for a bottle of aspirin.

"While you're cleaning up in Rio," Silas grumbled after he had tossed back three of the powdery tablets, "who's going to be minding the store here?"

"Gibson. He knows enough about DI to keep us rolling for a week."

"Sure, and after a week we'll be bankrupt. Anyway, his wife just had twins. He's like a zombie lately. He can't concentrate on anything. He's useless."

"Amanda will be here to help him out," Ethan

coaxed, hoping the mention of Silas's sister might assuage his fears about the management of Duran Industries during his absence. "Look, Silas, don't worry about it. It's only for a week. Amanda says you haven't taken a vacation since you were in college, and that you spent that one in the library researching your MBA thesis. If you don't take some time off soon..."

"I know, I know, I'll drop dead of a heart attack," Silas finished for him.

Silas rubbed a knot at the back of his neck and sighed. It was true that he'd devoted nearly every waking moment for the past ten years to making Duran Industries the major success that it was. When he'd taken over as chief executive officer upon his father's retirement, DI had been a prosperous business that manufactured household appliances and school supplies. In the ten years since Silas had taken charge, the company had contracted with other, more influential corporations and now produced everything from index cards to commercial aircraft. Company assets included orange groves, a satellite network, thoroughbred horses and a professional basketball team, among other things. Although his sister took an active part in running the business, Silas possessed controlling stock and could claim nearly all of the credit for the monster success he'd made of the corporation. Amanda had chosen to work from a public relations standpoint rather than with the actual running of the business, contending correctly that she was more of a people person than her brother was.

Three years ago, when Amanda married Ethan MacKenzie, a DI executive vice president, Silas, already aware of his new brother-in-law's capabilities and keen business sense, made him a partner in Duran

Industries. Since then, the two of them, along with Amanda, who also sat on the board of directors, had achieved great things with the company. They'd expanded to include factories and businesses in Canada and Mexico, and their most recent acquisitions in Brazil two years ago had led to opening a corporate office in Rio de Janeiro, a venture that was currently proving to be more trouble than it was worth.

"Ethan, I'll take a vacation when I get back, but right now I'm needed in Rio. No one, and I mean no one, knows what the hell is going on down there. Vasquez managed to make a complete mess of things before he left, and his desertion has only tripled those problems. I'll be leaving as soon as I can." Silas tossed files and legal pads full of scribbling into his briefcase and snapped it shut, an indication that the conversation was over.

"Silas, a week from Monday we begin that new deal with Don Thompson and his firm. That's going to need your attention, and after that, there are going to be a hundred other things that will require your presence in New York. There's no way you can get away then. Take your vacation now. You need it," Ethan added meaningfully.

Silas knew better than his brother-in-law that he needed a vacation. He also knew that his health was suffering due to stress and overwork. He hadn't told his sister or her husband about his frequent visits to his doctor lately, or the warnings Dr. Norton had wearily repeated each time he went. Nor had he mentioned the chest pains, the migraines or the abdominal discomfort he'd been experiencing for the past several months. He knew full well how badly he needed to spend this week at his beach house on Nantucket. Dr. Norton had been frighteningly explicit about the possible repercussions if he didn't. But business came first. And that was that.

"I guess Nantucket will just have to wait," Silas said as he prepared to leave the office.

"You're going to kill yourself," Ethan stated emphatically. "And you know Amanda will blame me when it happens. Are you trying to wreck my life, too?"

Silas smiled humorlessly. "Tell you what. I'll only take a commercial flight as far as Puerto Rico, then I'll fly myself the rest of the way in one of the company planes we're manufacturing there. I've been wanting to test one of those babies for a while now, and this is the perfect opportunity. You know how I love to fly."

"Poor substitute for a week at the coast."

Silas remained silent, and Ethan put up his hands in surrender. He knew that when the CEO of Duran Industries made up his mind about something, nothing short of tying him up with piano wire and locking him in a safe would change things. Ethan entertained that idea for a moment, then recognized the unrealistic nature of it. If Silas Duran wanted to throw himself into an early grave, that was his business. In the meantime, a problem in the legal department needed his attention.

The following afternoon Silas was behind the controls of one of the new twin-engine planes owned and manufactured by Duran Industries. Before him, the skies stretched clear and azure, below him, the turquoise Caribbean sparkled, dotted here and there by tiny green islands. He had left San Juan some time ago and estimated that he should reach the coast of Venezuela before long. He could refuel there and then continue on to Rio before nightfall.

Leaving New York had been a nightmare. He'd wanted to get as early a start as possible, so Silas had arranged for the company car and driver to take him to the airport. During the night, however, a steady snow had begun to fall, resulting in a late driver, tortuous driving conditions and an especially late arrival at the airport. Silas had missed his flight and been forced to stand by for the next one. Apparently even the power of big corporate executives was diminished and ineffective where commercial airlines were concerned. Waiting around the crowded terminal, drinking bad coffee and watching the snow plummet in fat, discouraging flakes, Silas made plans to buy the airline first thing when he got back and fire the belligerent ticketing agent who'd made him feel so impotent. He'd finally been granted a seat in coach only to discover his seatmate was a talkative matron from a tiny town in Puerto Rico who'd kept flashing fuzzy photographs of her many eligible daughters, describing in full detail their culinary and domestic skills. By the time he'd dealt with all the officials at Muñoz-Marin International Airport in San Juan, who moved unbelievably slowly and without concern, Silas was nearly suicidal.

But now, looking down at the tranquil Caribbean, he relaxed and breathed a little more easily. Silas loved flying. He enjoyed being in total control again after his miserable experiences of the day. It felt good to be so far removed from everything and everybody. Up here, he was alone and in command, his only company the clouds and sun. He almost smiled, then remembered what awaited him in Rio upon his arrival and why he was making this trip in the first place. His lips thinned, and he gripped the wheel angrily.

What had Vasquez been thinking, to just up and desert his prestigious and well-paying position with Duran Industries without giving notice, only to turn up a week later in the Falklands with that dancer? Responsible people didn't just shirk their business obligations that way. Silas detested irresponsibility and unreliability in people. Where was the sense of *duty* that he possessed and admired in others? No one seemed to know the definition of the word these days. Everyone seemed interested in just getting by. Lately, when the going got tough, the tough ran away. No one wanted to work anymore. No one wanted to excel in business. Everyone just wanted the easy life, he thought contemptuously. Well, not him. He wasn't afraid of hard work or responsibility, and he certainly wouldn't quit his job just because things got a little rough sometimes.

His attention was caught sharply when he noticed a strange humming in the plane's engine. He checked all the gauges, but found nothing amiss. Yet he gradually began to lose power, and along with it, altitude. He scanned the waters below him in search of a place to land, catching sight of a string of small islands. With any luck, one of them would have a clearing of some kind where he could put down. When a loud knocking accompanied the engine hum, Silas grew more concerned. The islands were becoming scarcer, and still he saw no place to land. He had nearly resigned himself to crashing into the ocean when he flew over the last of the tiny islands, far removed from the others, and saw that it contained a clearing of some sort. He couldn't believe his good luck when the clearing turned out to be a landing strip. An honest-to-God, cement-and-pavement landing strip! As Silas positioned the plane to descend, he lost power completely in one of his engines. When the plane slowed to a stop on the runway, he lost power in the other. He never noticed the man leaning against a small, brightly painted house by the side of the tarmac, because by that time his plane was silent and he was furious.

"Dammit," Silas said to no one in particular. "Don't tell me we're going to have to recall this entire line."

He emerged from the plane mentally reviewing the owner's manual in an attempt to determine the problem. Checking the engine and fuel lines, he could find nothing wrong. Eventually the islander beside the lean-to who had been regarding the scene with mild amusement sauntered toward him and peered intently over his shoulder. Silas started visibly, but the other man didn't seem to notice.

"Here is your problem, mon," the stranger stated, pointing to one of the more sophisticated pieces of machinery that kept the aircraft aloft.

"Who're you?" Silas demanded, angry that he'd been taken by surprise.

"I be Desmond, mon," the islander responded with an easy smile.

Desmond proceeded to go into a rather long and surprisingly well-informed explanation of why this specific mechanism wasn't functioning correctly, and offered in very technical terms some alternative ways to repair it. What he was saying was at odds with the manner in which he spoke. There was a gentle, mesmerizing quality in his speech, and he had the lilting, musical calypso accent indigenous to this part of the world. Silas thought inanely that the man should be talking about banana boats and steel drums, not mechanical failure in a private airplane. It was impossible to discern Desmond's age. His hair hung to his shoulders in dreadlocks, his sable skin was unlined. Yet his eyes carried a knowledge of tough experience and past hardships. A faded red shirt spilled over raggedy blue jeans, and he gazed at Silas without expression, as though he had been expecting his arrival all along.

"Do you know how to fix the plane?" Silas asked hopefully.

"No problem," Desmond assured him.

"How long will it take?"

"'Bout a week."

"A week?" Silas bellowed. "But that's impossible. I have to be in Brazil by this evening."

"Hope you a good swimmah, mon."

Silas narrowed his eyes irritably. "Why so long if you know what the problem is?" he asked, ignoring Desmond's attempt at levity.

"No parts. I'll have to get dem from St. Vincent, and de supply plane lands only once a week."

"When?" Silas asked.

"Yestahday."

"Meaning?" Silas was beginning to lose his patience with Desmond, beautiful speech patterns or not.

"Meaning dat dere's no plane until next Tursday, mon."

"I beg your pardon, did you say Thursday? Are you telling me I'm stuck here until Thursday?"

"Yah, mon."

Silas's hands wove savagely through his hair, clenching great handfuls of it. He really didn't need this aggravation. Not after the day he'd had. His head hurt again, and that nagging little pain in his chest was back, making its presence all too clear.

Desmond seemed to sympathize with his situation.

He clapped a hand warmly on Silas's shoulder and grinned encouragingly.

"Don't worry, mon," he assured Silas. "Dere's a beautiful hotel here with a fahntahstic restaurant. You will enjoy your stay here."

Silas's hopes picked up. If there was a hotel here, then there must be people—vacationers, maybe. With boats, yeah. And there must be a reception desk with, dare he say it, a telephone, right? He could call Ethan and have him send a rescue party for him. Maybe he could even hire someone to take him off the island on a boat if he couldn't reach Ethan. He couldn't be too far from the mainland.

"A hotel?" Silas prompted.

"Hestah, will take good care of you," Desmond promised.

"Hestah?"

"De manageah, mon. Makes a most delicious fish and fungi."

"Fish and fungi," Silas repeated, his mouth curling downward in distaste. "I can hardly wait."

"You will have a good time here," Desmond vowed, his face split by a broad white smile. "Wait and see. You will be glad Jah dropped you on dis island."

Silas ignored the prediction and instead asked, "How do I get to this hotel?"

As he gathered his briefcase and garment bag, Desmond gave him simple instructions. Silas was to take the path at the end of the runway until it became sand, then look to his right. The building he saw would be the hotel. Sighing in resignation at the unflappable islander, he began what he thought would be a short stroll to his accommodations. However, with every step he took, Silas became increasingly annoyed. It must have been eighty-five degrees, and he was still dressed in the dark suit he'd donned in New York in anticipation of his reception in Rio by several DI executives. He carried his jacket over one arm, but even in his shirtsleeves he was sweltering.

After walking for an estimated mile, the path began to narrow and Silas decided that heat prostration was inevitable. His aviator sunglasses slipped down his nose as droplets of moisture slid down his face in a steady stream, and his damp black hair plastered against his forehead. Perspiration stained the front and back of his expensive shirt, while dust and sand settled in the cuffs of his trousers. Desmond was wrong. He was not having a good time.

As the jungle seemed to close in around him, Silas began to wonder if maybe he'd crashed and died in the plane after all and had subsequently entered some sort of bizarre afterlife. There were sounds surrounding him he'd never heard before. Birds that laughed and screamed, things in trees that chattered and cried. Rustlings and whisperings near the ground alluded to things invisible to a mortal's eyes. Yet behind it all he sensed a serenity and stillness completely foreign to him. He considered himself an experienced man, yet here was an entire world he could never have known had he not been cast down into it.

Just when it seemed the jungle would swallow him up into eternity, two huge ferns parted as if of their own free will, and Silas stepped onto a beach. As suddenly as it had started, the jungle concert came to an end, replaced by sweet silence. What he saw made him stop and stare, mouth gaping, eyes wide. For the first time in his thirty-eight years, Silas was amazed. The scene before him was one which could have only existed in the book of Genesis. It was paradise.

A mere hundred feet away from him stood a simple structure Silas assumed must be the hotel. Beyond that was the most spectacular beach he had ever seen. Deserted, it was an endless stretch of pearly white that disappeared into the jade-and-ebony jungle. The ocean lapped at its shore, the waters blue, then green, then clear, as if the sun had tossed sapphires, emeralds and diamonds on the surface. Silas blinked. It was no dream. But it just might be Heaven.

The ocean breeze caressed his face like a lover's touch, beckoning him closer. Inhaling deeply, he filled his lungs with the salty scent of the sea and the exotic fragrance of the jungle blossoms behind him. It was as though he had entered another world. He was so far removed from telephoned problems and aspirin tablets that he might as well have left the planet. Suddenly his necktie was ridiculously uncomfortable, and he quickly reached up to loosen it. He hastened his step as he approached the hotel, ignoring the sand filling his eel-skin shoes.

The building he neared was just a construction of white stucco and bleached gray wood with yawning windows and weather-beaten shutters for doors. At present, the shutters were propped open by two massive potted palms, and Silas speculated that the proprietor rarely locked up at night. As he drew closer he caught strains of mellow reggae music escaping on the breeze, a plaintive, coaxing voice telling him not to worry about a thing, because every little thing was gonna be all right.

Inside the hotel, he felt as though he were still among the elements. What few walls there were had

been whitewashed and decorated with watercolor paintings of the ocean and jungle. The sparse furnishings
were bamboo and rattan, a few upholstered in a tropical
print of pink orchids and green ferns. To his left, Silas
saw a small sitting area, while to his right was a make-
shift bar and a series of small tables and chairs.
Apparently this was the "restaurant" Desmond had
recommended. Ceiling fans rotated slowly and hypnotically above him, their *swish-swish-swish* sounds main-
taining perfect reggae time. Plants tumbled from every
nook and cranny, swaying subtly, though as a result of
the breeze or the music, Silas wasn't sure. This world
had slowed to almost a standstill. There was no hustle
or bustle. There were no taxis threatening to run him
down in the street, no buildings making him feel claus-
trophobic, no board of directors breathing down his
neck for reports and results, no people making constant
demands and eliciting his contempt.

People. There must be people here, Silas thought. Or
at least a person. This Hestah person who ran the place,
where was he, she or it? Directly across from the door
by which he had entered was another that led to the
beach. Silas exited onto a wide veranda furnished with
more rattan and a striped hammock, long ago faded by
the sun and salt. The beach was as beautiful and as
empty as it had been the first time he'd glimpsed it.

Just as he was preparing to turn around and retreat
to the relative coolness of the hotel lobby, a movement
a few hundred feet up the beach caught his eye. Even
at this distance he could tell it was a woman, and she
was in no hurry to reach her destination. She approached him with languid, easy strides, ankle deep in
water that winked and lapped at her feet. As she drew
nearer to the hotel's entrance, he noticed she carried a

mesh bag full of live crabs in one hand, snorkeling gear in the other. He also noticed that she was tanned and curvaceous and very easy on the eye. A damp gold-and honey-colored braid tumbled carelessly over one deeply bronzed shoulder, brushing against her flowered bandeau top and skimming just above the waistband of her baggy khaki shorts. From one earlobe dangled two small gold hoop earrings, while the other sported one made from a small shark's tooth.

She stopped at the foot of the stairs in front of him, the ghost of a smile playing on her lips, her light brown eyes sparkling with laughter beneath tousled bangs. Silas's first coherent thought was one that centered on her tan line, or rather lack of one. His second was a realization that she was having a chuckle at his expense. His lips turned down in a frown, his eyes stormy behind the dark lenses of his Vuarnets.

"Don't tell me." She grinned at him. "Let me guess. You must have taken a wrong toin at Albacoiky on your way to Pismo Beach." It was a less than convincing Bugs Bunny impression, and Silas was more than a little peeved that she was finding humor in his situation.

Hester Somerset, meanwhile, was at a loss for normal conversation. She had noticed the man standing at the entrance to the hotel at about the same time he'd first observed her. As she'd neared, she'd experienced a wave of déjà vu that was almost overwhelming. He could have been any one of a hundred people from her past, a life-style she'd fled in near panic over two years ago. She'd lay easy odds that he was a corporate big shot who'd made his first million at twenty-nine and had his second ulcer at thirty. He reeked of money and power, from his expensive sunglasses to his designer loafers. Armani suit, she guessed. At least he had good taste. But he was probably as superficial and lacking in values as all the other vipers she'd met in the wonderful world of high finance.

Still, upon closer inspection, she had to concede that there might be something different about this particular specimen of businessman. A sense of real authority, self-assuredness maybe, tempered with a little less obnoxiousness than the executives she'd known at Thompson-Michaels. Arrogance probably, she amended. Although he was certainly good-looking. Sexy, even. She experienced an almost overpowering erotic response to him. His large size and apparent strength appealed to her baser instincts. The fact that he was standing several steps above her enhanced his well over six-foot height, but there was something more. Hester couldn't quite put her finger on it, but there was more that attracted her to this man than a suggestion of his sexual prowess. Something in his expression revealed a chink of vulnerability below his confident exterior. Despite his sneer of contempt at her bad Bugs Bunny impersonation, Hester recognized his uneasiness and uncertainty in his current surroundings. The thought that such a seemingly authoritative man could become so easily unsettled by her world of simplicity made Hester smile and feel a little powerful herself. Then out of nowhere, she wondered what color his eyes were behind his sunglasses. And what was he doing on the island in the first place?

"I need a room," Silas growled, his voice sounding harsher than he'd intended because of his thirst and the startling realization that he was intensely and uncomfortably attracted to this woman who appeared to have just risen out of the sea.

"No problem," Hester told him as she climbed the steps and brushed past him into the cool shade of the hotel. "How long will you be staying?"

Her seeming dismissal of him without a glance raised Silas's hackles. How dare she treat him as just another common hotel guest when he wanted fiercely to tumble her to the floor and have his way with her!

"Does it really matter?" he grumbled as he followed her into the kitchen and watched her fill the sink with water. "You don't exactly seem to be overrun with guests, do you?" In Silas's social and business circles, insinuating that someone's business was failing was an unspeakably vile insult. But this woman just laughed and submerged her crabs in the sink.

"Yeah, I guess you're right," she said mildly and smiled at him. "Want a beer? You look like you could use one. First one's on the house."

"Thank you," he managed to say. He was angry that a beautiful and damned desirable woman, who was tying his libido in knots, was completely unaffected by him. Not just unaffected, he corrected himself sternly, she was taking pity on him, for God's sake!

Hester walked out to the bar with Silas right behind her and reached into a small ice chest she kept there. She opened a long-necked bottle of Mexican beer and handed it to him.

"Do you have a glass?" he asked as he accepted the cool bottle, already wet with condensation. Hester smiled knowingly and reached into the cupboard above the bar for a pilsner and handed it to him. She herself put a bottle of mineral water to her lips and drank thirstily. That accomplished, she placed the bottle against her breastbone in an attempt to relieve the heat that coursed through her every time she looked at Silas.

Silas saw the act as a blatant and deliberate act of seduction and his lips drew downward as his hand tightened around the bottle.

"I'm Hester, by the way," she told him. "Hester Somerset. I manage the hotel. You're welcome to stay as long as you like. As you pointed out, we're not exactly booked up for the season."

"I'm only staying as long as it takes to get off this damn island," he informed her.

Hester frowned. "That's not a very positive attitude to take on vacation with you."

Silas yanked off his sunglasses and glared at her. "I'm not on vacation. I'm stranded."

Blue. Icy, piercing, beautiful blue. His eyes were the color of the Caribbean early on a brilliant, sunny morning. Hester could only stare for a moment, then rolled the bottle of mineral water from her chest to the back of her neck in an effort to cool another hot spot. The action left a trail of moisture on her brown skin that Silas wanted to follow with his tongue. Surely he was dreaming. No place on earth could be as gorgeous as this island paradise, and certainly no woman could be as appealing and arousing as this tempting little creature from the blue lagoon. Any minute now his alarm would go off, and he'd awaken in his Manhattan penthouse with just enough time for a cup of coffee before meeting with the board of directors. He took a long sip of beer from his glass and tried to concentrate on what she was saying.

"I wondered if that was your plane I heard or if someone dropped you off. Usually there's only Ford's plane on Thursdays. I was afraid maybe something was wrong with someone on the island."

"Then it's true? I'm stuck here until Thursday?"

Silas sank wearily onto a bar stool, looking beat and frustrated. Hester's heart turned over a little at the sight of a fallen giant.

"I'm sorry, Mr...."

"Duran."

She waited to see if he'd offer his first name, but when he just looked at her vaguely, she continued.

"Mr. Duran. Yes, well, Ford is our only connection to the outside world, and I'm afraid he only flies in once a week with supplies and mail. Or if there's a medical emergency he'll come to the rescue. Otherwise we plan our comings and goings according to his schedule."

"This is an emergency," Silas urged. "I have to be in Rio de Janeiro this evening. Tomorrow morning at the latest."

"Why? Are you donating a major organ to someone?" Hester asked skeptically.

"No, but I need to get to a very important meeting of my company there."

It figures, Hester thought. With him business would come first. And probably last, and everything in between.

"Sorry, that's not life or death," Hester told him.

"I'll pay him," Silas tried a different tack.

Hester shook her head. "Ford's not into money," she stated simply, and Silas thought the man must have a screw loose. "Besides, if someone's expecting you in Rio and you don't show up, they'll come looking for you. We can radio the Coast Guard to let them know you're here, and they can relay a message for you."

"You have a radio?" Silas brightened considerably.

"Well, of course I have a radio. It's sort of necessary around these parts."

Silas didn't like the way she was looking at him as though he were a silly child. He'd liked it much better when she was giving him the smoldering look she'd displayed when he removed his sunglasses. She wasn't any more unaffected by him than he was by her. She was just a little better at disguising it. He smiled predatorily. Too bad he'd be off the island soon. It might be a nice diversion to stick around and watch the temperature rise. Well, even though there was a way to contact Ethan now, it would still be impossible to get off the island before tomorrow at the earliest. And that meant there was still a hot, tropical night ahead of them.

Silas finished the last of his beer in one swallow, his cool blue eyes never leaving Hester's warm golden ones, his smile growing progressively more dangerous. She took a step backward as he rose from the bar stool and walked slowly and deliberately toward her. She found his presence very disturbing. Maybe she'd been on the island too long with too little contact with eligible members of the opposite sex.

He stopped a few inches in front of her, the look in his eyes hinting at any number of intimate ideas.

"Let's go have a look at that radio of yours, shall we?" he murmured provocatively as he took her arm and encouraged her to lead the way. "Then you can show me what you natives do when you get restless."

Back in New York City, traffic kept crawling, taxis kept honking, the wind kept biting and the snow continued to fall. It was as it had been that morning— crowded, noisy and cold. Inside the offices of Duran

Industries, Ethan MacKenzie sat quietly at his desk, twiddling his thumbs, smiling wickedly at his telephone.

"You're looking pretty smug," his wife remarked as she strode briskly through his doorway. "What happened? Did we just make another fast million at someone else's expense?"

"Amanda, my darling, you'd better be nice to me," Ethan told his auburn-haired, impeccably dressed wife. "You may just find yourself a widow upon your brother's return from South America."

"Well, then I'd better make sure your life insurance policy is in order," Amanda said dryly. "Can you give me an exact date for your imminent demise?"

"Oh, I'd say a week from today at the latest," he informed her.

"I see. Care to elaborate?" She perched herself on the edge of Ethan's desk while she awaited an explanation, affectionately smoothing back his blond curls with perfectly manicured fingers. "Last I heard, *he* was the one working himself to death. You were only suffering from a mild case of the working-lates."

"I just had the most curious telephone call from the U.S. Coast Guard," Ethan said. "It seems Silas's plane went down this afternoon over a tiny island somewhere around the Grenadines."

"Good God!" Amanda exclaimed. "Is he all right?"

"Yes, he's fine," Ethan quickly reassured her. "He managed to land the plane on an airstrip on the island. However, there's some kind of mechanical problem that can't be repaired until the local supply plane comes on Thursday. Consequently, your brother is in a rather bad mood. He wants someone to fly down and take him the rest of the way to Rio as soon as possible.''

"I would imagine so.'' She breathed a sigh of relief. "We'll send someone tomorrow morning, of course.''

"Well, we *could* do that,'' Ethan began, glancing mischievously at Amanda. "But I sort of told Silas it would be too difficult for us right now, and that he'd just have to stay there until something else could be arranged.''

"You didn't.'' Amanda jumped up from the desk and glared at her boyishly good-looking husband. She put her hands on her hips defiantly and said, "I can't believe you left him stranded there. Ethan, how could you?''

"Amanda, he's perfectly safe. The Coast Guard assured me that he's in no danger whatsoever. In fact, according to the crew of a cutter that knows the area well, he's at a great hotel on a perfectly gorgeous island.''

"Maybe so,'' Amanda conceded, "but that's beside the point. He...''

"Will have nothing to do but lie on the beach all day and relax all night,'' Ethan finished the statement for her.

"But he won't be able to...''

"Take calls, stare at a computer screen, worry about production, be frustrated by the board of directors. Don't you see? This is perfect. We've been after him to get away from it all, and he's gotten about as far away as he can get.''

Ethan watched as the realization of what this meant finally registered on his wife's lovely face. "It's the vacation he needs but refuses to take.'' She smiled.

"It's better,'' Ethan told her. "On Nantucket, he still

would have been on the phone constantly, being CEO from a few hundred miles away. For this week, he'll have absolutely no contact with the outside world. No phones, no television, no newspapers. He'll have no choice but to take it easy.''

"Oh, but Ethan," Amanda began. She was delighted that her brother would be getting a desperately needed vacation, but was stung with guilt about being so sneaky and underhanded about it. "We're being so bad by just abandoning him there. He's going to kill us when he finally gets back. By the way, how will he get back?''

"I had the Coast Guard radio a message to him," Ethan explained. "I said we'd have a problem getting someone down to him so he'll have to stay until the mail plane that services the island can pick him up. They said it comes every Thursday. Anyway, he can get a lift to the nearest populated island, or maybe even Venezuela. From there he can catch a commercial flight back to New York. In the meantime, the Coast Guard will relay a message that I'll be flying down to Brazil myself and leaving you and Gibson in charge here."

"Oh, he's going to be so mad," Amanda predicted. "But maybe he'll get a nice tan."

"Mad?" Silas shouted angrily, over two thousand miles away. "Mad? No, I'm not mad! I'm absolutely furious!"

Hester still sat on the stool in front of her high frequency radio, biting her lip worriedly. In hindsight, she supposed asking if he was mad was a pretty stupid question. She could tell by the way he was pacing and grumbling that the man was highly perturbed.

Her occasional radio exchange with the Coast Guard

usually left her in a good mood. They were a nice bunch of guys. The cutter that patrolled the area usually visited when they were in the vicinity and the crew would always come into the hotel for a few beers and a little R&R on her beach.

Today's radio contact, however, had not been pleasant. Although the radio operator in San Juan had been as genial as ever, it had been difficult keeping Mr. Duran from snatching the transmitter from her hand and shouting frustrated obscenities across the airwaves. He wasn't a happy camper at the moment. She'd have thought he'd be pleased he'd been given the opportunity to escape the rat race for a while. After all, this Mr. MacKenzie seemed to know what he was doing. Surely the business wouldn't fall apart because one of its executives was absent for a week. Mr. Duran must have some ego if he thought he was that vital to company stability.

As Hester watched him pace angrily back and forth, mumbling curses and planning the deaths of more than a few people, her own irritation began to grow. She switched off the radio and stood to face him.

"I don't see what you're so hot and bothered about, Mr. Duran," she snapped. "Geeze, you know, most normal people would give up a week's wages to be stranded here away from the demands of the workplace." She paused a moment in thought. "Come to think of it, I suppose most normal people do give up a week's wages to get away for a week." She stopped again when she saw Silas's expression, one that said furiously, "Huh?" She shook her head as if to clear it and continued. "What I mean is, why don't you just enjoy a week at the beach like any decent vacationer would? Are you so important that you can't be spared for a week?'' she added sarcastically. ''I mean, it's not like you own the company or something.''

''Yes, I do.''

''You do?''

Silas nodded but said nothing more. It was when she had said ''hot and bothered'' that he had looked up and become just that. He hated to say it, but she was beautiful when she was angry. The rest of her scolding speech had been lost on him as he'd become fascinated by the thin braided leather thong tied loosely around her ankle. He wondered if she ever wore shoes.

''Oh. Well.'' Hester cleared her throat for no reason except that she felt suddenly and inexplicably nervous. She just couldn't seem to look away from those intense blue eyes. ''Well, at least you seem to have capable people working for you. This Mr. MacKenzie seems to have everything managed very well.''

''Mr. MacKenzie is my brother-in-law, and I'm going to kill him upon my return.''

''Yes, well, I suppose that's your prerogative, of course,'' Hester told him. ''But why do you have to be the one to go on this important mission to Rio de Janeiro anyway? Why shouldn't your brother-in-law do it?''

''Because I can't seem to depend on anyone but myself these days,'' Silas responded testily. ''My number one man on the South American continent didn't show up for work last Monday because he was island-hopping with some mambo dancer, or limbo dancer, or samba dancer, or some kind of dancer!'' His voice grew louder with each type of entertainer he mentioned. ''Most of my executives in New York can't be relied on to run the business because they have families to deal with.'' He said the word ''families'' as if they were bad habits or felony charges. "Even my sister and her husband don't want to come in on the weekends. They'd rather spend time in the country."

"How despicable," Hester intoned with mock severity. "How dare those people want to live a full life instead of driving themselves into an early grave? That sort of behavior really is intolerable, Mr. Duran. I don't see why you keep them employed."

Silas threw her a black look that warned her she was entering dangerous territory.

"The point is," he began again slowly, as if speaking to a complete idiot, "that when one has a job that requires special dedication, one can't simply behave in an irresponsible fashion. I depend on my people to give me one hundred percent, just as I do myself. I can't abide negligence. People who abandon their duties just because things get a little rough sometimes are no more than feeble little whiners, and I want nothing to do with them." He paused, realizing that the vehemence of his statement would be lost and seem unnecessary to someone like the woman before him. Her biggest problems were probably which swimsuit to wear or how to keep her beach towel from blowing away in the ocean breeze. He sighed and said, "But then, what would you know about it?"

Maybe more than you think, Hester said to herself. For a brief moment during his tirade, she had been transported back to her Wall Street office, listening to Mr. Larsen chew her out for wanting to leave at her usual time when a particularly unreasonable client insisted on scheduling a meeting at well past the dinner hour. She hadn't gotten home until midnight that night. It had been 3:00 a.m. before she'd calmed down enough to fall asleep.

Out loud she said, "At any rate, you'll be needing a room. Do you want a view of the ocean or the jungle?"

"What's the difference in price?"

"There is none," Hester informed him. "Why do you ask?"

"Most hotels charge an arm and a leg for ocean-front rooms," Silas said patiently.

"Really? How strange." The only hotel Hester had ever been in was the one where she'd stayed during her month on St. Croix. She'd asked for a room with a view of the ocean there before she'd even said hello. At that point, price hadn't been a factor. She just wanted to look at the beach and the beautiful blue Caribbean.

Silas wasn't sure if she was just putting on an act or if she was actually as naive as she seemed. Just what was her story? What string of events had brought her to this utopia? Or had she been here since the beginning of time, awaiting his arrival, as primeval and mysterious as the rest of the island seemed to be? It struck him that there was an earthy quality about her that caused him to view her as ageless, almost mystic. It also struck him that the avenue his thoughts were currently taking led straight to a mental hospital. He had to get hold of himself.

"How much for the week?" Silas asked, bringing his thoughts back to something he could understand— dollars and cents.

"Oh, I don't know." Hester shrugged airily. "Let's see…six nights, say twenty-five dollars a night…"

"Twenty-five dollars?" Silas gasped.

"What?" Hester exclaimed in alarm. "Is that too much? The price includes all meals. Just as long as you eat what I eat. I don't want to have to be in the kitchen all day.''

This really was too outrageous for Silas. Here she had a potential Club Med on her hands and she was practically giving it away. He had business associates who would spend several thousand dollars a week just for a room in a place this secluded and idyllic. Not him, of course. He thrived in the city and could never be more than a few miles from one. And to have almost no contact with the outside world was simply unthinkable.

"Twenty-five dollars a night is fine," Silas said indulgently. "I didn't realize all meals were included in that price."

"But as I said, you have to eat when I eat, otherwise you're more than welcome to fix your own."

"Fine."

"So do you want the ocean or the jungle? They're both nice views."

"It really doesn't matter," Silas told her. The beer he'd consumed so hastily was making him sleepy, and he desperately wanted a shower.

"Ocean view," Hester decided after a moment. "You'll get a cool breeze and there are fewer mosquitoes. Follow me."

"Anywhere," Silas breathed quietly as she turned and headed toward the stairs at the end of the room. She had some way of walking, he'd give her credit there. A walk like that could start fights and stop traffic, he decided as he watched the casual sway of her hips, her long braid swinging from side to side like a metronome. Maybe a week in the tropics wouldn't be as bad as he'd anticipated.

"Are you coming, Mr. Duran?"

"Right behind you," he grated out as he picked up his briefcase and garment bag. And loving every minute of it, he added to himself.

Chapter Two

Hester showed Silas to a room upstairs that, as she'd promised, offered a magnificent view. The two windows were huge and without glass, their shutters, like the French doors leading out to the veranda, opening inward. Just beyond the veranda was a clump of palm trees whose leaves swayed and rustled in the cool breeze. The only other sound was the quiet splash of the surf only yards away. The room was painted a very pale green with white trim, and adorned with paintings like those in the hotel lobby. A white wrought-iron bed with a coverlet in the same soft green as the walls was pushed casually into one corner of the room, mosquito netting cascading from a hook in the ceiling surrounding it like a cocoon. The other furnishings consisted of a maple dresser and mirror, a matching maple rocking chair and a scarred cedar chest topped with a vase of flowers and an oil lamp.

"No electricity?" Silas asked when he saw it.

"I have power," Hester told him. "A small generator outside. I just like to conserve energy where I can."

Against the wall between the two windows stood an old writing desk and stool. The hardwood floor was polished to a golden sheen, and a woven rug of pastel colors lay at the center of it all. There wasn't much to it, but Silas liked it. It made him feel...calm. It was a sensation he hadn't experienced for a long time.

"Where's the bathroom?" he asked, looking around for another door. "I'd love a shower."

"Um, gee, that's kind of a tricky question," Hester hedged.

"What do you mean?"

"Well, we do have a shower. Sort of. But you can only take one after we've had a good hard rain."

"I'm sorry," he said, his voice rife with irritation, "but I don't follow you."

"See, Desmond rigged this great shower fixture outside. It's absolutely wonderful to shower outdoors. Very exhilarating."

"So?"

"But it has to be full of rainwater, otherwise the salt will rust the pipes. And we haven't had any significant rainfall for a while." Hester shrugged. "Sorry."

"Do you have a bathtub?"

"We're surrounded by it."

"The ocean," he stated blandly.

"Yes."

He drew in a deep breath and expelled it in exasperation. "The ocean," he repeated.

"There's a water closet at the end of the hall with a real flush toilet," Hester rushed on in the hope of appeasing him somewhat. "That was added some time ago. Porcelain piping, I think was used. Or was it clay? Anyway, there's a basin in there, and a few gallons of bottled water for bathing. Go sparingly, though. I usually only use it to rinse off the salt after I've bathed outside. In the ocean," she added.

"You actually *bathe* in the ocean?" Silas didn't try to hide his disdain.

Hester had had just about all she was going to take of his haughty attitude. "Look," she began through gritted teeth, "if you're trying to get me to lower the rates again, forget it. It won't kill you to bathe in the ocean a few times. It's like going swimming every day. For Pete's sake, it's only for a week!"

Silas became caught up with the image of her frolicking in the surf naked, sudsing herself all over before disappearing beneath the waves. Suddenly the idea of a dip in the ocean didn't seem so undesirable.

"You're right," he capitulated, the trace of a smile playing about his lips.

Hester gazed at him suspiciously, not quite believing he'd given in so easily. Maybe he could be reasonable after all when he wanted to be. He really did have beautiful eyes, she thought. How could she have considered them icy when in fact they were so warm? He had nice cheekbones, too, high and narrow. Maybe it was just that he was so tall and broad shouldered that made him seem so intimidating. At five foot three and one hundred and five pounds, she was easily overwhelmed. When she'd been at Thompson-Michaels she'd always worn three-inch heels to enhance her presence. That memory made going barefoot all the time even more enjoyable.

"Well, I'll leave you to it, Mr. Duran," she said,

bringing herself back to the present. "Try not to use too much water. Even though we're an island surrounded by it, it's still a scarce commodity."

"I won't use much."

Hester wondered if he ever smiled happily. "If you need anything, I'm never too far. When I'm not in the hotel, I'm on the beach. Or in my room."

"Which is where?"

"There are only eight rooms up here," Hester explained, "and mine is the one two doors down from you."

"How convenient," Silas murmured.

She was going to ask him convenient to what, but at that moment, Silas loosened the knot on his tie and began to unbutton his shirt. All the while, as he freed the pearly buttons from their fastenings, he kept his eyes on hers.

"Well, then," Hester said, swallowing, her throat suddenly dry. "If there's nothing else?" When he began to remove his shirt, she turned and started to pull the door closed behind her.

"There is one other thing," Silas said before she could leave.

"Yes?" She shouldn't have looked back. Upon seeing him shirtless, Hester's mouth went dry, too. He may be a workaholic, she thought, but he still takes time to work out. He had a tremendous physique, lightly muscled and firmly toned. Dark coils of hair covered his well-developed chest, sweeping down as far as the eye could see, and then some. Further speculation could have proved dangerous.

Silas's eyes glowed at the way she said "yes." He hoped she'd be using that word a lot around him.

"Can I have the key to my room?" he asked her.

"There are no keys."

"Why not?"

"No locks."

"What if someone breaks in?"

"Well, first of all, there's no one on the island who would do that," Hester assured him. "And secondly, even if someone did, they'd never get any stolen goods off the island without Ford knowing about it. He's very honest. He'd never transport any kind of contraband."

"What about boats?" Silas suggested.

"The General is the only one on the island who has a boat, and he never uses it. Just between you and me, I don't think he knows the first thing about boating, but he'd never admit that to anyone."

"The General?" he asked wearily.

"General Morales," she explained. "Retired from the Venezuelan army. You'll like him."

Silas was beginning to understand that this tendency of hers to say more than was necessary must be a result of her isolation from society. Whereas he had originally found it irritating, he was beginning to find it affecting him less negatively now.

"No, what I meant was what about boats from off the island that might come in," he elaborated.

"You mean like pirates?"

"Something like that, yes."

"I never thought about it," she confessed. "I guess we'll just have to hope it doesn't happen, won't we?"

"I guess we will."

Hester was about to leave again when Silas posed one last question.

"Does this no-locks situation include your door, two doors down from mine?"

"Yes," she told him hesitantly.

Silas smiled in satisfaction. "See you at dinner," he said, his voice full of promise.

That evening, Hester prepared dinner by the light of an oil lamp. Even though there was a generator to provide energy for the hotel, she rarely used anything electrical. The refrigerator and freezer took the bulk of her power, as she cooked on a portable propane camp stove. The occasional use of the ceiling fans and radio hadn't been a problem in the two years since she'd come to the island, but she'd continued to rely on oil lamps and hand wash her clothes to minimize the stress on the generator.

At the moment, she was preoccupied by thoughts of Mr. Duran. She'd been searching her brain's data banks like a computer ever since he'd told her he owned his own company. She probably should know his name, yet try as she might, she couldn't make any connections. To be honest, there wasn't a lot about her time in the business world that she could remember. It was as if that entire four-and-a-half year period of her life was a book she'd read long ago, and could now only remember in part. When she'd left New York, she'd been little more than a shell of a woman. She'd had no social life, no dreams or plans for the future, no friends or family. Even her past had been for the most part worthless, another forgotten book. She'd known the gamut of human existence, from being poor and unwanted in her grandmother's crummy tenement where she'd had nothing of her own, to being successful, wealthy and in demand, living in her own posh Manhattan condominium. At one point she'd been the wretched refuse of society, and at the other she'd had the financial community of New York City at her fingertips.

All in all, Hester had found the two life-styles frighteningly similar. The loneliness remained throughout it all, along with the emptiness. Most of the people surrounding her at Thompson-Michaels were as superficial, amoral and money hungry as the criminals and junkies in the old neighborhood had been. The only difference was that her colleagues drove better cars and drank better booze. Somewhere along the way, she had become one of them. Her only hope for salvation had been flight.

Her escape from New York was the real beginning of her life and development as a human being. The day she arrived in St. Croix was a symbolically beautiful one. The sun shone warm and brilliant in the sky, and the ocean sparkled outside her hotel window. Her first excursion was a shopping spree, her purchases consisting of nothing but swimsuits, shorts sets, sandals and sunglasses. On the street outside one shop, she stuffed the bag containing her silk suit and blouse into a garbage can. She'd done something similar with her briefcase at the St. Croix airport. Upon her return to the hotel, she stopped at the poolside bar to sip a piña colada, loving all four million and eighty-two calories the smiling bartender promised her it contained.

Everyone smiled here, she noted. And the music! It followed her everywhere. Steel drums, reggae and salsa were her constant companions all over the island. Clothes were brighter here, the buildings more colorful, the air cleaner, the people friendlier. It was impossible not to be in good spirits. Hester felt something that took her nearly three weeks to recognize as happiness. For the first time in her life she felt *good*. She *enjoyed* doing things. Life was *pleasant*. These were words that had never been present in her vocabulary before. She found herself smiling all the time, even humming snatches of reggae tunes she heard on the radio. She promised herself she would never go back to New York again. It would be impossible to exist in the demanding, heartless, stifling society of the city. Now that she knew there was an alternative to the emptiness and lifelessness she'd suffered for twenty-seven years, she could never return to her previous existence.

When her thoughts began to circle back to New York, Hester pushed them away and tried to concentrate on slicing a pineapple. By seven o'clock, she had finished making the fruit salad and was ready to begin steaming the crabs she'd trapped earlier, but she hadn't heard from Mr. Duran since their last questionable exchange. She suspected he was upstairs brooding about his predicament or doing some paperwork he'd brought along as a buffer against relaxation. God forbid he should take it easy. She decided to go up and tell him she'd fixed something and he was welcome to join her if he wanted. After making her way upstairs, she rapped lightly on his door.

"Mr. Duran?" she called softly. "Are you in there?"

When there was no response, she opened the door hesitantly.

"Mr. Duran?" she repeated.

This time she was greeted by what sounded like a muffled snore. Peeking around the door, she saw her guest sound asleep on his stomach, wearing nothing but one of her green-and-white striped towels wrapped around his waist. It looked as though he had returned from freshening up and fallen face first into the pillow, managing somehow to sweep the mosquito netting to the side. Hester stepped carefully toward the bed, taking inventory as she went. His backside was every bit as impressive as his front—smooth and lightly muscled. She felt a keen desire to run her fingertips over his shoulder blades and down his spine until the towel prevented her from venturing any farther. His face was turned toward her, and she marveled at the length and thickness of his eyelashes. In sleep, his lips were no longer thinned in exasperation, but full and enticing.

"Mr. Duran?" she said again, her voice barely a whisper. Why did he seem so much bigger when he was half naked and lying down? Since her vocal efforts to awaken him were having no effect, Hester reached out her left hand and placed it lightly on his upper arm. The sprinkling of hair there was soft and springy. Her palm lingered for a moment before her fingertips skimmed slowly up to his shoulder where his skin was cool and satiny. She shook him slightly and was about to utter his name again when his hand clamped swiftly around her wrist.

"Oh! You're awake," she exclaimed. Then when his grip on her tightened, she said, "Ow, Mr. Duran, you're hurting me."

Silas lifted himself up on his elbows and loosened his grip, unwilling to completely release his captive.

"Hester." He spoke her name sleepily as he expelled a deep breath. It was the first time he'd said it out loud, and she felt uncomfortable with the intimacy it suggested. "I forgot where I was for a minute. I can't believe I fell asleep. I never fall asleep that easily. Or sleep that soundly." He seemed surprised and puzzled.

"I think it's the climate. When I first came to the Caribbean, I found myself sleeping a lot, too." She twisted her hand in his grasp. "Would you please let me go?"

Instead of accommodating her request, Silas levered himself off the bed and stood facing her, all the while keeping a firm hold on her wrist. Hester found herself staring into his chest, inhaling great gulps of something wonderfully elusive and masculine.

"Why are you in my room, Hester?" Silas lifted her hand to examine her imprisoned fingers. Her hands were so small compared to his, her nails short and unpainted.

"I was going to tell you that dinner is ready. If you're hungry."

He wondered if her frequent innuendos were intentional, then decided they weren't. They were delivered with too much candor to be suggestive. Still, that didn't mean he couldn't make the most of them.

"Oh, I'm very hungry," he said roughly. He noticed that she looked everywhere but at his face. "It's been that kind of day."

"Fine," Hester mumbled, still all too aware of the heat in her hand where he lightly massaged her fingers. "I'll just wait downstairs while you get dressed." She tried to pull her hand from his, but he raised it to his mouth first and rubbed her knuckles lightly across his warm lips in a tantalizing manner. Hester sucked in her breath and met his eyes. Those beautiful eyes. Hungry eyes. They told her that his appetite included a desire for a lot more than she had prepared for dinner.

"What are we having?" Silas asked as if reading her mind. "For dinner, I mean." Reluctantly he released her hand, absently rubbing his own across his chest. Hester found the gesture fascinating, and the blush creeping into her cheeks probably told Silas exactly what she was thinking.

"Steamed crabs," she answered vaguely, her light

brown eyes once again lifting to meet his blue ones. Oh, boy, was she in trouble. She held her hand as if she'd been burned and started backing toward the door.

Silas wanted to ask her if steaming things was a specialty of hers, but decided it must be. That could be the only possible explanation for the feeling overwhelming him now. God, she was sexy.

"Steam away," he told her as she reached the hallway. "I'll be right down." His deep chuckle at her obvious discomfort in his presence followed her out of the room.

Hester slammed the door viciously behind her and stormed down the stairs, cursing and insulting Silas with every step. When she reached the kitchen, she nearly shattered every dish as she hurtled the dirty ones into the sink and the clean ones onto the table out on the veranda.

"Steam away," she mimicked. "Just who does he think he is, anyway? Just because he owns a corporation and has tons of money and probably a lot of people in New York jumping whenever he says move, doesn't mean he can throw his weight around wherever he goes. Things are a little bit different down here than they are in the Big Apple, and it's about time somebody set bad-tempered Old Man Duran straight with a good swift kick in the..."

"So set me straight."

The deep, angry voice came from behind her as she stood at the kitchen counter by the stove, and Hester closed her eyes in complete and utter embarrassment. She didn't have the nerve to turn around and face him, so she began plunking crabs one by one into the big steamer.

"I'm sorry, Mr. Duran," she mumbled sheepishly. "I didn't realize you were standing there."

"Obviously not."

Was it her imagination or did he actually sound a little hurt? She could understand if he was mad, but he didn't seem the type whose feelings could be bruised.

"I hope I didn't offend you," Hester said. "Sometimes my emotions get the better of me. I'll have to learn to control them a little more effectively."

By this time, Silas had moved to stand beside her, leaning his hip against the counter, his arms crossed at his chest. "Don't," he told her softly. "I seldom see any show of real emotion from people in my profession. It's refreshing really. Nice to know there's still a little of it left in the world. Besides, it was nothing anyone else wouldn't say behind my back. And I suppose I gave you a reason to be angry. I apologize, too."

Hester gazed at him then, not quite sure how to take what he had told her. He didn't seem the type to apologize easily, and his remark about others speaking badly of him in private seemed tempered with a what? Lonely quality perhaps? So instead of speaking, she braved a slight smile, and that seemed to work. Silas smiled back at her. It wasn't a big smile, but it wasn't bad. It was something they could work on. He had changed into baggy gray cotton trousers and a white shirt of some soft, breezy fabric. On his feet were white canvas slip-ons. He looked the epitome of a rich man on vacation.

"So you did pack some holiday rags," Hester teased. "I was wondering."

"Well, after all, I was going to Rio," Silas defended himself. "I may be overly concerned with my business, but I'm not entirely stupid. Say, don't they deserve a

fair trial or something before you boil them in oil?''
Silas indicated the crabs.

Hester's smile displayed perfect white teeth. Silas
found that he liked her smile a lot. Fortunately for him,
it was something she did frequently. He liked that, too.

"There really are a few things you ought to know
about the Caribbean, Mr. Duran,'' she drawled playfully.

"Oh?'' Silas joined in. "Like what?''

"Well, for one thing, the world moves much more
slowly below twenty degrees latitude,'' she informed
him. "It's called Island Time.''

"Is that a fact? I seem to have witnessed that particular phenomenon myself.''

"Also, the rules of the fashion industry are meaningless here.''

"That's another, very pleasant fact of life I noticed,''
Silas murmured, contemplating once again Hester's tan
line, or lack thereof. "But what does this have to do
with crabs?''

"Well, you see,'' Hester continued as she dropped
her last victim into the steamer, "among the other laws
of the Caribbean—the fun never ends, the music never
stops, and the rum flows freely and continuously—
there is also unfortunately no justice whatsoever for
edible crustaceans of any kind. Everybody around here
will tell you the same.''

Silas inhaled the spicy fragrance of the crabs as they
steamed above the wine-and-pepper broth and realized
he hadn't eaten since he'd left San Juan several hours
ago.

"Well, I can't say I'm sorry for the little rascals,''
he said lightly. "Better them than me.''

Silas couldn't remember the last time he'd actually

taken part in the preparation of a meal, but Hester had no qualms about accepting his suggestions for the sauce to accompany the crabs. When he offered to fix drinks, she asked for water instead, but encouraged him to help himself at the bar. Searching the cabinets, Silas found Jamaican rum, Puerto Rican rum, Antiguan rum and Barbados rum; rum from Martinique, Trinidad, St. Croix, Tortola and Montserrat. But no Scotch, his uncompromising usual. When he drank, it was always the same: his favorite brand of unblended Scotch over ice with just a splash of water. But it seemed all this hotel stocked was rum.

"Don't you have anything besides rum?" Silas called into the kitchen. "Something a little more… palatable?"

He probably wanted to say "chic" but was afraid of being labeled a snob, Hester thought. On second thought, he probably took pride in being a snob. Out loud, she said, "I keep having to remind you that you're in the Caribbean now, Mr. Duran. The customs are different. People even drink rum. Try the dark Barbados rum with tonic water. It's very refreshing."

Silas grumbled as he mixed his drink, something about peasants and primitive behavior. Upon tasting the concoction, however, his eyebrows lifted in surprise and his tongue did a little dance.

"Hey, this isn't half bad," he admitted upon his return to the kitchen. Hester put down the knife she'd been using to quarter a lime and approached him. She squeezed the juice of one quarter into his glass, dropping the remainder of it into his drink. Sucking the leftover juice from her thumb and forefinger, she said, "Now try it."

Her actions entranced Silas who took a large swallow from his glass. It was cold going down but did little to alleviate the heat coursing through him as he watched her. He couldn't seem to keep his eyes off her. She had changed into a pale gold gauzy blouse, the sleeves rolled to her elbows, the shirttail carelessly stuffed into her khaki shorts. Her long hair was still braided in a thick rope, but the shorter pieces around her face had escaped and glimmered in the lamplight like a halo.

Silas felt that if he reached out to touch her, she might disappear. Her beauty had an unreal, almost ethereal quality so different from the contrived, cosmetic splendor of the women he knew in New York. Hester was warm and inviting where so many city women seemed cool and distracted. Her ingenuousness and sense of humor were far more refreshing than any drink could ever be, offering him a very welcome change from the business opportunists and trend followers with whom he normally spent his evenings. There didn't seem to be any secrets to Hester Somerset; her approach to life was a carefree and straightforward one. He drank in her warmth and spirit, and it revived and intoxicated him more than all the rum in the Caribbean could.

They ate dinner together on the veranda by the amber glow of the oil lamp, its flame flickering now and again in response to the ever-present ocean breeze. Conversation was quiet and noncommittal, but after they cleared away the dishes they took their drinks down to the beach and sat near the water's edge. The warm surf lapped exhaustedly near their feet, trying to tempt them into an evening swim. After a moment, Hester's quiet voice broke the silence surrounding them.

"You know, even after two years here, I never get tired of this," she said in tranquil tones.

"Of what?" Silas asked. The balmy night air and two rum and tonics made him feel mellow and philosophical. He discovered he liked the feeling.

"Coming outside at night to sit on the beach. It's just so incredibly beautiful here. Not a day goes by that I'm not shocked by how gorgeous all this is." After a moment lost in thought, she said, "I grew up in New York."

"Did you? So did I. What area?" Silas wanted more than anything to find out about her past. It surprised him how badly he wanted to hear more about her.

"The Bronx." She indicated an area that was well-known specifically for its high crime rate and low quality of living.

"I've never been there," Silas mumbled, trying to hide his astonishment.

"I'm not surprised."

"But I know what it must be like."

"Trust me," Hester tried to keep the bitterness out of her voice. "You have absolutely no idea what it was like."

Silas remained quiet. She looked so young, he thought. Certainly no more than twenty-one or -two years old. She must have still been a teenager when she left, probably right out of high school. With no money for college, she probably didn't have any prospects for the future then. How had she finally found her way here?

"Where did you grow up?" Hester's question brought him out of his reverie and prevented him from asking her what had brought her to the island. "In a big house by the sea, I'll bet," she added.

"Long Island," he confessed, confirming her suspicions.

"Boy, we are from two different worlds, aren't we?"

"I refuse to apologize for having a good upbringing and a happy childhood," Silas snapped.

"I don't expect you to," Hester told him quickly. "I'm sorry. I don't normally get so uptight about my past. Sometimes I feel as though it happened to someone else entirely."

It must have, he thought. Because he couldn't imagine any way that the gentle woman next to him nervously digging her toes into the sand could have possibly survived the mean streets of New York City. Surely someone so sensitive and giving would long ago have been eaten alive.

"So just how big is this island?" Silas asked in an effort to change the subject.

"Not very," Hester told him. "About a mile wide at the center, I guess. Maybe two miles long. It's roughly oval in shape, though there's a small bay at the southwest curve. We're just above the southeast curve here."

"How many people?"

"When I first came here there were five besides me, but about three months ago, two marine biology students from the Sorbonne and their professor showed up to do a year-long study on some of the reefs surrounding the island."

"And you've lived here two years," he stated, shaking his head in disbelief at what she had told him earlier. Why would she isolate herself from the rest of the world at such an early age?

"Two years and one month, actually."

"How often do you get back to the States?"

"I haven't gone back. I haven't even left the island since I got here."

"You haven't been off the island in over two years?" He couldn't believe it.

"There's no need. Ford flies in every Thursday with whatever any of us needs. Every material possession I own is right here."

"What do you do to keep busy? Don't you miss things in New York?"

"Not really," Hester told him honestly. "I didn't do a lot in New York anyway. Although I do sometimes wonder what's happening on that TV show, *Strike Up the Band*. It was about the only thing I went out of my way to make time for."

"It got canceled."

"You're kidding! But it was so popular. I can't believe they took it off the air."

"Sorry."

"But that was my favorite show," she protested. "It was my only show. My only... That's terrible."

She seemed close to tears, Silas thought in wonder. He'd never watched the immensely popular show himself, but he remembered reading of its demise in the newspaper. As he recalled, the network's stock started to take a significant drop when it announced the removal of the show from its schedule.

Hester knew that Silas couldn't understand that his presence on the island had given her some ambivalent feelings about her existence there. His arrival and her conversations with him were stirring up memories of her life in New York and reminding her just how isolated and idealistic her life on the island was. At first, she had needed the seclusion to come to terms with herself and develop as an individual. But hadn't the metamorphosis been completed some time ago? For a while now, she'd been enjoying life on the island as any vacationer would. Had perhaps the time come to rejoin the rest of the human race? Now that she had identified herself and come to know and like the person she was, wouldn't it be appropriate to test that new self in more substantial surroundings? Did she want to spend the rest of her life alone on the island, or did she want to return to the real world and take a chance on a real life? Until now, she hadn't given it a thought. Then suddenly, with the arrival of Silas and reminders of her past, she was beginning to question her existence.

Silas sensed that her sudden meditation was creating some conflict inside her and sought to distract her.

"You never told me what you do here to pass time," he prodded.

"What? Oh." Hester's attention returned. "I read a lot, fish, snorkel, go crabbing, listen to music, do crossword puzzles, cook. I've also discovered that I love to paint. I never even knew I enjoyed doing things like that until I had the time for them."

"Are those your paintings in the hotel?"

"Yes." She beamed.

"They're very good," he said and meant it. "You use colors well."

"Thanks." It pleased her that he thought so, but confused her as to why she should care.

"Any other interests?" Silas found himself captivated by her, wanting to learn all he could.

"Well, since Professor Auclaire and her students have arrived, I'm developing a real passion for snorkeling and observing marine life."

"Really?" Silas lifted his brows suggestively. "A passion?"

"Jean-Luc is the one who got me interested in snorkeling. It's really amazing! There's a whole world down there you'd never know existed."

While Hester described—in uncommonly vivid detail—some aspects of the local marine life, Silas fumed, envisioning her lithe, tanned form barely encased in a bikini, swimming hand in hand with some young, blond, muscle-bound European geek in a Speedo.

"Jean-Luc?" he interrupted her in the middle of her favorite snorkeling story about an encounter with a moray eel.

Hester looked up, confused, and responded, "Yes. Jean-Luc. He's teaching me French, too."

"I'll bet he is," Silas grumbled and threw back the rest of his drink. He pushed himself up from the sand and returned to the hotel without a word.

Now what had she done? Hester wondered. Mr. Corporate-Executive-Type Duran was beginning to make her crazy. Just when she thought he might be okay, he turned on her for no reason. For the past hour and a half, they had shared some very pleasant moments together, and then out of nowhere, he gets angry and stalks off. Maybe he has a split personality, she thought. Or maybe it's just stress. God knows she had more than a nodding acquaintance with that. It could turn you into someone you'd never recognize, not to mention the type of person you never wanted to be.

She remained on the beach until her resentment cooled, then followed Silas's tracks back to the hotel. She found him searching furiously for something at the bar and offered her help.

"You're out of tonic," he accused, his blue eyes still a tempest of ill humor.

"No, I'm not. You're just not looking in the right place. Anyway, don't you think you've had enough?"

It was the wrong thing to say, she realized belatedly. Silas became even angrier and, if possible, more intimidating. She strode quickly to her back stock cabinet above the bar to retrieve more tonic water. As usual, the bottle Hester wanted was just beyond the reach of her fingertips. Silas saw her straining on her toes to get it, one bronzed, slender leg extended gracefully behind her, and something finally snapped inside him.

"Here, let me," he said softly and moved behind her. Not letting her step out of the way, he reached above her, easily plucked the bottle of tonic from the cabinet and placed it on the bar beside her.

"Thanks," Hester mumbled, feeling a tight shock in all the places where his body touched hers. How could she find him so attractive when only moments before she had thought him so exasperating? It made no sense. Yet as Silas remained behind her, his hands firmly gripping the bar on either side of her in an effective trap, her heart began to thump wildly.

"Turn around," he ordered gently. Hester did so slowly, still imprisoned within the boundaries of his arms. The room seemed to grow smaller and warmer by the second.

"Look at me." His voice, so deep and quiet, was casually coaxing, but his chest moved in and out in heavy breaths, and she knew he was as affected by the sizzling chemistry between them as she was. Since Silas stood nearly a foot taller than she, Hester was forced to tilt back her head to meet his eyes. She saw in them a passion and longing she knew must be reflected in her own. Silas's mouth curled into a knowing smile as he raised one hand to her hair, smoothing back her bangs.

Her hair was like satin, he thought. With his other hand he lazily stroked her lower lip with his thumb in a maddeningly tender way. Something squeezed Hester's stomach and put a match to her heart. She felt his warm breath on her forehead as he lowered his head to place a kiss there. Closing her eyes, she sighed as he brushed his lips over her temple, down to her cheek and jaw, and she made a helpless sound when finally, finally, his lips met her own.

Silas had intended only a light kiss on the forehead, but lost control after discovering that she was every bit as soft and vulnerable as he had dreamed. Her quiet moan, however, was ultimately his undoing. That slight, innocent sound, that utterance of surrender was too much for him to bear. What had started as a gentle brush of his lips against hers built steadily with every heartbeat until it was an insistent, hungry embrace. Silas took her mouth again and again, lost in his desire for her. He drove his tongue past her parted lips, tasting her deeply and passionately. His hands began a thorough exploration of her body, sweeping over her back and shoulders, strumming her ribs and cupping her fanny. When he wound one arm around her waist and the other around her shoulders, crushing her to his chest, Hester was too stunned, too overcome by longing to do anything but meet his kisses with a ferocity equal to his own.

Where had all this passion come from? she wondered. She had never experienced such emotions as these. Where would they take her if she let them run away, as they seemed to want to do? How soon before she completely lost control and did something she knew that she'd soon regret? As Silas's embrace became more possessive, his kiss more insistent, Hester realized the recklessness of it all, and knew that she must be the one to call a halt.

"Mr. Duran, please," she gasped as she put a hand on his chest in a futile effort to keep him at bay. The muscles she felt rippling beneath her fingertips almost caused her to reconsider her attempt to stop his advances.

"Call me by my first name, dammit." He continued kissing her temple, cheek and neck.

"I don't know your first name," Hester gasped out breathlessly. That seemed to do the trick, because Silas stopped kissing her and looked down into her eyes.

"You don't?"

"You never told me."

Silas was stunned that he had neglected to tell her his first name. He generally assumed people he dealt with in business already knew it, even though he rarely encouraged anyone to address him so informally. However, it seemed only natural that Hester should. How could he have allowed himself to be governed by one of his business rules where she was concerned?

"Call me Silas," he instructed her.

"Okay, from now on I will." She tried again to pull away from him. It only caused him to tighten his arms more.

"Say it."

"Silas," she said softly, ceasing her struggle and meeting his eyes. He smiled and eased his hold on her a little, still running his hands up and down her back. While he'd held her, he'd realized she wasn't wearing a bra, and the knowledge was driving him crazy.

His hands felt so good, so tempting, Hester thought. She knew if she stayed she'd be opening herself up to a potentially dangerous, if not destructive situation. Dangerous because she was so shocked at the immediacy and intensity of her response to Silas. She just couldn't trust her emotions right now. The situation could be destructive, too, considering her relative inexperience where the opposite sex was concerned. Silas was major league, and she'd barely made it out of sandlot. True, she'd had boyfriends since the time she was old enough to want one. But the only reason she'd ever wanted one was that it seemed to be the thing to do. She'd run with a pretty fast crowd in her teens, but she'd always managed to steer clear of unwanted intimacy.

Then, while at Thompson-Michaels, she'd had a brief affair with one of the other brokers, again only because she thought the time had come for her to join the ranks of the sexually initiated and have a lover like everyone else did. Her time with Leo Sternmacher was unremarkable and unfulfilling and ended when he was transferred to the West Coast. She'd never given another thought to wanting a man until now.

This was something she could not have anticipated. Never had she imagined herself capable of this impassioned, heated reaction toward a man she barely knew. Just his look was enough to make her feverish. His touch had the power to make her tremble, his kisses sent her into a frenzy. This was all untried territory, and it shocked her that she had made it to the ripe old age of twenty-nine without ever having experienced real passion. Silas did much more than fill the empty places inside her, he made them overflow and run wild with raw emotions.

Silas's hands were still slowly caressing Hester's back, moving lower with each circular motion they made. When he reached her waist, he paused for a moment, still looking into her eyes as if asking her permission to continue his exploration. She felt so good to hold, to touch. Her skin was soft and warm, vibrant as if the sun itself received life from her. His heart pounded and blood rushed through his veins as though he were a teenager and this was the first time he'd ever held a woman. She said nothing, but when he saw the naked desire on her face, he knew she felt as he did. His hands continued stroking her hips, lowered to her thighs, then cautiously cradled her derriere and drew her enticingly into the juncture of his legs.

Hester gasped when she understood the full magnitude of his arousal, and her expression registered her alarm. As her lips parted to voice her retreat, Silas interceded and kissed her again, exploring her warm mouth with his curious tongue. He freed her shirttail from her shorts and marveled at the silky skin of her back as he caressed it.

Hester became lost in a world of sensation, sparked by the touch of his mouth on hers and the continuous thrust of his tongue as he tasted her again and again. Wherever his fingers played on her body, they left behind a trial of fire. She was fast becoming an inferno that threatened to rage uncontrollably before finally consuming itself altogether. If she didn't put a stop to this now, she knew she would be burned to her very soul.

"Silas, we've got to stop," she panted against his shoulder when she had freed her mouth from his. She managed to work her hands up to his chest in a feeble gesture meant to push him away. Silas tasted her ear and kissed her neck one final time before looking into her light brown eyes again.

"What's wrong?" he asked dreamily.

"I think it's time we went to bed," Hester suggested, still a little dazed and not realizing the implication of her words.

"Great idea," Silas responded, his eyes glittering with the fire of anticipation. "Your place or mine?" He pulled her close again, raining butterfly kisses on her neck and shoulders, strumming her ribs. "I'll make it good for you, Hester, I promise. I know you haven't done much, uh, dating in the past two years, but tonight will be a new beginning."

"A new beginning?" Hester ground out through clenched teeth. His thoughtless, inane declaration made her furious. "A new beginning?" she repeated in disbelief. "Maybe that line works well with the women you know in New York, but don't you dare toss me in with them."

Silas pulled back and stared at her, clearly uncertain as to why she was so angry. "What do you mean, 'that line'?"

"We just met, Mr. Duran," she pointed out to him.

"Silas," he corrected.

"Mr. Duran," she repeated emphatically. "You can't possibly think that I'd...with you...before even...I could never...and *you*...!" Her colossal fury limited her vocabulary, but Silas got the gist of her meaning.

"Hester, I'm sorry. I didn't mean to imply anything. I only meant that, well, obviously something is happening between us. You can't deny it because I feel the way you respond to me. I don't know about you, but I've never felt this strongly this quickly about anyone before. There's something very different about you."

"I'm sure that's another line that you've used with great success," Hester replied testily, finally regaining command of her faculties.

Silas started to deny it, then realized uncomfortably that she was right. He *had* used that line with great success many times. The point was that this time he really meant it. It was a startling revelation. But now that he recognized it, how was he going to convince her that he was telling the truth?

Hester freed herself from his now-loosened hold of her and headed quickly toward the stairs. As she placed her foot on the first step, she turned to Silas one last time.

"You do seem to have a drugging effect on me, Mr. Duran, one that could prove addicting. And seeing as how I don't do much 'dating,' as you so tastefully put it, I think you're one bad habit that might eventually do me in." She paused, her gaze not leaving his, then added, "There are extra blankets in the linen chest at the end of the hall. It can get pretty cool here at night this time of year sometimes. Though I doubt you'll be needing a blanket tonight. Sleep well. Breakfast is at seven."

With that, she turned her back on a stiff-jawed Silas Duran, who watched her graceful ascension of the stairs, and agreed. It was going to be a warm night.

Chapter Three

Silas lay in bed awake for a long time that night. It seemed impossible that only the evening before he'd retired to his king-size platform bed in his Manhattan penthouse. He'd traveled light-years in only twenty-four hours. Normally he fell asleep to the drone of the air conditioner or furnace, with an occasional blaring of police sirens or car alarms somewhere in the street below. Here there was only the slight splash of the surf and the whisper of the palms in the breeze. Silas would have felt utterly at peace if it weren't for the knowledge of a certain enticing water spirit slumbering only a tantalizingly short distance away.

What a day he'd had! Flown two thousand miles, almost crashed into the ocean, landed on a nearly deserted tropical island in the middle of nowhere, hiked through the jungle, discovered paradise and found a goddess there waiting for him. Not his idea of a typical business day.

Inevitably his thoughts centered on Hester. She was a woman who could have stepped from a dream. Except that he never dreamed much about women. He dated a few off and on, when he attended social functions or needed an escort for a business-related affair, and although he'd been intimately involved with several women, none had struck any special chords. Yet in a matter of hours, Hester had tapped a mysterious spring of some unfamiliar emotion deep inside him. She was entirely different from anyone he knew, yet infinitely more appealing.

Why did she affect him so strongly so quickly? And what was he going to do about it? Her final statement tonight was clearly one that said ''back off,'' but that was going to be difficult. For a week, they'd be living in very close quarters, and whether she liked it or not, there was something pretty hot and heavy burning the air between them. Just how did she think they were going to keep their cool when this freight train named desire was running dead-on toward them?

Silas rose and wandered over toward the French doors. Outside the night sky was black, dotted with tiny crystal stars. He'd never seen so many stars. The thin, white line of the surf wound like a bright ribbon down the beach as far as he could see. All was quiet. His eyes settled on the open doors leading to Hester's room only a few yards away. It would be so easy to…

No, he chastised himself. He would wait. She wanted him as badly as he wanted her. He could feel it in the way she'd reacted toward him tonight. Her touch had been every bit as demanding and as sexually charged as his own. Sooner or later she would give in to her desires as he had to his. He only hoped it would be sooner.

Through the doors at which Silas gazed so longingly, Hester was entertaining similar thoughts. She'd tossed fitfully in her bed, tangled in sea-scented sheets, unable to erase the memories of the intoxicating way Silas had held and touched her. Her lips still tingled from his scorching kisses and her mind reeled as she thought again of his big, hard body pressed against hers.

"Boy, is it hot tonight," she mumbled under her breath.

Her thoughts spun with whys and what-ifs. Why was she so turned on by a total stranger? Why didn't she feel insulted by his advances instead of stimulated? What if they did make love together? Her experiences with Leo Sternmacher had been anything but earth shattering. Somehow she sensed that Silas's sexual technique would be explosive. With his knowing hands and sexy voice, he'd even managed to make the preparation of dinner seem erotic. What would it be like to be beneath him, his solid, full body crowding urgently into her smaller, softer one? To have his deep velvety voice describing all the luscious things he was going to do to her and what he wanted from her in return. He would be demanding and generous at the same time, his method thorough and pleasantly exhaustive. And at some point during it all, she would probably fall hopelessly in love with him if she wasn't careful.

Now where did that thought come from, she wondered crazily. She'd never been in love in her life, so how did she know she was even capable of it? Love was something alien, something that had never existed in her experience in any way, so why the sudden fear that it might become a problem? Besides, she was sure

Silas was the type of man who never let something as insignificant as love interfere in his relationships. After all, he had a corporation to run. Nothing, but nothing, was going to come before that.

Hester restlessly kicked the sheets into a heap at the foot of the bed. She had to stop thinking about Silas. He had disrupted her whole life in a matter of hours. How was that possible? She'd been just fine on the island until he came along. Hadn't she? Now that she gave it some consideration, was her existence on the island really enough? Had she really found the person she'd set out to find two years ago? If so, why did she remain in seclusion? Why didn't she return to mainstream society to discover whether Hester Somerset could handle it a little better than H.M. had?

"Oh, I'm so confused," she groaned quietly into her pillow. "What am I going to do?"

An answer was not to come to her that night. She dozed off and on fitfully until the first pink and orange fingers of light reached above the ocean. As usual, Hester woke with the sun, but this morning she felt exhausted, and for the first time in over two years, she had a headache.

Silas found her an hour later at the kitchen table, drinking coffee from a terra-cotta mug and stabbing violently at half a papaya. She wore a different pair of baggy khaki shorts today and a cutoff, sleeveless white T-shirt. Her hair was caught at her nape with an abalone barrette and streamed down her back in a dozen shades of copper and gold. As usual, she was barefoot.

"Good morning." Silas's greeting was like thunder in the quiet room. At the sound of his dark and honeyed voice, Hester jumped a little. Her nerves were still shaky from the previous evening's encounter.

"Morning." She tried to force brightness into her voice. "There's coffee on the stove and plenty of fruit. Eggs, too, if you want them."

"Coffee will be fine," Silas said, filling a mug for himself. "I never eat breakfast." He was well aware of the fact that she had yet to make eye contact with him.

"It's supposed to be the most important meal of the day," she informed him inanely.

"Hester."

He spoke her name like a boss would summon a secretary. She forgot about her papaya and turned in her chair to look at him. Despite his distant posture, he was impossibly sexy in dark blue designer shorts and a white polo shirt. His black hair was still damp from apparent washing, and a few unruly strands tumbled forward on his brow above tired blue eyes. Crisp black curls sprang from the V at his neck where his shirt was unbuttoned, and down the length of his muscular legs. Hester unconsciously chewed her lower lip.

"Hester, about last night," Silas began. He needed to clear the air.

"Please don't use that phrase," she pleaded, putting up her hand in protest. "It's trite and completely unnecessary. There's nothing to discuss."

"I think there is."

"Well, I can't right now. I have too much to do."

"Oh? Like what? Run to the supermarket? Pick up your cleaning? Take your cat to the vet?"

"I don't have a cat. Besides, there's no need to be sarcastic, Mr. Duran."

Silas glared at her.

"All right, Silas," she conceded.

"Thank you for that, anyway," he muttered.

"Actually, I am busy. I'm having a party tonight."

"A party?" Silas asked, surprise evident in his voice.

"The last Saturday of every month, everyone on the island meets at the hotel and we have a little get-together. You're lucky you came when you did."

"You're the second person who's told me I'm lucky to be here. I assure you, luck had nothing to do with it," Silas said caustically.

"That's not what Desmond says." Hester smiled sweetly, putting the memories of last night momentarily behind her.

"Oh, really? And when did you talk to Desmond?"

"He was by a little while ago," she told him as she popped a small piece of the papaya into her mouth and licked the juice from her fingers. Silas's gaze never left her hand. He wished her fingers were his own. "He used the radio to order your plane parts from St. Vincent. I hope you brought a credit card."

"Several. Desmond gets out early," Silas said grudgingly and sipped his coffee.

"Sometimes I don't think he ever sleeps. He said Jah had a special reason for dropping you here. There's no such thing as an accident. We'll just have to wait and find out what that reason is."

"Jah?" Silas asked. Hadn't Desmond said something to that effect yesterday?

"Desmond is a Rasta man."

"Is it painful for him?"

"No, I mean he's a Rastafarian." She laughed. Silas thought her laughter was one of the most beautiful sounds he'd ever heard. "The religion is based on the tenets of Christianity, but tempered with Caribbean and African influences. Jah is the name they give to God.

They're a very religious people. They put a lot of emphasis on loving one another and learning to live in harmony. Sounds like a nice idea, huh?''

"Yes," Silas agreed quietly.

"Anyway, Desmond thinks your life will be better and richer after you leave here, as a direct result of your stay on the island."

"Is that so?" Silas took another sip of his coffee. Like everything else on the island, it had an exotic, delicious flavor, much better than the silt he made at home.

"Good coffee," he commented for lack of anything better to say.

Hester grinned in a way that revealed a small dimple in her left cheek. Silas was enchanted.

"It's Puerto Rican. It's the best coffee on the planet Earth," she told him matter-of-factly.

"Compliments of Ford and his famous flying machine, I'll bet."

"We'd be lost without him."

For the second time in as many days, Silas felt jealous. He envied this man Hester needed and relied on. It must be nice, indeed, to be in a position to do things for her and be needed by her. He got the impression she was very self-reliant and seldom required aid from anyone. He hoped this Ford was grateful, then scowled as he considered the form that gratitude might take.

"What will you do when he retires?" Silas probed, trying to ascertain exactly what kind of relationship she shared with the other man.

"Oh, Ford won't be retiring for a while yet," Hester told him. "He's only thirty-two and in fantastic shape."

Silas wanted to shout, "How would you know?" at

the top of his lungs, but managed to stay in control. What was wrong with him? He'd never been jealous a day in his life where a woman was concerned. Hester brought out a primitive sort of possessiveness in him that Silas didn't understand. He wanted her all for himself, not sharing her with anyone, least of all French divers and rogue pilots. And if this was the way he felt after less than twenty-four hours, what kind of maniac would he be by the end of the week?

Before Hester returned to her preparations for the night's festivities, she led Silas to a small room off the lobby he hadn't noticed yesterday. Inside he found four walls of shelves overflowing with books. There were stacks of books on the floor, books on tables, books on chairs, everywhere. Even the window seat had been turned into yet another shelf of books.

"Welcome to the Island Library," she said, opening her arms in a sweeping and inviting gesture.

"This is what you meant when you said you read a lot," Silas guessed. "This is incredible."

"Ninety-nine percent of them were here when I came. A few are more recent acquisitions. No matter what you're in the mood for you'll find it here. Somewhere."

"How many have you read?" he challenged.

"All of some of them. Some of all of them."

"Clever."

Hester smiled again, revealing her dimple, and Silas grinned back at her.

He really should smile more often, she thought. He was quite…breathtaking when he did. As if to illustrate, she drew in a long breath before attempting to explain her system of cataloging.

"Fiction is on the left, nonfiction on the right. Beginning counterclockwise from the door it's mystery, comedy, historical novels, classics, drama, occult, biography, history, religion and science. With a few odds and ends thrown in. The ones on the floor are recent returns and those that I'm not sure can be cataloged.''

"Returns?"

"The others on the island are frequent borrowers of this particular library, especially Desmond and the General. And Diego, of course.''

"Diego?" Silas asked wearily. Would every man she mentioned be suspect to him and arouse feelings of jealousy?

"Diego Santos," Hester said. "He's a writer. He also owns the hotel."

"Diego Santos is a Cuban expatriate who won the Nobel Prize for literature last year," Silas stated numbly. No, he would not believe she was sharing an island with a Nobel prize winner.

"You know his work? He tells some terrific stories. You'll meet him tonight. All his books are on the window seat. Except for *El Barrio de Mi Papa*. Desmond borrowed that this morning."

"They're all in Spanish, I assume?" Silas asked.

"Oh, I forgot to ask if you speak Spanish," Hester said sheepishly.

"No. But you do, no doubt." Why was he not surprised?

Hester nodded.

"Diego's teaching you, right?"

"Actually his wife, Gabriela."

"Ah. I see."

"Well, I'm sure you'll find something to occupy your time," Hester finally said, excusing herself to the kitchen. "There's bound to be something here to interest you."

"No doubt about that," Silas assured her. He actually found several things that caught his attention, but settled on a Hemingway novel that seemed like appropriate island reading. He passed the remainder of the day, glued to a sand chair beneath a shady palm, completely wrapped up in the story. He hadn't read a novel for pleasure since high school and had forgotten how relaxing it could be to spend the better part of a day engrossed in a good story.

Silas had finished the book and was enjoying just sitting quietly on the beach when he became aware that Hester was near him. Her tanned bare feet peeked out from the sugary sand, the leather thong still wound around her ankle. A red-and-black flowered sarong was wrapped and knotted around her waist beneath a cropped black tank top. Her hair was unbound, shafts of gold, amber, copper and bronze cascading over her left shoulder. Tucked behind her right ear was one of the wild fragrant red blossoms he'd seen in the jungle. She was a vision standing there, looking like something wild and elemental, not quite ready to be tamed.

"Are you coming to my party or not?" she asked him teasingly.

Silas stood slowly and gazed down at Hester silently, then gently cupped her chin in his hand. He bent and placed a light, chaste kiss on her warm lips, now slightly parted in surprise.

"You're very beautiful, Hester," he stated simply.

"Thank you, Silas," she replied, puzzled. He seemed so serious and intense all of a sudden.

"So, you got a date to this shindig?" he asked on a lighter note.

"No." Hester smiled. "Usually I'm odd woman out, being hostess and all."

"Well, tonight may I offer my services as an escort? No charge."

"I'd be delighted," she confessed honestly.

"What time do the guests arrive?"

"In about half an hour."

"Are these affairs usually black tie?" Silas asked, carrying the charade as long as he could keep her smiling. The comings and goings of her dimple were fascinating.

"Black tie is strictly optional." Hester laughed. "Oh, Silas, I had no idea you could be so silly."

"Neither did I," he confided, and meant it. "Neither did I."

He changed quickly into his gray trousers, but this time donned a gray-and-white striped T-shirt. Feeling suitably tropical, he descended the stairs and found Hester putting the finishing touches to the lobby. Colorful paper lanterns were strung festively across the room, while each table sported a small candle lamp and arrangement of fresh jungle flowers. The bar and buffet were set up for easy self-service. Again the music on the stereo was reggae. Beyond the door and windows the blue-green Caribbean beckoned, and palms swayed and danced to the mellow music. Silas would recall the scene many times upon his return to New York as he watched the snarled traffic and hustling street crowds from his office window.

"You have a gorgeous place here, Hester," he told her softly, stopping by the door to the beach. "It's so relaxing, so serene. Like no place I've ever seen before."

Hester strode over to stand beside him and nodded

in understanding. The long silvery-white beach and green, green jungle only enhanced the clear turquoise beauty of the ocean. It was like living in a postcard. "I know how you feel," she said. "I'm still astounded by how lovely it all is. Nothing man-made even comes close."

Silas was quiet for a moment before asking the question that had been bothering him since he'd first laid eyes on her. "What are you doing here, anyway?"

"What do you mean?"

"You said you grew up in the Bronx, but somehow you came to this island and never left it. That's a pretty big change. How'd it come about?"

The last thing Hester wanted to do right now was get into a discussion of her past with Silas. She had guests coming, after all, and as a hostess, it was her responsibility to keep everyone happy. After the way Silas had gone on about his man in Rio and the irresponsibility crisis at Duran Industries, she didn't think he was going to like what she had to say about leaving her job without notice and rejecting her obligations there to escape to a simpler existence. Especially when he learned that she had done it on the morning of perhaps the most important contract signing the company had ever known.

"I didn't like the way the weather kept changing in New York," she said evasively. "Seems like every year at about the same time it would get really cold. Sometimes for months at a time. I finally had to move south."

"What about your life there? Career? Friends? Family?"

He would put career first and family last, she thought sardonically. "I wasn't close to my family," she told him. "I never knew my parents. My grandmother raised me until I was a teenager."

"But what about...?"

Silas never got to finish his question because at that moment they were joined by Desmond and Diego and Gabriela Santos. Hester was glad to see them for a variety of reasons, not the least of which was that their appearance bailed her out of an uncomfortable situation. She didn't want to lie to Silas, but she didn't want him to know about her past, either. It would only make what was already a bizarre and uneasy situation even more difficult. She enthusiastically greeted each of her guests with a kiss on the cheek and introduced them to Silas.

"Señor Santos." Silas gripped the writer's hand in greeting. "It's a privilege to meet you."

"Oh, please, call me Diego," the white-haired man said warmly. "I am very pleased to meet you as well. Desmond has explained your circumstances to us. It is very fortunate that you found our island when you did." He had an agreeable, open face and smiled frequently and without reservation. Silas liked him immediately. The woman at Diego's side was introduced as Gabriela Santos, a robust woman with piercing black eyes and flaming red hair coiled into a chignon. A brightly flowered muumuu flowed to her ankles, effectively disguising her ample figure. She, too, was easygoing and full of laughter, and obviously delighted at Silas's sudden materialization on the island.

General Ruben Morales and his wife, Teresa, arrived shortly thereafter. Like Diego, the General was dressed in white pants and a *guayabera* shirt. But where Diego was somewhat short and heavyset, General Morales was tall and fit, taller even than Silas. To make up for the considerable loss of hair on his gray head, the General had grown a bushy moustache that all but covered his mouth. Though not as inclined to laughter as the others, he made Silas feel comfortable and disposed to conversation.

Teresa Morales was as small as her husband was large, and although quieter and more reserved than the others, she was every bit as friendly. Silas noted throughout the evening that the Moraleses rarely left sight of each other. They seemed a very devoted and loving couple.

By the time Hester had served rum and tonics and rum punches to everyone, the biologists had arrived. Silas was at last able to meet the notorious Jean-Luc Reynard, as well as another student, Nicole Boulanger, and their professor, Fabienne Auclaire. He nodded briefly and politely to the two women, but his attention was centered fully on their male companion. The picture he'd carried in his mind was disturbingly accurate, except for the Speedo. Tonight Jean-Luc wore tight, faded Levi's and a form-fitting olive drab T-shirt. Studying his youthful, handsome face, Silas guessed his age to be about twenty-three. The little creep. He watched Hester greet the Frenchman with a kiss as she had all the others and nearly shattered his glass with his angry, white-knuckled grip. He was really going to have to do something to alleviate his jealousy. Like make savage love to Hester over and over again until she could think of nothing but him, craving only his touch, whispering only his name. He wanted to bury himself deep inside her with such an intensity as to make her forget all other men. He was startled that he wanted her so badly. It meant he was losing control of his emotions. And more than anything else, Silas hated not being in control.

Despite his disturbing thoughts and the annoying presence of Jean-Luc, Silas enjoyed the evening more than any he could remember. The parties he went to in New York were usually dry and business related, or else society fund-raisers of some kind. Either he spent the entire evening making deals with stone-faced, mercenary-minded men, or he was trying to survive the advances of false-faced, mercenary-minded women. Either way, he went home at night feeling as though he'd been an object of someone's opportunism or lust, be it financial or sexual.

Because of his wealth, business position and social standing, people often tried to use him to forward their own lives through deals, design or deceit, whatever their ultimate motives were. Here, however, no one wanted anything from him except engaging conversation and pleasant company. Silas was happy to comply. He spent much of the evening sitting on the veranda with Diego and General Morales, staring at the ocean, absorbed in Diego's stories of pre-Communist Cuba and in the General's accounts of Latin American politics. Silas basked in the warmth of new friendship, sipping his rum and tonic and puffing contentedly on the Cuban cigar Diego had given him.

"This is one fine cigar, Diego," he told the writer. Then he added somewhat wistfully, "You can't get these in the States, unfortunately."

"There is nothing as satisfying as a cigar from Havana," Diego announced decisively after a deep draw from his own. "Especially when it is enjoyed in such surroundings as these. Beautiful island, good friends, interesting conversation. And a lovely woman with whom to share it all. We are indeed very lucky, are we not, Ruben?''

''As usual, Diego, you have put my own thoughts into words,'' General Morales responded. ''Tell me, Silas, are you a married man?''

Silas's head snapped up in surprise. ''What? Me? No. No, I've never been married.''

''Why not?'' Diego asked.

Silas shrugged. ''I've never given it any thought, really. My job is very demanding. I don't have much time for a family.''

Diego made a clucking sound of disapproval. ''No job is as important as a family,'' he stated knowingly. ''You should make time.''

Silas wanted to protest, to defend his choice of his life-style, but something in Diego's voice prohibited him. It was the absoluteness of conviction with which he spoke. Maybe the man knew what he was talking about, Silas thought. Then immediately he corrected himself. Diego knew what was right for Diego. Silas knew what was right for himself. And he wasn't a family man. Was he? No, certainly not.

As Silas wrestled with personal choices, Hester was inside the hotel with the other women, lounging about the lobby. Normally she was the most active member in the conversations the women shared once a month, but tonight she was noticeably quiet. Gabriela, understanding the probable reason for Hester's preoccupation, but wanting to draw her out, ventured a comment she was certain would get results.

''Well, I don't know about you, Teresa,'' she said playfully after a comfortable lull in the discussion, ''but if it weren't for Diego, I might be a little envious of Hester and her new man.''

"My what?" Hester gasped, nearly dropping her rum punch.

"I know what you mean, Gabriela," Teresa replied, ignoring Hester's reaction and enjoying the game. "He reminds me so much of my Ruben when he was that age. So virile and overwhelming."

"Please, you two." Hester laughed nervously. "Quit kidding around. He'll hear you."

"Who's kidding?" Nicole joined in spiritedly. "He's the best-looking man I've seen in a long time."

"Don't let Jean-Luc hear you say that, Nicole," Fabienne cautioned. "You know it would break his heart."

It was no secret on the island that Jean-Luc was hopelessly smitten by the dark-eyed, chestnut-haired Nicole.

"He can hardly keep his mind on his research as it is because of the heartless way you snub him," Fabienne added. "Besides, you're much too young for Monsieur Duran. I think he needs a decidedly more experienced woman. Like me."

Hester couldn't disguise the panic in her expression. Fabienne was about Silas's age, and very attractive with her dark auburn hair and green eyes. She was also very articulate and intelligent. And French. What more could a man possibly want? Did Silas like the scholarly type? He probably didn't have a lot of prerequisites where women were concerned. As long as the word, "yes," or *"oui,"* occurred frequently in their vocabulary. Was Fabienne planning on testing her theory?

"Hester, don't look so alarmed. I was only joking. It's obvious that you and Silas harbor a *grand passion* for each other. I couldn't turn his head if I wanted to."

"I have no idea what you're talking about, Fabienne." Hester shrugged unconvincingly. "There's absolutely nothing between Silas and me."

Four female faces turned to Hester and accused silently, Oh really?

"Well, there's not," Hester insisted. "We have nothing in common, and we disagree about everything."

"Some of the great romantic classics begin that way, you know," Gabriela informed her loftily. "You're in very good company, literarily speaking of course."

"But books and real life are two entirely different things," Hester protested.

"Don't be so sure." Teresa smiled mysteriously and lifted a hand to tuck a few salt-and-pepper curls behind her ear. "Remember the story I told you of how I met Ruben?"

"You're right, Teresa. But then you and the General are a rather exceptional couple."

"That's true," Teresa sighed.

"Why Madame Morales," Nicole said with a hint of discovery in her voice, "your eyes are positively twinkling. You never told me the story."

"Some stories are best kept for more appropriate times, dear," Teresa replied cryptically. "Right now I think I'd like to dance with my husband."

Both Teresa and Gabriela collected their husbands and turned the cotton dhurrie rug in the lobby into a dance floor.

When Silas joined Hester on the sofa, he had a strange expression on his face.

"What's wrong?" she asked him.

"Wrong? Nothing's wrong. Everything is frighteningly perfect here. I just can't shake the feeling that I've left the planet Earth and found Shangri-la."

''What makes you think you haven't?''

Silas raised his eyebrows at that, unable to answer truthfully. He watched the two older couples dancing slowly, embracing one another with such obvious and deep affection. He thought about what Diego had said earlier about families and felt a sudden emptiness within himself. What would his life be like in twenty-five or thirty years? he wondered. If he were to retire from Duran Industries when he turned sixty, as his father had, what would he do? He didn't think he'd take an interest in horse breeding as his father did. Amanda and Ethan already had plans to sail around the world together, jumping ship wherever they found a potential adventure. But Silas didn't consider himself much of a sailor. The few times he'd been out on their boat, he'd gotten violently ill. The Moraleses had retired to the island ten years ago and spent their time simply enjoying each other's company. What would Silas do? And who would take over the business if he did retire? When he died, so would the Duran name. Even if Amanda had children, which she'd made clear was highly unlikely, they would be MacKenzies, not Durans. No, he would probably run DI until they carried him out feet first. Why retire when there was nothing to retire to? He might just as well work himself to death.

Thoughts such as these usually brought on Silas's inevitable headaches, chest pains and stomach knottings. But this time, he noted with awe, they were nowhere to be found. In fact, he hadn't felt the tiniest twinge of his normal physical ailments since he'd arrived at the hotel. For someone whose regular diet lately seemed to consist of pills in brown plastic bottles and tablets in shiny aluminum foil, this was a significant development. Although Silas had packed all his prescriptions, he hadn't felt the need for any of them.

"Care to dance?" he asked Hester, surprising them both.

"No, I don't think so," she said. "I don't dance very well."

"How can anyone not dance to this music?" Silas was insistent. "It's wonderful."

"Oh, so you like de raggedy everyday stuff, do you?" Hester inquired in her best calypso accent.

"Desmond said it was called reggae," Silas said, somewhat confused.

"Same ting, mon."

"I've never heard of it before. I like it."

"Honestly, Silas, for such an experienced man, you sure have missed out on a lot in life. Pick up some Bob Marley tapes when you get back to New York. It will do wonders for your attitude."

"Bob Marley, huh?" he mumbled, distracted. He was beginning to agree with her that he had missed out on plenty in his life. "Come on, let's dance. You deserve to party, too, you know."

Before she could decline again, he took her hand and pulled her to her feet. By this time Nicole and Jean-Luc were among the dancers, and Desmond was now Gabriela's partner while Diego took Fabienne for a spin around the dance floor.

To ensure a little privacy among the crowd, Silas guided Hester to a corner of the lobby that was obscured by large potted plants. No one seemed to notice their retreat. Silas drew her closely into his arms, leaving not even a breath of space between them, and Hester's senses reeled at once again being so near him. He smelled of the tropics, his big body warm and hard against hers. She let her fingertips play lightly up and down his muscled back and sighed when he tightened his hold on her.

Silas's lungs filled with the sweet fragrance of the blossom behind her ear, and his fingers tangled in the silky strands of her hair. He pulled it gently until her head tipped back to expose the soft skin at the juncture of her neck and shoulder. Bending his head, he kissed her there, kisses so whisper light, Hester wondered if perhaps she had imagined them.

They danced on in silence for some time, getting used to the feel of each other's bodies, becoming familiar with all the intricacies that made them so different from each other and at the same time so complementary. Hester became lost in Silas's embrace, forgetting everything except the strong arms that held her so tenderly.

Her thoughts and feelings of intimacy were invaded when General Morales and Teresa reluctantly began saying their good evenings. Before long everyone had called it a night and set off for home.

After Silas and Hester cleaned up the postparty remains, they retired to the veranda for a nightcap. The evening was warm and balmy, and the Caribbean lapped quietly at the shore.

"It's remarkable," Silas commented after a few moments of companionable silence, "that on an island so tiny, with such a small population, there's such an abundance of experience."

"What do you mean?" Hester asked, liking the relaxed atmosphere the two of them were able to enjoy together.

"There's such a variety of people and past lives. Everyone here has an interesting story to tell. If I invited nine business associates to my home, I guarantee it would be one repetitious and dull evening.''

''How so?''

''Everyone I know lives the same way. They all have similar experiences, identical to my own. There would be nothing to learn from the conversations. Except for maybe a few investment tips.''

Not knowing how to respond, Hester remained quiet and took a sip of her drink.

''Tonight I heard just about everyone's story but yours, Hester. Just what chain of events landed you here? You're a puzzle to me. What made you leave New York for destinations south?''

''Silas, trust me when I say you wouldn't understand.''

''Was it a man?'' he asked levelly, bracing himself for her answer. Somehow he wasn't sure he could handle it if she were carrying a torch for some jerk who'd abandoned her.

''No, it was nothing like that,'' she assured him. Then she thought about that long ago July evening that had caused her to change her way of life in the ghetto. She thought about Micky Scoletti and added quietly, ''Not in the way you think, anyway.''

''What then? Tell me.''

''Look, just suffice it to say I was unhappy and needed a change of scenery,'' she said sharply. ''It's really much too late to go into it tonight.''

Hester rose abruptly from her chair to leave, but Silas caught her wrist before she could flee. Still seated, he held her firmly and took a long sip of his drink before speaking.

''I'll let it go for now,'' he told her, his blue eyes silver in the moonlight as he looked up at her. ''But

I'll know what brought you here before I leave this island. I intend to know everything about you.''

He continued to hold her wrist as he set down his glass and stood to face her, pulling her roughly toward him, encircling her waist with his other arm.

''I intend to discover even the most intimate details about you,'' he promised.

With that his lips came down to claim hers in a searing kiss that caught her by surprise and left her breathless. When her lips parted in shock, his tongue entered her mouth and casually explored, then retreated to trace a delicate line around her lips. Hester was certain that she would melt from the heat he sent coursing through her body.

''You look so beautiful tonight,'' he whispered reverently when he finally pulled away. His eyes blazed with hunger, and Hester could feel the stirrings of his arousal against her abdomen. She closed her eyes as she felt all the strength leave her legs.

''You look so native, so savage in that outfit,'' Silas continued ''All evening I could only think about unwrapping you to see what's underneath. I want you, Hester. Right here, right now. Let's make love on the beach.''

''Silas, this is crazy,'' she protested. But she, too, wanted desperately to lose herself in his arms. His touch did things to her that she'd never felt in her life. She wanted to be careless and let her emotions run wild to see where they would take her. She'd never felt such desire before she met Silas. Now she wanted to let it run its course, to know the full extent of unbridled passion. But it was still too soon, she reminded herself. She needed to remind him, too. ''We barely know each other,'' she ground out, trying to sound confident of that fact, even if she wasn't.

"I think we both know enough to realize there's something between us that's too strong to ignore." His fingertips skimmed teasingly at the hem of her short tank top, moving inch by leisurely inch across her ribs until his hand rested below the swell of her breast, luxuriating in the velvety softness of her skin. Cautiously and tenderly, he cupped her breast with his big palm, weighing its heaviness. Hester allowed a groan of need to escape her.

Silas smiled predatorily and rubbed a callused thumb over the rigid peak of her breast, already hard with anticipation. He couldn't stand denying himself any longer. When Hester closed her eyes and rolled back her head in surrender, he lifted her top to expose the soft globes. He was right about her lack of a tan line. Her breasts were full and beautiful, and as bronzed as the rest of her. Silas growled like a hungry animal and lowered his head to take first one then the other into his thirsty mouth. While he suckled the turgid peak of one breast, his hand roamed freely over the other, gently squeezing its fullness and caressing its pebbly bud.

Hester buried her hands in Silas's dark, silky hair and held him there, overcome by the sensations his tongue and fingers excited. His other hand splayed across the small of her back, urgently pressing, arching her back in a way to bring her closer so that he could fill his mouth with her softness. She was so warm and inviting, insistent even, as she pulled him closer to her. Silas lost himself in his ministrations, unable and unwilling to let her go.

Slowly Hester grew unconscious of the world around

her, lost completely to physical sensations and the pleasure Silas's mouth was giving her. Never in her life had she felt so all consumed. Her mind and senses were entirely out of control and she wasn't sure she wanted it any differently. Her fumblings with Leo had never prepared her for an onslaught such as the one Silas was creating inside her. She felt like a hot rushing river, helplessly winding toward a waterfall that went crashing into an unknown abyss. She had to do something to slow her runaway emotions before she went hurtling toward certain disaster.

"Oh, God, Silas," she cried when she was able to find her voice. "Stop it. You're driving me crazy."

"Good, it's working," he rasped heatedly against her warm skin and went back to enticing her with his tongue.

Hester's fingers in his hair loosened and her hands fell defeatedly to his shoulders. "Please, Silas," she finally sobbed. "I can't handle this. It's just too much for me to endure."

At the sound of desperation in her voice, Silas paused. Still holding her, he straightened and looked down into her face. When he saw the fear in her overly bright amber eyes, he began to understand. Slowly, without breaking eye contact, he pulled her top back into place and lifted his hands to her shoulders. Hester blinked, and two fat tears escaped, making a silent journey down her cheeks.

"It's been a long time for you, hasn't it?" he asked quietly. "And I'm pushing you too hard."

"It's just…" Hester began, then faltered.

"Shh," Silas coaxed, using his thumb this time to brush the tears from her face. "You don't have to explain anything."

She drew a ragged breath and took a step back from him, turning to stare at the ocean and the moon's watery reflection on the waves.

"I'm obviously not as experienced as you are," she stated simply, her voice trembling a little.

"Hester…"

"No, let me finish. I've only been sexually involved with one man, and it was a very brief, very unfulfilling affair. I'm not used to the kind of fireworks I feel when you touch me. My reactions to you frighten me. A lot." She hesitated before she finished reluctantly, "Especially when I realize this type of thing is such a standard, sort of commonplace experience for you."

Standard? Commonplace? He wanted to shout at her that she shook him to the very depth of his soul! He was no more accustomed to the explosive feelings she aroused in him than she was to the fireworks she described. Her accusation left him speechless. He had to find a way to make her understand that despite his somewhat numerous liaisons, he'd never, in any way, found someone to spark his emotions, not to mention his libido, the way she had. But he was too shocked at his own reactions to be able to reassure her that she touched him as no one else ever had.

Hester mistakenly took his silence to mean that her assumptions about him were correct. That she was, in fact, just another sexy piece he wanted to enjoy for a little while. If she had turned to confront him, she would have seen the desperation and confusion on his face, but she didn't. Instead she quickly muttered, "I'm sorry," and ignored Silas when he called her name as she fled to the safety of her room. For the first time since coming to the island, she wished she had a lock for her door.

Chapter Four

Sunday morning dawned bright and beautiful, just as the two days before had been. Only two days since he'd come here, Silas marveled as he stood at the French doors in his room. Again he beheld the vista of blues and greens before him, and again he was stunned by the sense of tranquillity that surrounded him like a warm embrace. Despite the late nights and sexual tension he'd been experiencing, he felt calmer and more rested than he had in some time.

A sound below him brought his attention down to the wide path that led from the hotel to the edge of the ocean. Hester emerged from the building in a pale yellow maillot, her braid swinging temptingly above her fanny. In one hand she carried her mask and snorkel, in the other her swim fins and mesh bag.

"Good morning," Silas called down to her, hoping

she didn't harbor any ill will toward him after last night's steamy interlude.

Hester thought it incredible the way just the sound of his rough morning voice could send her temperature skyrocketing. She'd hoped to get away from the hotel while Silas was still asleep and stay clear of him for as long as she could. After last night, she wasn't sure how she was going to behave normally around him. However, it seemed she wouldn't be given the luxury of escape. The barracuda had caught her, and now she would have to let nature take its course.

Reluctantly she stopped and turned to meet his eyes. Wearing only white silk pajama bottoms, he was quite intimidating and unbearably sexy. Muscles bunched in his forearms where he leaned on the veranda railing, and rippled poetically everywhere else she could see. The crisp black curls swirling about his chest and plunging down his abdomen made her fingers itch to bury themselves there. His sleep-tousled hair added a soft, vulnerable quality to his otherwise self-assured stance. How could she still feel badly toward him? He looked so...lovable.

"Good morning, Silas," Hester said with resignation. Since leaving New York, she had become a faithful follower of the what-will-be-will-be school of thought. Silas was going to be here for another four days and nights. She might as well try to make the best of it.

"You're out early," he told her, relieved that she was speaking civilly to him.

"I'm in the mood for seafood salad, and I need some crabmeat. Early in the day seems the best time to go crabbing around here. You can catch them off guard because they're just turning in."

"Late night partying types, are they?" Silas commented.

Hester nodded, uncertain whether she should extend an invitation to him. If he accepted, and they wound up spending the day together, it could get awkward. Eventually they were going to have to face their feelings for each other. Or at least, she would have to face her feelings toward him. Would sooner necessarily be better? She'd rather avoid it for as long as possible. She wondered if there was any chance she could spend the rest of the week with the Moraleses.

Silas saved her the trouble of deciding by volunteering his services as an assistant, but cautioned, "I've never been snorkeling before. You'll have to teach me. And hold my hand." He smiled that delicious smile of his and promised to be right down. Moments later he appeared at the door in a pair of pale blue trunks, one of Hester's turquoise beach towels thrown over his shoulder. The colors must have enhanced the blue of his eyes, because they seemed to spark brighter as they blazed over her from head to toe. He was magnificent, Hester thought, her face growing warm as memories of last night assailed her. Such thoughts, and the sight of him now, reinforced her suspicions that he would be a devastating lover.

"There's some extra snorkeling gear in the closet by the stairs," she told him, hoping her voice didn't betray the direction of her thoughts. "Help yourself." Then as an afterthought, she shouted after him. "Get some sunscreen from the bathroom, too. At least SPF 8. Stronger if I have any left." To herself she muttered, "You're going to need it."

While they trekked up the beach, Hester explained the basics of snorkeling to Silas, including proper breathing techniques and the correct way to wear his mask. The reef where they'd be crabbing was a coral one teeming with life very near the shore. The water remained shallow quite a distance out from the beach, so there was little danger of currents or large predators.

"Actually there's a much nicer spot for snorkeling," she admitted. "It's up the beach in the other direction. But that's where the biologists are working, and I try to keep out of their way."

"When will they be done with their study?" Silas asked.

"It's a year-long look at the reefs around the island, so I guess it will be about nine months before they head back to civilization."

"Civilization," he repeated. "Sometimes I wonder. Especially where cities like New York are concerned. At times it can be the most primitive and brutal place on earth."

Hester nodded in agreement, but was surprised that the statement had come from Silas. It sounded more like something she would have said herself.

After they'd gone about a quarter mile up the beach, Hester dropped her towel and headed immediately toward the water with her mask and fins. Silas did likewise, but followed uncertainly. The water was cool and clear, barely making even the tiniest of swells. Even where it was chest high, he found he could look down into it and see his feet as though peering through flawed glass. He watched Hester deftly slip into her fins and mask, then tried to imitate her actions with equal dexterity. After struggling for a few moments and ducking involuntarily below the surface a few times, Silas finally managed to work his feet into his fins and yank the mask over his head. He heard Hester's muffled laughter at his antics, but stoically chose to ignore it.

"See that area over there where the water looks dark?" she asked after he'd gotten accustomed to his gear, gesturing toward a large shady place in the water near them. "That's where we'll be snorkeling. Don't touch any part of the reef, because some of the corals are as sharp as razors. They can look harmless, but they're not, and some sting like crazy. Anemones, too, can sting, even though they look like flowers or other corals, so be careful. There are a lot of fish, some of them pretty big, but they won't bother you. To them, you're just another fish, bigger and clumsier, and not nearly as attractive as they are." At this comment, Silas made a face at her, but she continued with a smile. "I'm going to try to grab a few crabs from the floor if I can, but that takes a certain technique and months of practice, so don't try to help me unless you want to get pinched. Hard. Okay?"

Silas nodded dumbly, trying to remember all the rules of this new game.

"Any questions?" Hester asked one last time.

"Should I just go back and wait for you on the beach?" Silas inquired hopefully. Maybe this snorkeling thing wasn't such a good idea after all.

"No, just be careful." She laughed. "I think you're really going to enjoy this. We'll be right below the water's surface, so if you want to ask me anything, just tap my shoulder and we can come up."

"Okay," Silas agreed with more confidence than he felt. "I'm ready."

They wet their masks and lowered them onto their faces, testing them for leakage. On the count of three they submerged, and Silas found himself caught up in a world like none he could ever have imagined. It took him a few minutes to get used to the fins on his feet, and more than once he found himself with a mouthful of saltwater where fresh air should have been. But once he mastered his equipment, he allowed himself to swim about freely.

The reef wasn't an overly large one, but it contained more color and movement than Silas had ever seen. Almost immediately upon submerging he was surrounded by a school of tiny silver fish. Sunlight filtered through the water in wavy rays, creating speckles of light all over the ocean floor. Everywhere he looked were splashes of bright color. Fuschia sea fans swayed gracefully all along the reef, dotted here and there with fiery crimson anemones. A huge dun-colored brain coral squatted at one end of the reef, surrounded by smaller, purplish-gray mushroom coral. On the reef itself, corals of ocher and amethyst danced in the ocean current invitingly. Silas found himself wanting to reach out to them, but stopped when he remembered Hester's warning.

There were fish, too. Lots of fish. Some were over two feet long, but as promised, kept to themselves. Brilliantly colored damselfish cruised around him in blues, purples, oranges, silvers and reds, their expressions bored in contrast to the riot of colors on their bodies.

There was a surreal quality to the place, Silas thought. Sounds were muffled, movements slow, the light abstract. He felt weightless and graceful, as if in a dream. If he'd been awed by the beauty of the island, he was even more astonished at the wonders he found in the ocean.

He was so caught up in the experience that he actually forgot about Hester until he saw a hermit crab scurrying across the ocean floor. He looked around and saw her at the other end of the reef, her mesh bag billowing out behind her, already containing several crabs. He swam to her and placed his hand softly on her bare back. When he pointed to the surface she nodded, and they swam to where the water was shallower before they came up.

"So what did you think?" she asked when she'd stood and removed her snorkel, pushing her mask to the top of her head.

"I've never seen anything like it!" Silas exclaimed animatedly. He'd removed his mask altogether. "The colors are unbelievable! I never imagined anything underwater could be so alive. It's like an entire beautiful city unto itself down there."

Hester laughed openly, and to Silas it was a musical sound.

"What's so funny?" he asked.

"You," she confessed, grinning at him.

"What about me?"

"Look at you. Big, powerful corporate CEO, owner of all he surveys, overwhelmed by a simple coral reef the same way a little boy would be."

"So?" Silas challenged. "Are you making fun of me?"

"Of course not. It's just the incongruity of the whole thing. I think it's so wonderful that you have the ability to see the beauty surrounding you, Silas. Too many people spend their entire time on Earth ignorant of the most basic gifts life has to offer. It's nice to know you aren't one of them."

It was then that Silas realized his desire to have her extended far beyond his physical need. She had voiced exactly what it was about herself that he found so irresistible, the reason she so fascinated him.

"But I was one of them," he stated plainly. "Until I came here. Until I met you." He gently pulled her mask from her head and gathered her weightless body into his arms. "You put things into a whole new perspective, Hester. I don't think I'll be quite the same man when I go back to New York."

When she saw he meant to kiss her, Hester grew resistant. She still hadn't come to terms with what had happened last night and didn't want to become even more confused. She slipped from his arms and said evasively, "I think a trip to the islands leaves everyone with a new outlook on life. Don't worry, I'm sure it will only be temporary. You'll be yourself again in no time." Quickly she added, "We'd better rest for a while. We've been down nearly an hour." She hurriedly turned and headed toward the shore.

Silas was stung by her comment that suggested he would resume his old habits once he returned to his job in New York, and it caused him to sound angry when he said, "An hour? That's impossible." Reluctantly he followed her out of the water still smarting from her prediction and the fact that she had eluded his kiss. "How can you tell it's been an hour when you never wear a watch?" he bit out stiffly.

"I just know," she retorted, similarly perturbed that their moment of peace had too fast become a time of antagonism again. "Look at your own watch if you don't believe me."

Silas checked the expensive gold timepiece he had carelessly dropped onto his beach towel earlier. They had been in the water for nearly an hour. He grumbled something unintelligible, lay down on his stomach and closed his eyes.

"You'd better put on some sunscreen if you're planning on staying in the sun," he heard her warn.

"I never burn," he informed her.

"Famous last words."

When it appeared that he intended to lie there unprotected, Hester fished the lotion from under their drying gear and filled her palm with a generous amount. As she began rubbing it gently onto Silas's back, he turned his head to face her and growled, "Just what do you think you're doing?"

"Silas, you're fewer than fourteen degrees north of the equator. Does that mean anything to you? Like maybe the sun's rays might be just a teeny bit more intense and harmful than they are on Long Beach?"

"There's really no need to be sarcastic, Hester."

She relented somewhat, but still wanted to emphasize the importance of protecting his skin from the dangerous intensity of the sun this far south.

"Your skin might not be as lily-white as mine was when I got here," she told him, "but you could burn every bit as badly as I did."

"You got a bad burn?" Hester's heart skipped two beats when she heard the obvious concern in his voice.

"I was a little overzealous, and I paid for it by being sick for days. I don't want to see the same thing happen to you."

She squeezed more of the fragrant lotion into her hand and turned her attention from Silas's back to his shoulders and arms. His hard muscles beneath her fingertips flexed and relaxed, the coarse hairs on his arms springing softly in response to her touch. Her breathing grew a little erratic as she decided a man's arms had to be his sexiest physical feature. Especially the arms of this particular man.

"This sunburn you got," Silas continued their conversation, his voice now noticeably less gruff.

"Yes?" Hester prodded as she began to put sunscreen on his long, lean, muscular legs.

Silas made a contented sound before asking, "Did you get that before or after you started sunbathing topless? I couldn't help but notice last night that you have a great tan. All over."

Hester told herself the reason she lost her grip on the bottle was that her hand was so slippery from the lotion. She quickly picked it up again and finished her task, trying to hide the color she knew must be rising in her face.

"I, uh," she stammered. It was impossible to meet his eyes. "When I first got here, I couldn't resist the urge to go native. Everything was so primeval and lush. My nearest neighbors were a good mile away. I started going swimming and even on fruit-picking excursions into the jungle topless. It was an exercise in freedom. Very exhilarating, too, I might add."

"I can imagine." Boy, could he imagine.

"Since the biologists have come, though, I've tried to be a little more, uh, decorous. They have a tendency to show up unannounced sometimes."

"Please don't let *my* presence inhibit you," Silas urged, his good humor returning quickly now that he saw that he still had the ability to unsettle her.

Hester shot him what she hoped was a killing look and started to replace the cap on the bottle of sunscreen. Silas turned then to lie on his back, placing his hands comfortably behind his head.

"Aren't you going to do my front, too?" he queried, grinning smugly.

I ought to just let him fry, she thought, but instead of recapping the bottle, she knelt and oozed more of the sunscreen onto her hands, slowly and sensuously massaging the lotion into his chest. His skin was already warm from the sun, attracting her hands like a magnet, and the rough hair on his chest tangled around her fingers as if trying to trap them there. Like his arms, his chest was lightly corded with muscles, and it struck Hester that perhaps she had been too rash in thinking a man's arms were his sexiest feature.

As her hands kneaded lower toward his belly, Silas felt his heartbeat quicken wildly. Wherever her hands touched, he burned, a sweet fire that threatened to rage out of control. When her wandering fingers neared the waistband of his trunks, he suddenly caught her wrists sharply and lifted them only a hairsbreadth from his body. As her eyes met his, Hester saw the passion that dilated his pupils until only a ring of blue surrounded them, as the Caribbean enveloped the island.

They stared at each other for a long time, then Silas, still imprisoning her wrists, slowly and deliberately pulled her down to him until her lips were close enough to capture with his own. His kiss was fierce and unpracticed, a completely instinctive response to the desire she'd raised in him with her caresses. Hester returned his kiss with equal abandon, as aroused from their physical contact as he, realizing how impossible it was to resist him. She wanted him, too, and knew she would ultimately submit to the yearning her body and heart felt so acutely for this man. It was going to happen, she decided. Her need for Silas was as much a part of her as her own heart was. She would allow herself to be swept away by her emotions for now and enjoy her few days left with him. She wouldn't let herself think about the time when he would be gone. Not yet.

Silas's kiss intensified, and when Hester felt his tongue dart out over her lips she parted them, inviting the invasion by entwining it with her own. Once Silas understood that she was welcoming his overtures instead of trying to deny him, he became ravenous. He rolled her over onto her towel so that she lay stretched out beneath him, his muscular thigh wedged snugly between her own. With his left hand, he trapped her arms above her head, while his right went exploring on its own, cupping and massaging first one breast, then the other. Hester arched her back eagerly, which brought her into hard contact with Silas's thigh. Her gasp was swathed in his kisses, but he comprehended its meaning. He stroked his hand down her rib cage, across her belly, then lower, to where the heart of her femininity ached for his touch. Tightening his grip on her wrists, he tentatively caressed her there, and Hester gasped again, rolling her head back deliriously.

Silas lifted his head to study her face as he stroked her a second time, then a third. Hester moaned helplessly, her eyes glazed with passion. With sure fingers, he gently pushed aside the fabric of her swimsuit. Long fingers pressed tenderly against her velvet softness until she sighed. "Oh, Silas." He smiled at his effect on her and kissed her again, his tongue deeply penetrating her mouth at the same moment his fingers ventured farther. She arched her back feverishly higher against him, feeling the surging strength of him straining against her.

"Oh, God, Hester. I want to make love to you,"

Silas panted as he finally broke their kiss. "Say that's what you want, too."

Hester was completely dazed. Once his hand had dipped below her waist, she had become a quivering mass of raw nerves, a being whose life's purpose was to receive erotic pleasure. She heard Silas's voice through a silver fog of passion and knew she should respond. Yet her own voice had escaped along with her good sense and she could only lie there wanting him.

"Let's go back to the hotel," she heard him say a little more clearly as he released her wrists and arranged her swimsuit back into place.

"Last night you wanted to make love on the beach," she finally managed to whisper.

"Too much sand. I want you in a cool bed where I can set you on fire. Someplace where we can enjoy each other all day. And all night."

Making love with Silas for hours sounded like a good idea to Hester, too, and she nodded her assent.

"I'd like that, too, Silas," she told him with a shaky smile.

They held each other quietly for several minutes until they calmed down to a point where they could stand on legs that didn't tremble. She looked over at the spot where she had dropped the mesh crab bag, only to realize belatedly that she had neglected to tie it shut. All but one of the crabs had made a jailbreak, leaving little crab tracks as they beat a hasty retreat back to the sea.

"Looks like we'll be having light meals today," she said as she turned the bag upside down and freed the remaining crustacean.

"Oh, I wouldn't necessarily say that," Silas contradicted. "I intend to satisfy a very big appetite when we get back to the hotel." His eyes and smile were full of promise as he collected their towels and snorkeling gear. "And I intend to take all day to do it."

They walked back down the beach toward the hotel hand in hand, trading heated glances all the way. Occasionally they stopped to embrace when the inches of distance between them became intolerable. By the time they reached the hotel they had worked up a tremendous hunger for each other. But when they entered the lobby to find Diego and General Morales seated comfortably at the bar amid curls of fragrant cigar smoke, they realized there was a hitch in their plans.

"Silas!" Diego greeted him companionably. "We came to invite you to go fishing with us this morning."

"Fishing?" Silas asked distractedly.

"Yes, fishing. Every Sunday Ruben and I shore fish from Hester's beach. It is by far the best fishing on the island, and she is generous enough to make a delicious lunch for us, too." Here he paused and offered a winning smile to a flustered Hester.

General Morales added, "Today we thought we would ask you to join us. It is very relaxing and gives us men a chance to talk of things women do not find so interesting. No offense, Hester, of course."

"None taken, General," she replied automatically. In her preoccupation with Silas, she had completely forgotten the older men's Sunday-morning ritual. She grinned sheepishly at Silas and almost laughed out loud at the crestfallen expression on his face. He looked like a little boy who'd been told his family wouldn't be going to Disney World this summer after all.

"Uh, that's very kind of you, General Morales," Silas began, his mind racing with polite excuses.

"Please, call me Ruben."

"Ruben," he corrected. "But I've never been shore fishing and I'd probably just be in your way."

"Nonsense!" Diego protested. "You will enjoy it. We brought all the extra equipment you'll need."

The two men stood, their intentions stated. Silas was clearly about to be shanghaied into an afternoon of male bonding whether he liked it or not. Under other circumstances, he would have welcomed the diversion. But the knowledge that he would be casting his line into the cool Caribbean when he could instead be plunging into Hester's warmth held little appeal for him. Even if he did manage to turn down the invitation, his day of uninterrupted play with Hester would be slightly inhibited by the continued presence of two fishermen quite near on the beach.

Hester's thoughts seemed to echo his own as she sighed in resignation and said, "I'll put some sandwiches in the fridge for your lunch. There's plenty of fruit, too. I have some things to do around here, so I'll leave you gentlemen to enjoy your afternoon."

"I'll just go put on a shirt," Silas said with what he hoped sounded like eagerness.

"Don't forget the sunscreen," Hester called mischievously after him.

The afternoon on the beach passed quickly with Diego and Ruben, and Silas eventually became quite adept at the sport of shore fishing. By the end of the day, Gabriela and Teresa came looking for their husbands, agreeing to stay for dinner when Hester suggested the six of them dine on part of the day's catch.

Throughout dinner, Silas and Hester gazed at each other, seemingly unaware of the other couples. For Silas, the day had been an agonizingly long one, his thoughts constantly turning into erotic daydreams of what he would be doing to Hester if they'd been alone together. In his mind, he would take her back to his room and slowly peel her swimsuit from her salty, sun-warmed body, freeing her hair and weaving it through his hands until they were lost in the golden tresses. He would carry her to his bed, lower her onto the cool crisp sheets and enter her deeply as he followed her down. Then Diego would ask him about his work at DI, and he'd be abruptly returned to reality.

For Hester, the day had been a question-and-answer session with herself. If she were honest, she had to admit she'd felt somewhat relieved that Diego and General Morales had shown up for their usual Sunday recreation. She decided she needed to explore her feelings more fully before committing herself to Silas. Committing? What did commitment have to do with anything? The man would be gone from her life in a matter of days. Where was the commitment in that? How could she have fallen so hard, so fast, for a man she barely knew? For a man whose type she'd so disdained before? Because he wasn't like any other man she'd ever met, a voice inside her said. He made her feel good when he was around. He made her laugh. She liked his perception and intelligence. Not to mention that she seemed to find him impossibly sexy.

Maybe she was falling in love with Silas. That would explain why she was beginning to enjoy her everyday existence on the island even more than she did already. Since he'd come to the hotel, her life seemed to have taken on a new dimension. In just three days Silas had made a difference. Her last thoughts before sleeping were fantasies about him, just as her waking concern was whether or not he was awake. And she really did like being around him. Even if things sometimes got a little tense.

Gabriela and Teresa sensed what was going on at the table, even if no one else did. They hustled their husbands through dinner and hurriedly helped Hester clean the dishes. When they saw that Diego and Ruben had cornered Silas on the veranda for cigars and an after-dinner drink, the two women began an agitated discussion in rapid Spanish that was too quick for Hester to follow.

"*¿Estos hombres que creen?*" Gabriela finally turned her attention to a befuddled Hester. "What do these men think? I am so sorry our husbands have behaved so stupidly today. Men are so blind where love is concerned."

"Sometimes," Teresa amended benevolently. "Like today."

"What do you mean?" Hester asked, still perplexed.

"Any fool can see that these feelings between you and Silas are, er…"

"In the advanced stages," Teresa supplied for the other woman.

Hester blushed. "I didn't think it was that obvious."

The older women exchanged approving glances.

"Do you think Silas feels the same way I do?" Hester ventured the question, hoping a second and third opinion might help clarify the situation a little.

"It's obvious he wants you," Teresa stated simply.

"Yes, but I wonder if he cares for me."

"Perhaps you should ask him that."

"I'm afraid to."

"Why?" Teresa challenged. "The worst he will say is that he doesn't. Which I find very unlikely. And even if he does, he'll be gone in a few days and you can forget him. At least you won't have to worry about it anymore.''

''I'll never forget him,'' Hester vowed quietly.

''Or perhaps he will say that he does care for you,'' Teresa offered.

''And then what do I do?'' Hester wailed. ''He's still going to leave on Thursday. If there's anything between us, that'll just make it more difficult. Either way, it's going to hurt.''

''You could go with him,'' Gabriela suggested.

Hester's eyes widened in alarm. ''Go back to New York? No, I can't, Gabriela. I don't think I could survive in a city that huge and cold again. It was bad enough when that was the only life I knew. Now that I realize there's so much more, living there would be even more unbearable than before.

''But I thought New York was a very much admired city,'' Gabriela said.

''Most people love it,'' Hester agreed. ''But for me to go back would be like committing suicide. There's nothing there for me but bad memories and a lost identity.''

Gabriela looked to Teresa for help, but the other woman shook her head and said something softly in Spanish. Teresa had shared many hours of conversation with Hester since the younger woman had come to the island, and she knew of the unhappiness Hester had experienced in the city.

''Feeling the way you do,'' Teresa pointed out, ''if Silas leaves without you, you will have only sad memories and a lost identity here. At least this time in New York, you would have him. That would make a difference.''

''Even if Silas did invite me to go back with him,''

Hester posed the hypothetical question, ''which he hasn't, who's to say it would last or turn into anything permanent? Just how long would I have him?''

''For as long as the two of you are happy together,'' Gabriela said.

For as long as they were happy together, Hester repeated to herself. When she thought about it, she might even be happy with him in New York. But what would happen when he grew tired of her? When he met another woman who caught his eye? There must be other women in his life. Silas wasn't the type of man to fall in love with just one. Especially with one like her, who would clutter his way of life instead of complimenting it. He needed a woman who had flash and style, who could hold her own in a variety of situations. Hester had been away from the mainstream for over two years, mixing with no one but a handful of other expatriates from reality. She could barely hold her own with Silas as she did on the island. How could she expect to perform in his social and business circles, populated as she was sure they were, by barracudas and innocent-looking but deadly anemones? She'd probably wind up as stressed out as she'd been before. And when Silas finally did decide he was tired of her, which he was bound to do eventually, she'd be alone again. Only then her pain would be greater, her loneliness more unbearable. The next time she left New York, she wouldn't be escaping a life she despised, but cast aside by the man she probably loved. The next time, even a tropical paradise wouldn't be enough to heal the wounds of despair.

''Hester?'' Gabriela's voice brought her out of her reverie. ''What are you looking so unhappy about?''

''I think I'm falling in love with him,'' she responded helplessly. And it was precisely because of that love that she knew she couldn't return to New York with him. She'd rather end their time here, while he still wanted her, than watch as his desire for her left his eyes and wandered to someone else. "I couldn't go back with Silas," she added. "Anyway, I don't know why I'm even considering it, because he certainly hasn't mentioned it. It's crazy to think that he would. This is just another fling to him. He can't possibly expect anything long-term to come out of our time together. That just isn't his style. He has a job to get back to, after all."

Hester closed her eyes and massaged her temples, wishing she had an aspirin. Already the real world was invading her peaceful existence in the form of confusion and headaches, two things she hadn't suffered on the island before Silas's visit.

"Would you two mind saying my good-nights for me?" she asked the two women. "I'm suddenly very tired, and my head feels like a bowling ball fell on it."

Teresa and Gabriela nodded sympathetically. Hester went to her room and collected her things for a nice, cool wash, then retreated to the bathroom. Since there was no lock on the door, she wedged a flat piece of wood into a gap in the doorjamb in a way that made it impossible to open the door. It was a bit of jury-rigging she'd developed one evening some time ago when the overly festive crew of the racing yacht *Rogue's March* out of Grenada had anchored off her beach and spent a night at the hotel. It had proved effective in keeping the reveling regatta winners on the right side of her bedroom door. Now it would work toward keeping Silas's distance until she could sort through her muddled emotions.

Downstairs, Teresa and Gabriela collected their husbands and announced their desire to leave.

"But the night is still young," Diego objected.

"No, my darling," Gabriela corrected, "it is very late. It is time for us old people to be in bed." She sent her husband a meaningful look.

"Well, perhaps you are right," Diego finally agreed, though still uncertain as to what was going on.

Teresa had better luck with her husband. One expressive glance from her suggested to Ruben that the situation was indeed what she had described to him the previous evening.

"Well, Silas," he clapped the other man on the shoulder. "We will see you again before you leave, I am sure."

"Without question," Silas assured him. To Teresa he asked, "Is Hester still in the kitchen?"

"No," she told him hesitantly. "She went upstairs. She said to tell everyone good-night, that she was tired and going to bed." She watched Silas's expression reflect first bewilderment then doubt. "I believe she mentioned a headache," Teresa added nonchalantly.

"A headache?" Silas's attention snapped to Teresa angrily. "She said she had a *headache*?"

The older woman grinned satisfactorily. "Yes. Rather a bad one, too."

Silas said a hasty good-night to everyone then raced up the stairs two at a time. A headache? She had the nerve to try to keep him away with some tired excuse like a headache? After what they'd shared on the beach that afternoon? He'd give her something to ache about all right, but it wouldn't be her head. It would be much lower and much more acute. An ache that only he could ease.

He didn't bother to knock at her bedroom door, but instead threw it open, ready to tumble her to the bed and kiss her senseless. But her room, lit softly by the oil lamp on her bedside table, was strangely empty. The double bed itself was still made, its peach coverlet undisturbed.

His gaze roamed, taking in every aspect and detail. This was Hester's room, he reminded himself. Everything that was important to her, indeed everything she owned, was in this tiny space. It was bigger than his own room, and much homier, washed in the golden light of the lamp. Several of her paintings adorned the whitewashed walls. Books were stacked haphazardly in bookcases of varying size and texture. Her writing desk was covered with papers and magazines. Plants hung from the ceiling, cascaded from shelves and sprang from several terra-cotta planters on the floor. As in his room, French doors opened onto the veranda, but here the entrance was veiled by delicate lace curtains that now swelled slightly from the evening breeze. Where his room created a sense of calmness within him, Hester's enhanced that tranquillity with the inviting warmth he knew was such an integral part of her.

He stepped cautiously to a low dresser, cluttered with delicate, feminine things—perfumes and powders, seashells and sachets. Perfume. Who would Hester wear perfume for on the island? He lifted the small crystal bottle and removed its stopper, waving it below his nose. It smelled beautiful. It smelled like Hester. She had been wearing it at the party. For him? He quickly pushed the thought away and replaced the bottle among lotions and lace. No, if she'd been wearing it for him, she wouldn't be hiding from him now.

Dammit, where was she? He was growing steadily

angrier, first because she'd tried to dissuade him with an imaginary headache, and now because she had disappeared on him entirely. A soft splashing noise at the end of the hall caught his ear. She was bathing. Perfect for his plans. Now he could just pull her from the water closet and take her on the hallway floor. This might turn out better than he'd thought.

He closed her bedroom door quietly behind him and marched with great intent and a savage little smile to the small room at the end of the hall. He turned the knob of the door and pushed, but it wouldn't budge. With mounting indignation, Silas realized that Hester had locked the door against him. Now she'd gone too far. Doubling his fist, he pounded furiously on the door.

"Hester, let me in. We need to talk."

His deep, booming voice held just a touch of a threat. Just enough to convince her she'd been right to wedge the door shut.

"Silas, I'm washing," she said tiredly. "I'll be out in a little while."

"We need to talk."

"We will," she promised. "But first I have some thinking to do."

Silas paused, perturbed that she was avoiding him, but wanting badly to be with her. "I'll be waiting up in my room," he told her. "You won't sleep tonight until I've had some answers. Among other things."

After a few moments of silence, when Hester thought Silas had returned to his room, she heard his voice again on the other side of the door. This time there was none of the arrogance, none of the menace. This time there was only solicitude and uncertainty.

"Why did you lock me out?" he asked her softly.

"Why are you keeping me away from you? I won't hurt you, Hester. I couldn't."

"Oh, Silas," she whispered to herself after she was sure he was gone. "If only I could believe that was true."

Chapter Five

A half hour later, Silas, dressed only in his white silk pajama bottoms, leaned against the veranda railing outside his dark room sipping a rum and tonic. His anger at Hester's escape had subsided, replaced by a desire simply to talk about what was happening between them. His attention was diverted from his musing when he heard a small noise coming from the direction of Hester's room. Since she had evidently finished her evening ablutions, Silas considered this a good time to confront her.

He padded silently and deliberately toward the open French doors of her room, only to hesitate before entering her quiet sanctuary. Through the slowly fluttering lace curtains, he could see her setting about her nightly rituals. She wore a short flowered kimono, her hair twisted atop her head and caught with combs like a geisha's. He knew she couldn't see him lurking out in the darkness, and he chastised himself at the prospect of having become little more than a Peeping Tom. Yet something within him prevented his revealing himself. He was fascinated. He'd never really watched a woman prepare for bed in an asexual, unpretentious manner. He'd watched women remove their clothes and climb into his bed often enough before, but never had he viewed a woman preparing for bed in such an unaffected way. For the simple reason that Hester wasn't trying to be enticing, Silas found her actions all the more stimulating.

Hester hummed quietly as she turned down the bed. Silas almost gasped audibly as she nonchalantly untied and discarded her robe to reveal her nakedness. The smooth lines of her perfect form beckoned to him, and he was about to enter until he realized she was getting dressed again in a man's tank-style undershirt and white cotton panties. Seeing her dressed, or rather undressed, in something so similar to what he wore under his own clothes made Silas's blood run hot and fast in a fashion that no woman in silk and lace had ever inspired. His grip tightened on his glass when she freed her long hair and began to brush it. With each languid stroke of her shimmering tresses, a little explosion went off in Silas's midsection. Maybe their talk could wait until morning. For some reason, Silas had other, more pressing, matters in mind right now.

Hester had just finished braiding and binding her hair when the ice cubes shifted in Silas's glass, the small clinking sound ominous in the otherwise silent night. Immediately she turned from her mirror to the veranda doors.

"Silas?" she asked quietly.

Without a word he parted the curtains and stepped

into her room. Her cheeks were flushed with heightened awareness, the peaks of her breasts hard and vividly revealed beneath the light fabric of her undershirt. The soft expanse of her abdomen revealed below made Silas's fingers itch to stroke it.

"How long have you been out there?" Hester demanded faintly.

"Long enough."

If possible, her cheeks pinkened even more, her soft lips parting in chagrin. In embarrassment, her honey eyes dropped to stare at the floor.

"A gentleman would have made his presence known as soon as he realized the situation," she stated primly.

Silas smiled ferally. "You should know by now that I'm no gentleman, Hester. Polite behavior didn't get me where I am today. I take advantage where I can and use what resources I find available."

"Like me," she assumed out loud, her eyes still lowered.

"No," he denied, knowing it wasn't true in this case. If she were just anyone, he could have seduced her and walked away. But she wasn't just anyone, and he didn't want to walk away. "No, not at all like you," he told her.

"I don't believe you," she said and turned away. "Go back to your room, Silas. Let's just forget that this morning on the beach ever happened."

In a few quick strides he stood behind her, looming over her like a thundercloud. He set his drink on her dresser with a thud, splashing some of its contents onto the surface. Then his strong hands gripped her shoulders and spun her roughly around to face him, yet still she refused to meet his eyes.

"I can't forget it, Hester," he said urgently, his fingers sinking desperately into her warm skin. "And I don't want to. I want to make love to you from now until…" He left the statement unfinished, unwilling to consider his limited time with her. "I want to make love to you," he repeated, hauling her fiercely into his arms. "Tell me that's what you want, too."

Hester shook her head mutely, still unable to look at his face, fearful that she might lose control and give into the passionate longing that coursed through her.

"You can't deny you want me," he accused. "Because we both know you do. Tell me you want me, Hester. Say it."

"No," she whispered weakly.

Silas's hand gripped the end of her braid and wound it around his fist like a length of rope until his hand splayed at her nape. With a less than gentle tug, he brought her head back until her face tipped up to meet his.

"Say it," he insisted gruffly. "You know it's true."

Gazing into Silas's blue eyes, seeing his desire and knowing it reflected her own, Hester could no longer deny her heart. Even though her brain told her it was certain disaster to give in to her emotions, her heart had already surrendered completely to her love for him. She wanted him all right. She wanted him in her heart, in her bed and deep inside her. She was so overcome by yearning, her voice sounded gritty and low when she spoke.

"I do want you, Silas. I want you so bad."

"Bad, huh?" His triumphant grin and the victorious glimmer in his eyes set her heart racing. "Well, I'll do my best to be as bad as you want."

What had she let herself in for? Hester thought, panicked. She was way out of her league where Silas was concerned. A small thrill of fear, tempered with desire, sent her pulse thumping.

For a moment Silas only looked at her, drinking in the wantonness glowing in her eyes. When she unconsciously parted her lips in a silent demand, he lowered his head to hers and kissed her deeply, drinking in the honeyed warmth her mouth offered him. His tongue entered her mouth again and again, reaching farther, tasting more with every penetration. Only the need for breath ended his plunder. Then his lips went to her forehead, her cheeks and her neck. His one hand remained wrapped in her hair, forcing her to return his savage kisses. His other hand dropped from her shoulder to her breast, kneading and fingering the soft flesh through her shirt.

Hester returned Silas's fevered caresses with equal abandon. Her tongue joined with his in a dance of sexual celebration, her hands traveled of their own free will over the corded muscles on his bare back. His big, hard body was so unlike her own and drew her touch like a lure. She was completely immersed in her discovery of him. While one hand stroked the smooth planes of his back, the other tangled itself in the dark curls on his chest.

Silas made a wild noise in the back of his throat and lifted his lips from hers to murmur, "Yes, that's it. I love the way you touch me." While one hand still caressed her breast, the other freed itself from her braid to grasp her wrist, which lay against his chest. During a particularly penetrating kiss, he urged her hand downward and under the waistband of his pajamas. Hester cried out in protest when he gently cupped her hand over his hard length, but when he sighed in ecstasy and she saw the look of pleasure on his face, she gently closed her fingers around him.

"Oh, God, Hester," he moaned and pulled her closer. For a time they touched each other, reveling in the rapture brought on by simply embracing. Then slowly, cautiously, silently, Silas backed Hester toward the bed, and waited for some indication from her to continue. Her gaze held his as she grasped her undershirt, pulled it over her head and dropped it to the floor.

Silas swallowed hard. "Are you sure you're ready for this?" he ground out in a last attempt at being valiant, hoping to God that she wouldn't change her mind. "It's been a long time since something like this has happened to you."

"Silas, nothing like this has ever happened to me," she told him. "I've never felt the things you make me feel." She placed her hand softly on his chest. "I'm more than ready for this. It's something I've wanted for an eternity and didn't even know it."

Another impediment to their union suddenly struck Silas. "You could get pregnant," he realized with surprisingly little alarm. "I didn't exactly come prepared for a party."

"No, it's okay," Hester assured him. "The timing is wrong for anything like that to happen."

"Are you absolutely certain this is what you want?" he asked her again.

"What's the matter, Silas? Are you turning chicken?"

A fire blazed in his eyes as he untied the drawstring at his waist and let his pajamas pool at his feet. Hester's heart quickened at the sight of him naked and ready for her. She stepped out of her panties and he drew her roughly against his hard length. With one long and probing kiss, they lowered themselves to her bed, all raw nerves and tingling sensations.

In the winking yellow glow of the lamplight they joined, Silas entering her not with a ferocity she might have expected, but with a tender easing of his strength into her softness. At first he felt a tightness in her that was a result of her relative inexperience and time, and he thrilled to know she was so uninitiated. Gradually, as her body grew accustomed to his invasion, she opened to him and he thrust deeply inside of her. Hester gasped and moaned in surrender as Silas's thrusts grew faster and harder until both of them were consumed by the inferno burning around them. As they clung together in the afterglow of their loving, the still night slowly enveloped them, silent save their quietening breaths and mumbled words of contentment.

Just when they thought they had calmed to a point of satiation, desire rose again, and they succumbed with a fury that surprised them both. Throughout the night they pleasured each other, every encounter a little more erotic and intense than the one preceding it. Finally exhaustion claimed, and satisfied and depleted, they slept soundly and dreamlessly in each other's arms.

Hester awoke first in the gray light of a cloudy dawn, held securely in Silas's possessive embrace. She lay with her back to his warm chest, each thump of his heart a reminder of the previous night's endless exploits. His heavy, steady breathing told her he was still asleep, with one muscular leg draped over hers and one big hand gently cupping her breast. She had never felt more cherished, more…loved. Yet she knew Silas was not a man who loved freely. Despite the way he'd made her feel last night, the possibility that he felt as she did this morning did not occur to her. A single tear escaped from beneath her lowered lashes, followed quickly by another, then another. Soon her pillow was damp with melancholy tears.

She knew she was in love with Silas. Wildly, hopelessly, recklessly in love. Some time during the night, amid tender caresses and quiet murmurings, it occurred to her that this new and alien feeling she was experiencing must indeed be love. And it went deep. Straight through the bone to some inner, previously undiscovered part of her that she would have sworn did not exist. Silas made her feel desirable and needed. But more important than that, he made her feel as though she were special. In Silas's arms she surpassed her existence as one of millions of pin-striped, overstressed executives or even as a carefree beach bum. During the night she had become a sentient, individual being, discovering parts of herself she had never even begun to know. Silas had unchained a new Hester, one who was able to love.

Yet almost as quickly as she realized her capacity to love, the object of her affections would be torn from her. In a few days, Silas would leave her world to return to his own. He would be going back to high finance, corporate functions, industrial deals and stressful living. And then a new revelation taunted her. He'd also go back to women who fit that sort of life-style. Hester remembered all too well what kind of women rich, powerful men in business wanted. Flashily painted, long-legged, slow-witted ones. The kind with dangerous curves, no moral fiber and even less vocabulary. The kind she wasn't two years ago, and certainly not the kind she was now.

Of course he'd made her feel special last night, she

berated herself. He'd probably had more than enough practice at it with plenty of willing subjects. Hester began to wonder what Silas saw in her in the first place. He's on vacation, she reminded herself viciously. She was convenient, and let's face it, more than willing. The man wasn't an idiot after all. Why should he turn down what she so freely offered? With that, she became angry—at herself for being so stupid and vulnerable, and at Silas for taking advantage of that vulnerability. She swiped furiously at the tears on her face, the motion awakening Silas. His arms tightened around her, pulling her close as he nuzzled her neck and kissed her hair. Without a word his hand on her breast dipped lower to her belly, pausing at the soft thatch of curls just below. Hester held her breath, feigning sleep.

"I know you're awake, Hester," Silas murmured lazily in her ear. Then with a childlike quality in his voice he asked, "Can we do it again? I just can't seem to get enough of you. You're addicting."

He rolled her toward him so that she was on her back and lowered his head to kiss her. But when he saw the mixture of emotions on her face, first passion, then anger, then sadness, he paused.

"Hester?" he asked guardedly. "What's wrong?"

"Nothing," she responded blandly. "What do you want for breakfast?"

"Don't give me that. Something's bothering you. What is it?"

"Nothing's wrong, Silas," she snapped. "Everything's just perfect for you, isn't it? This has turned out to be a real peachy-keen vacation. You've got sun, surf, fishing buddies and a willing little piece of action on the side when you want it, right?"

"What?" Silas was genuinely confused, and getting

a little angry himself. He rose on his elbows menacingly above her. "What in the hell are you talking about? After last night, how can you wake up and still be mad at me? What did I do now?" His voice grew more threatening with each question.

"You took advantage of me."

"Advantage of you?" Silas roared in disbelief. "Advantage? How could I be taking advantage of you when you wanted this just as much as I did?"

"Did I, Silas? Did I really want it?"

"You know you did. You practically begged me for it."

He had effectively climbed on top of her during the heated exchange, one hand planted on her pillow on either side of her head, his heaving chest within inches of hers. He had only to close those few inches between them to join their bodies in the impassioned embrace they'd enjoyed mere hours before.

Hester stared into his blue eyes, loving the way his hair had been mussed by her fingers and his lips reddened by her kisses. She couldn't stay mad at Silas, because she knew what he said was true.

"You're right," she confessed abruptly, letting her anger leave her body on a deep breath. "I did. I wanted you more than anything else in the world. I still do."

Silas relaxed a little, but was still uncertain about her confusing mood swings. "Then why are you so mad?"

"I'm scared, Silas," she whispered, unable to keep the tremor from her voice.

He nibbled her lips in a tender kiss and said, "Why? What are you afraid of?"

Hester just shook her head silently and squeezed her eyes shut. It did no good. Again, helpless tears tumbled down her cheeks. How could she tell him she was scared because for the first time in her life, she felt love, love for someone who would ultimately abandon her? How could she describe the magnitude of her loneliness once he had returned to New York? She had been alone before, in her life in the city, but her loneliness had been for something she did not know. Now she knew. Now she understood what love and companionship were, and now her solitude would have a definite meaning. She was scared that anguish would replace happiness once Silas was gone. Last night, through their lovemaking and her emotional response, she had become whole. When he was gone, she would be left in pieces again, and this time she doubted her ability to rebuild her life.

But how could she explain these things to Silas? She would have to reveal her past to him, and that included her desertion of Thompson-Michaels. She didn't want to risk the disappointment he would feel at her behavior. Even though she knew there was nothing to be ashamed of, she was certain he would misunderstand her actions. And then when she did voice her fears to him, it would only serve to drive a wedge between them, inhibit the few days they did have together.

Hester decided quickly that since her loss was going to be great and soon in coming, she might as well make the best of the brief opportunity she had. She would keep her feelings secret and attempt to enjoy their short time to its fullest. What was the old saying about loving and losing? That it was better than not having known love at all? But the decision did little to still her anxiety or stop her tears.

Silas was overwhelmed when he saw the drops of sorrow escaping Hester's normally laughing eyes. He didn't understand why she felt sad when they so recently had enjoyed the peak of human emotion. He felt helpless. What could he say or do to comfort her when he didn't know what was wrong? Instinctively he lowered his body to hers, gingerly kissing the moisture from her face, his hands cradling her chin and jaw. Eventually Hester kissed him back, her pain becoming passion with each caress of his lips. As thunder rumbled outside and rain began to patter softly on the veranda, Silas deftly parted her legs and eased himself into her welcoming warmth. He thrust hard and deep until they were both utterly lost in their desire and need for each other.

At midmorning they dressed in their discarded clothing and went to the kitchen to fix breakfast. Silas had mentioned something about needing their strength, and both had decided perhaps nourishment might be a good idea. Outside the sky was thick and slate, dousing the ocean and island with a continuous deluge of rain.

"How often does weather like this occur?" Silas asked between bites of fresh pineapple, papaya and mango.

"Hardly ever," Hester told him. "Especially this time of year. Usually summer is the rainy season."

"How long do you think it will last?"

"Who knows? Rain down here is very weird. Maybe an hour. Maybe all day."

"Gee, that's too bad." Silas grinned wickedly. "That mean's we'll have to stay inside all day long. However will we keep ourselves occupied?"

Hester smiled back at him. "I'm sure you have at least one idea," she said.

"At least."

They returned to bed after breakfast, remaining there

all day, making love furiously, as if to cease would be to die. Only when they were too exhausted to do anything but lie in each other's arms did reality return. Once again they found themselves in Hester's bed, naked and damp with slowing passion, their ardor momentarily spent.

Silas lay on his back, clasping Hester to his heart. Her unbound tresses streamed across her shoulders and pillow, a handful of the silky gold clutched desperately in his grasp. As she fell into a light sleep, his fingers wove through her hair and a dozen thoughts assailed him at once. What was he going to do? The sun was setting on another day in paradise, reminding him of his impending departure. In seventy-two hours he'd be back in the States. Back in his apartment with all the modern conveniences. Back to friends with whom he had something in common. Back to his position at Duran Industries where God only knew what had been fouled up in his absence. Funny, though, how he really hadn't missed electric lights, telephones and air conditioning. And strange, too, how Diego and Ruben, not to mention Hester, held more appeal for him than his colleagues he'd known since college. And especially odd was the fact that he hadn't given DI a single thought since that first evening with Hester.

Still, he couldn't very well walk away from his responsibilities in New York. That would make him no less contemptible than Vasquez in Rio. Silas's innate sense of duty prohibited him from doing anything as rash and impulsive as staying on the island. As much as he might want to. And he knew that as much as he cared for Hester, eventually he would need to return to New York. Getting away from it all for a while was fine. But Silas thrived on the hustle and bustle of the city. He might complain about it, and there were days when he swore he'd do anything to escape the noise and pollution, the crowds and the crazies, but the truth was he needed the city and its endless movement and change. The island was a wonderful escape, but it wasn't real. He had to have the constant challenge of his job to survive. It simply wasn't in his nature to relax and be peaceful for long periods of time. He was a predatory animal whose instincts needed continuous honing for making deals and breaking banks. He was a ravager, not a lover, and he needed the quarry of the city in his pursuit for power and success. He had no choice but to leave Thursday. He had to get back in the game.

This is what Silas told himself that rainy evening—and that evening, he believed it was true. He, too, fell asleep after a while, awakening sometime after dark to find himself alone in Hester's bed. After fumbling around for his pajama bottoms and wristwatch, he dressed hurriedly in the silent room. The rain had stopped, but stubborn clouds remained, obscuring the moon and stars, making it impossible for him to see what time it was.

When he found the bathroom empty, he descended the stairs to the kitchen in search of Hester. A pale yellow light flickered there, and the aroma of fresh coffee lingered, but otherwise, there was no evidence of her. After pouring a cup of coffee for himself, he strode through the lobby to the door that opened onto the beach. He sensed more than saw Hester sitting out there, but found her easily nonetheless. In the darkness she was little more than a black shape, but somehow a little light glinted off the gold in her hair.

"What time is it?" Silas asked as he lowered himself into the damp sand beside her.

"I don't know." Her soft voice parted the darkness. "Well after midnight."

"That would make it Tuesday morning," he pointed out what they both realized. Hester said nothing. She didn't need to be reminded of the quickly passing time. Soon enough, Silas would be gone.

"You know, you never have told me how you managed to get from the streets of New York to the beaches of the Caribbean," Silas began, hoping to finally get a straight answer from her.

"That's a very long story, I'm afraid."

"Is it one you're willing to tell?"

Hester shrugged noncommittally. She knew Silas wasn't going to give up until she'd told him something of her past. "One day I woke up and decided my life had gone to hell in a hand basket," she said simply. "So I left."

"Aren't you skipping a few little details here and there? After all, you said this was a *long* story."

"My life in New York was completely vacant." She sighed in resignation. "I did nothing but work, had no friends or family, not even a cat. I'd never even been outside the city. So I chucked it all and bought a plane ticket south to St. Croix. One-way. First class."

And she probably used her life savings and hocked everything she owned to do it, Silas thought.

"And from St. Croix?" he prodded.

"I spent about four weeks on St. Croix," Hester continued dreamily. "Boy, that's a beautiful place. Have you ever been there?"

"Once, when I was in college. Some friends and I went for spring break."

It figures, Hester thought sarcastically. Out loud, she said, "I had a wonderful time. Loafed on the beach. Got a tan. Got a passport," she added proudly. "That was a big moment in my life."

When the moon finally emerged from behind a cloud, Silas could see the wistful expression on Hester's face. It must have been a tremendous change for her to experience. From a dirty, dangerous inner-city neighborhood that bred hopelessness and horror, to an idyllic island in a crystal sea where the sun always shone brightly and the serenity of a warm breeze was a constant companion. Small wonder she hadn't returned to New York City.

"Anyway," she went on, pulling herself from her reverie, "One day, purely on impulse, I hired myself out as a crew member on a chartered yacht traveling to Tobago. We put in here one night, and in the morning they left and I didn't."

"You just jumped ship?" Silas asked incredulously. Such spontaneous behavior was a mystery to him. He couldn't imagine doing something that would alter the course of his life without weeks or even months of careful forethought.

"Diego needed somebody to run the hotel," she explained. "I needed a job. It worked out perfectly. Besides, any of the guys on the *Urizen* will tell you that I wasn't much of a sailor. They weren't too sorry to see me go," she told him sheepishly.

"Diego just hired you on the spot?" Silas went on in disbelief. "He didn't check your references? What had your job been in New York? Did you have any experience in hotel management?"

"Whoa, Silas." Hester's laughter bubbled up without restriction. "Calm down. I keep telling you things

are different down here—less rigid, more laid back.
Diego and Gabriela and I hit it off immediately. They
didn't need my credentials. Diego's writer's instinct, as
he calls it, sensed I would be perfect for the job. He
knew I wanted seclusion and peace of mind, and this
job would be perfect for that.''

"So he just put you to work."

Hester nodded. "Besides, even if he didn't trust me,
what was I going to do, steal from him? There are
rarely any guests anyway. The hotel was on the property he bought from General Morales, that's all. He's
a writer, not a resort manager. I think he only fixed the
place up because he couldn't stand the thought of a
nice building in disrepair on such an otherwise beautiful island.''

"Just how long have the others been here?" Silas
asked, curious to know more about his newly adopted
social circle.

"Well," Hester began, relieved that she had suc-
cessfully sidestepped his question about her life in New
York, "I've told you about the biologists. Diego and
Gabriela came here about ten years ago from Miami.
That's where they fled when Castro took power in
Cuba. Once their children were grown and in college,
they decided they wanted to get away from city life.
While they were visiting Diego's brother in Venezuela,
they looked into the possibility of buying property on
a small, unpopulated island in the Caribbean. A realtor
representing General Morales led them here. The General wanted to sell part of the island so that he and
Teresa wouldn't be so isolated. He's also the one who
furnished the landing strip and pays Ford to make his
weekly visits. When the Moraleses met the Santoses,

they got along famously and the General sold a quarter of the island to them.''

"Originally Ruben and Teresa owned the island?'' Silas was now very interested.

"Yes," Hester told him. "And by the way, he doesn't let many people call him by his first name. Only those he carries a lot of respect for.''

Silas's eyebrows lifted in surprise at her statement. "I wondered why you always referred to him as 'the General' and never called him Ruben.''

"He's never issued the invitation to me," she said without malice. "I suspect much of it has to do with my youth and the fact that I'm a woman.''

"You don't seem offended by it.''

"I'm not," Hester said honestly. "General Morales is from an entirely different culture than mine, that's all. He certainly means no contempt or superiority in desiring the use of his title. It's just the way things were where he was brought up. If he was arrogant or disdainful about it, then I would be offended.''

Silas understood her reasoning. Before he had become CEO at Duran Industries, he had been required to deal with others in much loftier positions than his own. Only when others paraded their higher rank as if it made them supreme did Silas resent or lose respect for them. Those who simply handled their positions as jobs that must be done commanded a respect from Silas he was more than willing to give.

"How did Ruben and Teresa come to be here?'' Silas asked, returning their conversation to its original subject matter.

"I'm not too sure of the entire story," Hester said with a note of longing in her voice, "but it's all terribly romantic.''

"How so?"

"Well, I can only tell you the framework of the story from what Teresa had told me. I'm sure there's a lot more embellishment she could add if she wanted."

"I'm intrigued," Silas confessed. "Tell me more.

"Let's see." Hester thought for a moment about where to begin. "Both the General and Teresa are from a small village in Venezuela. Apparently his family was a very rich and powerful one that had been in the country since the time of the conquistadores. They practically owned the entire town. They also owned this little island. The big house at the other end, where the Moraleses live now, was like their vacation home in the old days. To see it, you'd think it was once a plantation house. It's gorgeous. Anyway, General Morales was a dashing army officer when he first met Teresa."

"Who was?" Silas urged her to continue.

"Who was a peasant girl from the village. She worked at his parents' hacienda as a servant."

"This story sounds a little familiar."

"Oh, it is," Hester assured him. "It has all the makings of a terrific novel of a forbidden love affair. Not only was the class difference a tremendous obstacle, but Teresa was also the daughter of unmarried parents. A big taboo in such a strict tiny community."

"That does create a problem."

"Wait, that isn't the half of it," Hester told him, her eyes sparkling merrily as she, too, became caught up in the story she loved. She had spent so many hours in Teresa's home when she had first arrived on the island, listening with her elbows propped on the older woman's kitchen table, chin in hands, eyes wide with wonder at the tale revealed to her. "Not only was her mother a lowly, unmarried peasant girl when Teresa was born, but it turns out her father was a very notorious outlaw along the lines of Robin Hood. He was wanted by the local authorities literally for robbing from the rich to give to the poor.''

"So the plot thickens," Silas said.

"Teresa was very unpopular in the town for a variety of reasons," Hester went on. "The circumstances surrounding her birth, of course, her paternity, the fact that she wasn't ashamed of herself like any decent illegitimate child should be, and most importantly, because she was very beautiful and high-spirited. It really ticked people off that she enjoyed life so much despite the misery they tried to force her into."

"I can see how that would ruin some people's day," Silas said, only half joking. He'd met more than enough people who thrived on making others as unhappy as they were themselves.

"At any rate," Hester continued, "General Morales fell madly in love with her at first sight and pursued her relentlessly. But Teresa resisted because she had high morals and because she held so much disdain for the upper class. The excesses of his family when so many people in their village were starving angered her. She wanted nothing to do with what he represented."

"So what finally got them together?"

"He kidnapped her."

"He what?"

Hester smiled broadly. "General Morales snuck into her room in the servant's quarters one night and literally carried her off. He put her on the back of his horse and they rode off into the night. Then he put her on the family yacht and had his crew strand them on this island.

"That's incredible."

"He kept her here with him for months. All she'd brought with her was her nightgown, so she was pretty much at his mercy. He didn't force her to do anything she didn't want to. In fact, he practically killed her with kindness. He wanted to prove to her that he wasn't avaricious or heartless the way many of the upper class were. So he arranged things in a way that would compel her to get to know him better." Hester was quiet for a moment, indicating she was finished with her story.

"So what happened?" Silas demanded.

"She fell as madly in love with him as he was with her," Hester told him.

"And?"

"And they lived happily ever after. More or less."

"But what happened when they went back to the village?" he asked urgently. "How did his family react?"

"His father had died when he was a teenager, so General Morales was effectively the head of the household. He announced he was marrying Teresa and whoever didn't like it could, quote, 'Get the hell out of my house.' No one wanted to lose their job, and his mother and sisters didn't want to lose their social standing, so no one took him up on his offer. As far as the townspeople went, well, they were pretty shallow, as you've already guessed. They knew how powerful his family was and didn't want to cross him. So, externally anyway, no one gave them any problems. But the General and Teresa knew they had no friends. They knew privately that people sneered and hated them both."

"Why would they even stay around someplace

where they were so unhappy?'' Silas wondered. ''They should have just stayed on the island.''

Hester stared at him, amazed. ''Why, Silas, I'd think you of all people would understand that. General Morales had a duty to perform. He was a high-ranking officer in the Venezuelan army with a lot of responsibilities. He couldn't just chuck them all and escape to an island paradise with the woman he loved. He had an important job to do. At least that's the way he saw it.''

''But…'' Silas was shocked to find that he wanted to echo Diego's words that no job was that important. Of course the General had to return to his village and his position, Silas reminded himself harshly. It would have been sheer folly to just up and desert his obligations as an officer.

''Once he retired, he and Teresa moved here permanently,'' Hester told him. ''Their children and grandchildren come up from Maracaibo to visit them two or three times a year.''

''That's a great story,'' Silas muttered when he realized Hester had concluded it.

''Diego is always saying he's going to write his next book about the Moraleses' story,'' she smiled.

''Why doesn't he?''

''Because he respects their privacy and would never exploit their love for each other.''

Silas nodded, then another thought struck him. ''How did the hotel get here?''

''That's also a very interesting story.''

''You're just full of those tonight.''

''Despite the small size and low population, there's a rich history on this island. I lived in the biggest, most progressive city in North America for a long time and never heard stories or met fascinating people the way I have here.''

He had to agree that in his thirty-eight years he was hard-pressed to think of anyone more interesting than the inhabitants of this little island, too.

''The hotel?'' he asked again.

''Right. Diego and Gabriela decided it was too big to live in, so they had a smaller house built a little way up the beach. But Diego couldn't stand the thought of a nice old building standing vacant and useless, so he turned it into a hotel, such as it is.

''Originally, though, when General Morales's great-great-grandfather, I believe it was, bought the island, he built the big house at the other end, not only as a retreat for the family vacations, but also as a refuge in case war broke out. That was way back in the late 1700s or early 1800s.''

''This hotel is almost two hundred years old?'' Silas asked, almost choking on a swallow of coffee. ''That's unbelievable.''

''No, the Morales home is almost two hundred years old,'' Hester corrected. ''The hotel is a mere one hundred and fifty years old. Give or take a few years. It was built by the General's great-grandfather for his mistresses.''

''Mistresses?'' Silas asked with interest. ''As in more than one?''

Hester nodded. ''He had a veritable harem that he didn't want to leave on the continent when he took his family on vacation. So he built a second building at the other end of the island to secretly keep his girlfriends hidden from his wife.''

''This is great stuff, Hester,'' Silas interjected. ''Networks kill for this kind of miniseries fodder.''

Hester laughed. "I know, but Teresa swears it's all true."

"So you're telling me I've been sleeping in a room that was once devoted to experiencing all manner of earthly delight and sensual pleasure?" Silas thought for a moment, his eyes growing warm with remembered passion, then said, "Yes, well, I suppose I've had my share of those, too."

Hester said nothing, but stared at the sky over the peaceful ocean. It had lightened to a dark lavender, a promise of a clear day. She, too, was preoccupied with thoughts of shared embraces and lingering caresses.

"Would you like some more coffee?" she asked after a moment.

"I can get it," Silas said quickly, gathering the two stoneware mugs. When he returned he continued their discussion. "What about Desmond?" he asked.

"Desmond is an enigma, really. He doesn't say much about himself, but there's something about him that makes me feel like he's suffered some great tragedy in his life. Something that ultimately resulted in his coming here to either escape it or try to deal with it. He's a friend of General Morales. I don't know where they met. They're both pretty tight-lipped about it. He knows all about machinery of every kind, especially airplanes, but I don't know where he learned it."

"Yes, I was impressed by his knowledge of aircraft. He discovered the problem with my plane in the blink of an eye. And it's a fairly new model. Not much had been written about it for public consumption."

"Like I said, he's an enigma."

Together Silas and Hester watched the sun emerge from the sea, warming the sky with subtle shades of pink, orange and yellow, until finally a crisp blue sky evolved, cloudless and perfect, as if apologizing for yesterday's stormy weather.

"And I thought Broadway shows were spectacular," Silas said with quiet reverence when the sun finally brightened the sky with its appearance.

It was Tuesday morning on the island. In forty-eight hours, Silas would be leaving. He should be rejoicing that soon he would be back in his beloved New York. Why then, did he feel a panic such as he had never known that at the end of forty-eight hours, his freedom would be coming to an end, instead of returning after a week of forced imprisonment? Why did he sense a foreboding at his return to his career and the life-style he had chosen and enjoyed? To the way of life he *needed* in order to survive? Silas felt concerned and confused. Was he returning to what he most needed and desired for his life, or was he in fact leaving it behind?

Chapter Six

At midmorning on Tuesday, as Hester and Silas sat side by side on the beach, enjoying the sun and each other's company, two mounted riders appeared some distance up the beach.

"It's the General and Teresa," Hester said. "They go riding every day."

Hester went into the hotel to prepare some iced tea, returning with a bamboo tray full of refreshments that she placed on a folding table beneath a palm.

"Good afternoon, Hester, Silas," the General greeted them warmly. "Is it not a beautiful day today after yesterday's foul weather?"

"Gorgeous," Silas agreed, his eyes falling on Hester. She was once again clad in her khaki shorts and bandeau top, her hair pulled back in a long ponytail and bound with a gold ribbon.

She blushed and looked at Teresa who smiled a knowing and satisfied smile.

"I fixed some iced tea and fruit," Hester told the older woman. "I thought you both might need cooling off after your ride. There's water for the horses in the trough, too, after all the rain."

As General Morales went to water the horses at the trough that had been constructed along with the building nearly a century and a half before, Teresa greeted Silas.

"Have you been finding enough to keep you busy?" she asked. Silas thought he saw a slight twinkle in her eyes. "I'm sure our little island must seem very boring and backward compared to New York City."

"On the contrary," Silas told her, "I've been discovering all sorts of fascinating things to do here. And last night, Hester filled me in on some of the local history." He tried to manage a little twinkle in his own eyes as he smiled at her. "It's really very interesting. I understand you and Ruben have a very beautiful home."

"Oh, yes!" Teresa enthused. "It's quite lovely. There's rather a colorful history behind it."

"So I hear."

Teresa's smile broadened as she said, "Yes, well actually, some of the most scandalous stories have not yet been made public. Perhaps someday, Hester, I shall tell you of the peccadilloes of Ruben's father. Now there was a man who..."

"Teresa," the General's voice came from behind them, laced with mock severity.

Teresa only grinned and said, "Well, maybe sometime next week you will come visit me at the big house."

"You bet I will," Hester laughed. Then she sobered suddenly as a thought struck her. "It's too bad you have to leave so soon, Silas. You really should see the big house. And the interior of the island. We've spent all our time on the beach when there are some really beautiful spots inland."

"Thanks, but I got a much closer view of the jungle than I wanted on the hike from the airstrip," Silas muttered dryly.

"But you were overdressed and dragging luggage then," Hester reminded him. "Not to mention the fact that you were in a pretty crummy mood that day."

He had been in an awful mood on Friday, hadn't he, Silas remembered. Hard to believe, considering the high spirits he had enjoyed since then.

"Why don't you take him on a tour of the island today?" Teresa suggested.

"How?" Hester wanted to know. "We should start early in the morning if we're going to walk. It's too hot now."

"Take the horses," the older woman told her. "Let them rest here for a little while, then you can go on horseback."

"But what will you and the General do?"

"Go fishing," General Morales answered as he returned to the group. "I can use the gear you have, Hester."

"And I shall make use of the library," Teresa added.

Hester turned to the handsome man beside her. "How about it, Silas? You know how to ride?"

Silas looked at her and said smugly, "I learned at a very prestigious riding school in New Hampshire when I was a boy. How about you? Can you hold your own on horseback?"

Hester responded with equal smugness. "I learned from a high-ranking officer of the Venezuelan cavalry. General Morales taught me."

"I think you will both be fine," the General told them, clapping them each on the shoulder in a fatherly gesture. "Now did I hear someone mention iced tea?"

"Help yourself," Hester invited.

The four of them spent the remainder of the morning in leisurely conversation. At a little past noon, Hester donned a baseball cap and sunglasses and pulled herself up on the back of Teresa's gray mare, Bianca.

"Aren't you going to put on shoes?" Silas asked her from his perch on the General's black stallion, Bolivar.

"Silas, I haven't worn shoes in two years," Hester told him mildly. "My feet would probably reject them."

"But if we're going to be in the jungle..."

Hester was touched by Silas's concern for her welfare. She smiled at him winningly and vowed, "I'll be fine. Trust me. I go into the jungle barefoot all the time. It's walking as God intended."

Silas frowned in disapproval, but didn't argue. His own feet sported trendy tennis shoes that complemented his white shorts, red T-shirt and expensive sunglasses.

He still looks like a businessman on vacation, Hester thought. She suspected he would never be able to completely cut loose from his career. There would always be a part of him that was Silas Duran, CEO of a Fortune 500 corporation, responsible and respected, powerful and patrician. A brief stay on an island where bumming around was the rule of thumb would never take that out of him.

They rode up the beach at a slow lope for a while,

the warm Caribbean waters splashing playfully around the horses' hooves. When they reached the camp of the French biologists, they found them on the beach with their diving gear, collecting specimens, and stopped for a quick chat.

"Hester," Jean-Luc greeted her excitedly, his blue eyes glittering to rival the ocean behind him. "I found the most perfect specimens of *Dipleura* and *Madrepora*. I cannot wait to show them to you."

"That's terrific, Jean-Luc!" Hester exclaimed. "Now you can really take your studies of coral in depth and illustrate your discoveries in your thesis."

"Oh, they are both perfect," the young Frenchman stated proudly. "I will begin studying their behavior immediately."

Silas's lips thinned to a grim line as Hester and the young student exchanged biological rhetoric. A jealous pang shot through him at the realization that soon he would be gone, but Jean-Luc would remain, enjoying conversation and recreation with Hester. He had never so envied another human being. Jean-Luc was practically a boy, still a student, who had no job, no social connections, no money and no material possessions. Why did Silas feel such an intense desire to switch places with him? Because then Jean-Luc would return to the responsibilities and pressures that awaited him at DI. And Silas could stay on the island collecting starfish and seashells, basking in the heat of the sun and the warmth of Hester's company. It was a thought that distracted him throughout the remainder of the day.

Hester and Silas left the group of divers to their research and turned the horses toward a path that headed inland. As they rode deeper into the jungle, the air grew heavier, the light more sporadic. Sounds were muffled and loud at the same time. Occasionally dappled spots of sunlight would appear along the path they were traveling, a reminder that they were still outdoors. Jungle birds called out their irritation at the invasion of their abode, shrill songs mixed with macabre laughter. Thick green leaves on some of the trees were enormous, big enough to use as area rugs. The jungle smelled like life—rich and pungent, excessive and strong. Silas inhaled deeply, feeling a purging sensation, as if the aroma of nature expelled the last of the city smog from his lungs.

"Where does this path lead?" he asked after they'd ridden for some time in companionable silence.

"Eventually to the big house, but there's a place along the way I want to show you," Hester told him.

"Is this the only highway on the island?"

Hester glanced over her shoulder at Silas and smiled. "There are actually two, uh, roads, I guess is the best word, though they're really not much more than bridle paths. This one goes roughly north and south, while another farther on goes east and west. The east-west road is fairly overgrown because no one uses it much. But the General and Teresa use this one pretty frequently when they come to visit. The most densely populated section of the island is the southeast. Desmond lives more toward where the roads intersect, but there's the path that leads from the airstrip to the hotel that he keeps clear, so he never uses the road at all."

"So you have two roads and a path that make up your traffic system here," Silas summed up.

"Considering the fact that two people on horseback constitutes rush hour, I'd say that's more than enough."

"True."

As they rode along, Silas had to amend his earlier views of the jungle. It was indeed a beautiful place, as peaceful as the beach. How could he have thought it so menacing before? It was so primordial, the essence of the earth. He could imagine a time when early man had to pit himself against the elements, savagely struggling for survival in a primitive, instinctive existence. A time when the only things of importance were food to curb one's hunger and a mate to procreate the species.

Procreation. Silas grinned slyly as he leered openly at the side-to-side motion of Hester's curvaceous bottom atop the slowly moving Bianca ahead of him. Now that was something he really would have enjoyed about prehistoric life. Especially with Hester. She'd make a great mother, he speculated, indulging in an uncharacteristic fantasy. He could envision her round with his child, wearing some of those cute little maternity overalls he often saw pregnant women wear these days. But Hester had said there was no danger of her becoming pregnant now. He didn't know why, but somewhere deep inside him, that realization disappointed him. He was still puzzling over this disturbing revelation when Hester called over her shoulder to him.

"We'll stop here for a little while to rest and give the horses a break. There's a beautiful place I want to show you."

Silas dismounted and led Bolivar to the tree where Hester was tethering Bianca. Her face was flushed from the heat of the day, and tendrils of her hair had escaped their bond, framing her face in amber wisps below her baseball cap. Silas couldn't resist her. Placing his big hands on her slender neck, he tilted her head back with his thumbs and kissed her. It was a kiss of longing and promise, a kiss that said too much time had passed since they had last touched. When it was over, Hester felt shaky and hot, desire bubbling over in her heart.

"How can I want you again so soon after..." she began. "I mean after all the times we..."

"I know," Silas interrupted her, drawing her body against his in a warm bear hug. "I feel that way, too."

For a moment they only held each other, then Hester took Silas's hand and led him through a small clearing in the brush.

"Where are you taking me?" he asked, following with obvious reluctance. "To some ancient native voodoo burial ground where you can work more of your spells on me?"

"Silas, what are you talking about?" Hester muttered as she picked her way through the trees.

"I keep thinking of you as some kind of fairy or water nymph," he confessed.

"What?" Hester gaped at him.

"Well, look at you," he defended himself. "The way you look and dress. You always seem to have flowers or something on your clothes." His hand pointed to her bandeau. "The colors you wear are all nature's colors. You're very natural."

"Silas, every color reflects nature," Hester informed him.

"You know what I mean. You just seem to be so much a part of your surroundings. I keep finding it harder and harder to believe you come from the streets of New York."

"That's a nice compliment, Silas. Thank you." Hester blushed. She wasn't used to receiving praise. "I only wish it were true. Unfortunately, I'm no more a child of nature than you are.'' After a moment, one of his statements returned to her. "A nymph, huh?''

Silas cleared his throat roughly. "Yes, well, you know the kind that run around in the forest or in the ocean. Naked. Wanton. Mischievous. And very curious about mortal men.''

Hester cocked her head to the side. "I guess I can see where you might find a few similarities there.''

"Now let's see about presenting an accurate picture.''

As they continued through the jungle, Silas again marveled at her. She must be a chameleon to be able to adapt so completely from one way of life to another. He hadn't intended to ask her about her time in New York, because she seemed so unwilling to discuss it, but before he could stop himself, his curiosity got the better of him and he suddenly spoke out loud.

"Was your life in New York very awful?'' he asked.

Hester paused before answering, not really surprised that their conversation had taken such a turn. "No worse than some,'' she told him philosophically.

"Will you tell me about it?'' Silas requested. "I'd really like to know.''

Hester considered for a moment before deciding a description of her childhood wouldn't reveal enough of her past to allow his discovery of her job at Thompson-Michaels and ultimate breach of duty. So with a shrug, she began.

"I never knew my mother,'' she said in a flat tone. "She was only fifteen when I was born and ran away from home shortly after the blessed event. My grandmother, a widow who probably nagged her husband into the grave, raised me by herself.''

When there was no response from Silas, Hester continued, trying to reflect indifference and leave the bitterness in the past.

"Lydia, that was what I called my grandmother, was not a very nice person. She drank a lot, living off welfare and social security. And she was pretty abusive verbally, but she never raised a hand to me physically, something for which many of my friends envied me. They usually sported some nasty bruises and wrenched limbs."

"That's barbaric," Silas muttered.

"It was a way of life in my neighborhood. It still is for a lot of people. Anyway, by the time I was ten, I had joined a gang of older kids, most of them twelve or thirteen. We cut school all the time, not that anyone noticed, and I started smoking and committing a few crimes, shoplifting, mostly. Nothing heavy-duty like a lot of other kids were into."

"Heavy-duty?" Silas was almost afraid to ask.

"Drugs, extortion, burglary, even prostitution," Hester told him. When she saw the shocked look on his face, her heart went out to him. She knew it was appalling, but she'd grown up with it so she could deal with it matter-of-factly. Silas's childhood had been spent at expensive private schools and riding camps. She knew rich kids sometimes faced problems of alcoholic parents or friends on drugs, but usually not as early on or in such an extreme as street kids did. And she was fairly certain none of Silas's school friends had turned to a life of crime. Not until they were out of college, anyway. And then it was probably strictly of the white-collar variety.

"Oh, Silas I'm sorry," Hester said as she took his hand and held it. "I didn't mean to depress you, but you asked."

"No wonder you wanted to get away from it." He sighed. "I'm sorry you had to go through all that. I wish I'd known you then."

"I'm glad you didn't." Though she was moved by the fact that he seemed to care so much. "Let's change the subject. Look, this is what I wanted to show you."

They had cleared the jungle and stood on the beach of what appeared to be a small tidal pool. The water was clear and turquoise in color, as still as a bath. A sparkling white beach surrounded it, with sand as soft as powder. Opposite where they stood was an opening in the jungle where the water disappeared back into the trees.

"What is this place?" Silas asked.

"There's a lagoon on the southwest side of the island," Hester explained. "Off the lagoon there's a small stretch of water, almost like a stream that empties into this pool. It's the best place in the world to go swimming." She removed her sunglasses and baseball cap invitingly.

"So what are we waiting for?" Silas wondered, stripping off his shirt and removing his tennis shoes.

At the sight of his bare chest and the dark curls that arrowed down to his shorts, Hester's blood ran a little thicker, a little faster. Silas seemed to understand the effect his seminude state had on her and smiled arrogantly. Well, two could play at that game, she thought.

"Ever been skinny-dipping, Silas?" she inquired sweetly, reaching behind to untie her top.

Silas's smile fell somewhat, his eyes catching fire when he saw what she was planning to do. "No," he responded roughly. "But this has been a week for new experiences, hasn't it?"

His eyes never left her as she untied and removed

her bandeau, swinging it hypnotically at arm's length between thumb and forefinger before letting it drop carelessly to the sand. Hester smiled seductively and Silas felt himself growing hard at the vision she created standing topless on the beach. His palms grew itchy, wanting to cup her full, tanned breasts and caress the erect peaks. Instead he remained still while she proceeded with her private striptease. Deftly her hands traveled to the buttons of her shorts, and with the unfastening of each, Silas's heartbeat grew a little more erratic. By the time her shorts fell around her ankles and she stood in nothing but her cotton panties, his senses were going haywire. Hester saw plainly the extent of his discomfort clearly outlined in the tightness that appeared in his shorts. She reveled in her power over him, but at the same time was a little frightened by it. If standing before him partially clad brought about such a strong response, how would he react when she touched him?

"Let's go swimming," she suggested breathlessly, wanting to prolong the anticipation of the moment when they would again become one. She quickly shed her underwear and ran into the calming waters of the saltwater pool. Swimming immediately to its center, she ducked below the surface, letting the blue-green water cool her heated skin. When she emerged, she found herself face to face with Silas, his black hair wet and sleek, his eyes seeming even bluer as they absorbed the color of the ocean. Where the water in the center of the pool came up to Hester's neck, it was only chest high to Silas. Tiny liquid crystals clung to the curls spiraling across the wide expanse of his chest, and little rivulets of water streamed slowly down the corded muscles of his arms. As she noted the light dusting of freckles on his shoulders, it occurred to Hester that he was getting a nice tan. How can any one man be so breathtaking? she wondered, admiring the flawless beauty of his physique. Through the clarity of the water, she could tell he, too, was naked, and she knew the perfection of his body extended to what lay below sea level. A thrill went through her as Silas took a step toward her and placed one palm over her breast.

It was all so erotic, this loveplay in the tidal pool. The movement of the water seemed to stimulate even more her already sensitized skin. Her nerves danced as Silas's touch was magnified tenfold, and she closed her eyes in order to concentrate more fully on his caress.

Just as Hester had made a thorough perusal of him, Silas had been making a little inspection of his own. He could see her brown naked body clearly through the rippling water, soft and round where his was hard and solid. She was so beautiful. He'd never met a woman he could simply look at continuously and never find a fault or disguise. Generally when he was with a woman, he found himself wondering what she would look like without makeup or expensive clothes, asking himself whether she perhaps had something to hide. With Hester, he didn't need to ask the question. She was honest and open, without deceit or pretense. When was the last time he'd met someone so genuine whom he could trust implicitly? Not for a very long time, he realized.

As she stood motionless in the water, wet and desirable, Silas felt both physically and spiritually drawn to her. Almost involuntarily he'd approached her and touched her, and it was as if someone pulled a string inside him so tightly that he would snap.

"God, Hester," he ground out. "I don't understand

what you do to me. You only have to look at me and I lose control." His fingers closed more possessively on her breast, and he stroked his thumb back and forth across her nipple, watching mesmerized as it hardened and became erect under his ministrations. "I could go on forever just touching you. You're so soft and... perfect."

"No, not perfect," she acknowledged as she placed her hands on his shoulders for support. Her knees were weak from the hot sensations speeding through her with his caress.

Silas pulled her closer and bent to draw her breast into his mouth. His lips closed over the rigid peak and suckled it, his tongue taking up the motion that his hand now performed on her other breast. With slowly pursing and unpursing lips, Silas began a sweet torture that turned Hester into a raging inferno. She let her head roll back and became completely consumed by the fire inside her. Silas smoothed his other hand over each vertebra as he followed the downward direction of her spine. When he came to the end of the line, he cupped her soft derriere, using her weightlessness in the water to pull her up into close contact with his pelvis. Hester gasped when she was forced to recognize how ready he was for her. She wrapped her legs around his waist, instinctively inviting him to join her body to his.

"Do you feel that, Hester?" he whispered as he lifted his head but continued to stroke her breast and buttocks. "That's what you do to me." He removed one of her hands from his shoulder and encased it over his solid length. Hester opened her eyes, alarmed by the fierce passion in Silas's expression and at the extent to which their mounting desire for each other had ascended.

"Yes, it is a little scary, isn't it?" Silas said raggedly when he saw her alarm. "Out here in the jungle, we're like two animals enslaved to our instincts." His lips took hers in a furious kiss. "Open your mouth, Hester," he demanded as his head descended again. His tongue plunged deep, penetrating her mouth again and again as his hand opened and closed over her breast. "That's it," he gasped against her cheek before kissing her deeply again. As her hand brushed over him, his tongue tangled with hers in a primitive dance.

"Silas, please!" Hester finally cried out when she was able to end the kiss.

"What?" Silas urged. "What do you want? Tell me."

"I want to feel you inside me," she said frantically.

He vaguely remembered his earlier concern for precautions, but Hester's insistent hip action was completely destroying any coherent thoughts he might entertain.

"Silas, please," she repeated with quiet urgency. She was too caught up in the heat of the moment to feel his slight hesitation. "Make love to me. Now."

She released him and returned her hand to his shoulder, then loosened her legs a little from around his waist to facilitate his entry. That motion, along with her flushed cheeks, parted lips and shining eyes, caused Silas to forget all his good intentions. With both hands, he gripped her buttocks and thrust himself deep inside her. Hester's fingers dug into his warm skin and both lovers cried out at the intensity of their union. Silas began a rhythm that went deeper with every stroke. Repeatedly he branded her his until they both felt as though the water were simmering around them. Slowly their fever built to a raging boil until Silas exploded inside her. Hester's own climax followed immediately amid a burst of flaming colors, and she clung to him, gasping for breath.

She came very close to uttering, "Silas, I love you," but checked herself at the last moment. That was the last thing he wanted or needed to hear, she told herself. In two days, he'd be gone. She didn't want him to remember her as a lovesick beach bunny cooing over him.

When their heart rates had steadied, Silas lifted Hester into his arms and carried her to the beach. Stretching out alongside her in the sand, he cradled her head in one hand and splayed the fingers of the other open across her belly. The sun was already warming her skin with its kiss. His eyes gazed down at her beneath a tumble of wet black hair. Hester raised her hands to his face and delicately traced his cheekbones and lips with her index finger. Silas closed his eyes and sighed.

"What are you thinking about?" she asked him after a moment of peaceful silence.

He opened his eyes reluctantly, looking both troubled and tempting. "I'm thinking how hard it's going to be to leave here on Thursday."

Hester's smile fell at the mention of his departure. She had been trying to forget about their limited time together. "Then don't leave," she suggested hopefully. "Stay here on the island."

His short laugh was laced with bitterness. "That would be nice. But completely unrealistic. I have too many obligations. I can't just abandon them."

"Sure you can. Just call your sister and brother-in-law and tell them you're not coming back."

"If only it were that easy. Look, I don't expect you to understand the enormity of my responsibilities at DI. You can't imagine what kind of problems would arise if I were to simply abandon my duties at work."

Hester was tempted to respond, "Oh, can't I?" but something held her back. How would Silas react if she were to reveal her past desertion of her own business obligations? She was certain he'd be disappointed and angry with her. If he'd been disillusioned by his man in South America with whom he'd only been a business associate, he would certainly be disenchanted with her after all they'd shared. Why promote bad feelings between them when he would be leaving soon anyway? She decided it was best just to keep quiet and enjoy the time they had left. Let him remember her as his child of nature on an island paradise—not as a fallen executive.

As they lay side by side on the beach, soaking up the afternoon sun, Silas began to think about what Hester had told him of her childhood. No wonder she didn't want to leave the island and go back to New York; she had nothing to return to. Yet as repelling and terrifying as the picture she'd presented to him had been, he found himself wanting to draw her out, to learn more about what her life had been like there and the specific reasons for her departure. Propping himself up on one elbow, he turned to face Hester and asked, "What happened to make you leave New York?" He hoped this time to receive a more complete answer than one which concerned the weather. "I mean really. Was there some particular reason for it, or was it a combination of things?"

Hester opened her eyes and met Silas's gaze, her mind racing in an effort to step around the truth. She didn't want to fight with him, but she knew an admission of her actions at Thompson-Michaels would lead to just that. So she answered evasively, "I just couldn't stand what my life had become. I guess it was a lot of things. I had no family, no real friends, I hated my job, I hated where I lived. There was just nothing in New York for me. I was very unhappy, so I left in the hope of finding something better."

"You must have been very young," Silas decided incorrectly. "Did you leave right after you graduated from high school?"

Hester realized Silas must think her very young indeed, much younger than she actually was, to mistakenly assume she'd left New York shortly after her high-school graduation. She wanted to laugh and cry at the same time. He'd just offered her the perfect way out of a potentially uncomfortable situation. She could tell him about her life before she graduated from college and let him draw his own conclusions. She wouldn't be lying to him, really. She'd simply be withholding a few details. It was harmless, actually, she told herself. They had no commitment to each other, and he'd be leaving on Thursday. Why shouldn't she be a little selfish in wanting to preserve the rapport and regard for each other they had established? So she rolled onto her stomach and cupped her chin in her hands as she began.

"After high school, I moved out of Lydia's apartment and into another one by myself. With every passing year, she'd become more and more abusive until I couldn't stand it anymore. I had already decided, when I was fourteen, that I was going to get out of the ghetto if I had to lie, beg, borrow or steal to do it."

"What happened when you were fourteen?" Silas asked.

"My boyfriend was murdered," Hester told him hollowly.

"What?"

"His name was Micky and he was sixteen," she said. "And I guess what I felt for him was the closest thing to love I ever knew." Until now, she added silently. "He was handsome and intelligent and determined to rise above the type of life we all had."

"Was he in the same gang as you?"

"No, he was way too smart for that. In fact, he was always trying to talk me into getting out, but I was too scared of losing the only friends and identity I'd ever really had, such as they were. Anyway, I wish I had listened to him. He was killed because of my association with that damned gang." Hester lifted a handful of sand and watched meditatively as it sifted through her fingers. Her thoughts were carried back to that evening half a lifetime ago that had changed her irreparably. The night she'd lost the only good thing that had ever happened to her until she'd left New York, and met the man who now lay beside her, wondering about her past.

"So what happened?" Silas prodded.

"One night a bunch of us were at the schoolyard just sitting on the swings talking," she said as she looked at a point past his shoulder. "Micky was there, too. Even though he wasn't a gang member, the others liked him and knew he was my boyfriend, so they let him hang out with us when he wanted to. He was on one of his rampages again about going to college and getting out of the slum. We were so captivated that none of us even noticed when a car kept circling the block. It was full of Crimson Blades. I didn't even recognize their colors until it was all over.''

"Crimson Blades?''

"A rival gang. We were the Guardians. The Blades were our worst enemies.'' She emitted a humorless chuckle and said, "It all sounds so stupid now. A bunch of kids with malevolent names making war on each other because they think it makes them seem tough and grown-up. How could I have been such an idiot?''

"Maybe because you *were* a kid,'' he said quietly. "You were only following the examples set for you. You didn't know there was another way. A way out.''

Hester's eyes, full of sadness and frightening memories, met his. "Micky knew. He had so many plans. He really could have made it out. But the Blades fixed that. On their final pass by the schoolyard, somebody in the car fired a gun. To this day I don't know why. Maybe they'd just stolen it and wanted to see if it worked. Well, it did. One bullet. That's all it took. Micky died immediately. We never even found out which one of them pulled the trigger.'' A lone tear fell from her eye and she quickly swiped it away.

"Hester, I...''

"Anyway,'' she cut him off, "that night I decided to make some changes. I wasn't going to wind up like Micky, and I wasn't going to let his dream of escape go unfulfilled. The next day I quit the gang and got a job after school to save some money. And I started going to school every day, making sure I got good grades. My teachers were astounded. After I graduated, I moved to a neighborhood that was barely a step above the old one. Between the cockroaches in the cupboard and the fistfights in the corridor, it was hard to tell the difference from Lydia's place. So I got a second job as a bartender at a cocktail lounge called the Satin Dragon. It was pretty sleazy, but the money was good.''

She paused when she saw Silas shaking his head as if to clear it. ''What's wrong?'' she asked him.

''I don't mean to be rude, but you were a bartender in a strip joint? That's unbelievable.''

''It wasn't a strip joint,'' she defended. ''Well, not exactly.''

''Excuse me, Hester, but I'm having a little trouble picturing you in that sort of life-style. It's just impossible, after seeing you in this Garden of Eden setting, being perfectly serene and living the laid-back life of an islander, to visualize you pouring cheap gin under a neon sign.''

''Silas, you asked,'' she reminded him, feeling more than a little insulted by his obviously repulsed attitude.

''I know, and now I wish I hadn't,'' he muttered in distaste.

''Well, I guess that's pretty typical,'' she sneered.

''What's pretty typical?''

''The rich never do want to be confronted by the fact that there are a vast number of people condemned to a life of poverty.''

''Is that a fact?''

''It is if your reaction is any indication.''

''Just what are you saying, Hester?''

''We've been getting along great up until now,'' she pointed out. ''But as soon as you find out about the state I used to live in, as soon as you see *exactly* the extent of my hand-to-mouth existence, you're suddenly offended by me. You just can't accept the fact that some people have to live a life of constant need where they work demanding, crummy jobs in a struggle to survive.''

Silas met her accusing eyes, not certain he could contradict her.

''Or maybe you recognize the truth in what I say,'' she continued, ''and you feel guilty because you've always had whatever you want just for the asking.''

''I told you before that I won't apologize for my background,'' he said roughly, not denying her allegation.

''And I told you I don't expect you to,'' she assured him. ''But I also don't expect you to find fault with me because I was poor. I won't apologize for my background, either. I don't resent you because you're rich, do I?''

''Don't you?''

''Well, maybe at first,'' she conceded. ''But not anymore.''

''I can't change my past, Hester,'' Silas said, taking her chin in his hand. ''And I wouldn't if I could. I'm sorry if I sounded like an awful snob. I suppose in a lot of ways I am. It just shocked me. After all the ugliness and brutality you've witnessed, you're still such a warm, generous, gentle and happy person. I can't say that about myself, and I've had every advantage life can offer. You're right. I do feel a little guilty. I apologize for reacting the way I did.''

Hester thought about what he said, then ventured a small smile. ''Apology accepted,'' she said, then lifted her face to his in a tender kiss to seal the agreement. ''And don't say you're not warm. Why, you should see your shoulders and nose. You have quite an impressive sunburn.'' She was relieved to be able to turn the conversation away from herself and her unpleasant past. "We'd better get dressed and get back to the hotel."

"But you promised to show me the big house," Silas protested, beginning to feel his shoulders burning now that she mentioned it.

"There's no time now. We have to return the horses so Teresa and the General can get home." Hester noted the slump of his shoulders and acquiesced somewhat. "I'm sorry, Silas," she said softly. "We just don't have enough time."

"I know," he agreed. Both of them realized it wasn't just for the Morales home that they needed more time.

Chapter Seven

When Hester and Silas returned to the hotel later, their moods were noticeably more somber than when they'd left. Even the General's proud display of his day's fishing success could not lighten their dispositions. When Teresa was informed that the two young people had not made it to the north end of the island and the Morales estate, but had instead spent the afternoon at the tidal pool, she smiled discreetly and proposed an alternate plan.

"Perhaps we can have a gathering at the big house tomorrow," she suggested. "Since Silas must leave Thursday morning, tomorrow's get-together can be a little farewell party for him."

"An excellent idea, Teresa," General Morales chimed in. "We have not entertained for quite a while. It will be a welcome celebration."

Hester had been looking forward to spending her last

day with Silas alone, just the two of them, but Teresa's idea did have merit. Her last hours with Silas were going to be difficult ones, and maybe with the buffer of friends surrounding her, his imminent departure might not weigh so heavily on her heart.

"That's generous of you, Teresa." Silas smiled. "I'm flattered."

"Nonsense, Silas. It's been such a pleasure meeting you, and you've fallen in with our little circle quite naturally. It's only right that we give you a proper send-off. Besides, it will give the rest of us another excuse for a party. This time of the year is so lacking in holidays."

After saying their goodbyes, Teresa and Ruben promised to spread the word about the following day's festivities. Ruben was kind enough to leave two cleaned groupers behind for Silas and Hester to have for dinner. As they watched the Moraleses' retreating forms disappearing down the beach, Hester turned to Silas, her arms crossed defensively over her bare midriff.

"Well, I don't know about you," she said, "but I could use a shower before we tackle dinner. After all that rain, the tank should be pretty full. In fact, I'm sure there's more than enough water for two."

"Now that you mention it, I am feeling a little sandy myself. Mind if I join you?"

"I was hoping you'd say that."

Hester went upstairs to collect fresh towels and shampoo, then led Silas down a narrow path behind the hotel. The path ended in a small clearing that housed a tiny wooden stall. Beside it was a huge metal tank, slightly rusted, that had been cleverly rigged to gather rainwater. Between the two fixtures was what looked like a foot pump with pipes connecting them. Hester opened the door to the shower, and Silas saw that it contained a shower head and a long piece of fraying rope.

"To get wet," Hester explained, "you pull the rope. Then you get yourself all sudsy. Then you pull the rope again to rinse off. It's all very scientific."

"I see," Silas said, but was wary nonetheless. "Are you sure this is going to work?"

"No problem. Just be sure you don't use up all the water to get wet and then have nothing left for rinsing."

Thus assured, Silas reached behind his back and grabbed his shirt in his fist, pulling it over his head in one swift movement. As he stood before her bare chested, his black hair falling forward, the smell of the sea surrounding him, Hester felt her heartbeat quicken. He was so big, so seemingly overpowering. Yet she knew he possessed a capacity for tenderness that many men never had. The sun had left his skin brown and warm, the lines in his eyes fanning out more distinctly now after several days on the beach. As if of their own accord, her hands buried themselves in the hair at his temples and pulled his head down to hers for a searing kiss. Raising herself up on tiptoe, Hester pressed her mouth urgently against his, and Silas responded with a growl, seizing her in his arms and crushing her to his hard form. Their lips fought a battle of possession, capturing and plundering, neither quite surrendering to the other. He spread his hands over her shoulders to massage and relax, then dipped them lower in a frenzied caress. When his fingers found the knot in her bandeau they quickly untied it and let it drop to the ground between them. Her breasts thus freed from their confinement, Hester pressed wantonly against Silas, loving the feel of his hairy chest against the soft skin of her own.

Her kiss deepened as his fingertips skimmed lightly over her braid, loosening the scrap of fabric that bound it. He unwove the long tresses until they draped around her in wavy shafts of gold and copper. That task completed, his hands traveled to her breasts, thumbing the already stiff peaks into hard pebbles.

"I love the way you respond to me," he murmured between kisses. "You feel so good, Hester. So right."

"Oh, Silas." She sighed as her hands tried to encircle his hard biceps and her mouth rained kisses on his neck and chest. If she felt so right to him, couldn't he love her, too? Why couldn't he say it? Why couldn't he at least feel it?

"Silas, I..." she began. Hester wanted desperately to tell him how she felt, but something inside prevented her. A tiny fear that he might reject her if he knew the true nature of her feelings.

"What?" he whispered against her ear, reminding her that she'd left her statement unfinished.

"I...I want you. So much it hurts."

"I know how to make the pain go away," he promised.

"Me, too." She smiled, her momentary hesitation vanishing as she found a flat brown nipple nestled among the black curls on his chest. Softly she flicked the tip of her tongue against it, then drew it fully into her mouth.

"Oh, so that's what it feels like." Silas groaned. "Now I see why you like it so much." His hand closed over her breast gently, kneading its fullness, her nipple caught between the V of his index and middle fingers.

"Oh, yes," Hester whispered, lost in the massage of his rough palm over her skin.

They remained in their heated embrace for some time before Silas grinned wickedly and said, "Honey, as nice as this is, unless you want to take off like a rocket on July fourth, I suggest we take our shower. A nice, cold shower."

Reluctantly Hester released him and they separated to remove the remainder of their clothing, leaving it in a careless heap on the ground. Despite the tepid temperature of the water that cascaded over them at the tug of the rope, their bodies remained heated and sensitive throughout their shower, their senses alert to every nuance their bodies underwent. After Hester washed and rinsed her hair, she turned to face the stream of cool water one last time. As she let the last of the salt and sand wash away from her, she felt Silas move behind her, one hand fondling her breast, the other cupping the heart of her femininity. She placed her palms flat against the wall, lost in pleasure as he playfully nipped and kissed her neck and shoulders. Just when Hester thought she would die from the rapture and delicious sensations Silas had aroused in her, she felt him straighten behind her. As he turned her to face him, his eyes never left hers and he whispered incredibly erotic promises into her ear. Then he placed his hands firmly over her thighs and slowly entered her, pulling her body closer to his as he sunk deeper into her warmth.

Even rockets in July didn't reach the heights to which Silas carried her. As the last of the water rushed over them like a sheath, they traveled farther into the cosmos together, stars and planets rushing past them in a blur of variegated light. When finally they reached the center of the universe, a sudden, blinding light engulfed them in its intensity and heat. For long moments the lovers basked in the glow of their culmination before slowly and unwillingly descending back through the heavens to the real world below. When Hester was able to remember who and where she was, she wrapped her arms desperately around Silas's waist and buried her face in his chest. He held her tightly against him, shuddering at the magnitude of his response to her.

"Silas," Hester said softly when she found her voice, "I've never felt like that in my entire life."

"It was a first for me, too, sweetheart," he replied, stunned to realize that he'd twice addressed her with an endearment. It was completely out of character for him to use such words, but with Hester they came so naturally. Again he felt puzzled over why she should raise such a reaction in him when others hadn't.

For a long time they held each other, weak and trembling from the peak of arousal they had reached, and with the fear that came with not understanding their emotions.

It was after dark when they finally got around to preparing dinner, a meal consumed in quiet awareness of their shortening time together. They retired early to Hester's room, climbing silently into bed, pulling the mosquito netting around them as if that could keep the world at bay. They slept peacefully throughout the night in each other's arms, waking only when the morning sun crept stealthily into the room, violating the closeness they had cherished all night, bringing the rude reminder that their last day together had arrived.

After eating breakfast, they walked the two miles to the Morales home, following the shoreline this time instead of taking the jungle road. It was another perfect day, sunny and warm with a steady, cooling breeze. Back in New York it was probably snowing, Silas thought. Strange that only hours away it was probably cold and gray, a biting wind whipping people off balance. Actually he really didn't mind winter weather so much, as long as it didn't inconvenience him. When he was younger, before he'd taken over at DI, he used to love to ski. He hadn't been for such a long time. He'd have to get away from the office for a weekend to hit the slopes when he got back. Maybe he could talk Hester into coming up for a short time to join him. He completely forgot that the couldn't stand people who rejected their working obligations in favor of a weekend in the country. Yes, the weather on the island was nice, but Silas liked a change of seasons, especially good skiing weather.

"Don't you ever get bored of the weather being the same all the time?" he voiced his thoughts out loud.

"What do you mean? It's gorgeous!" Hester pointed out the obvious. They were halfway to the Morales', walking barefoot, hand in hand through the surf. Silas dangled his tennis shoes casually by their laces in his other hand. Hester hadn't bothered with any. She'd hitched the skirt of her sundress well above her knees and tucked it into her belt. Silas had rolled his khakis up to his shins and let the tail of his dark blue polo shirt fly carelessly in the breeze. Hester thought they probably looked like a magazine ad for the Virgin Islands. "How could I ever get tired of this weather?" she added, tilting her face up to drink in the rays of the warm sun.

"Don't you ever miss the change of seasons?"

"We get a change of seasons here."

"You do?"

"Sure. In the summer it gets humid." Hester's smile told him she was teasing, but Silas insisted on being serious.

"That's what you consider a change of seasons? Humidity?" he asked, demanding a straight answer.

"All right," she relented. "Yes. Sometimes I miss the change of seasons. Why?"

"I don't know," he hedged. Just why had he asked? "I was just wondering if maybe you ever thought about moving back to the States again. Permanently."

Hester shrugged. "I don't know. If I did, it wouldn't be to a city. I don't think I could function in a crowd again. I like the idea of living on an island. It's so calm, so safe. It would take something much more important than my own welfare and peace of mind to inspire me to return to the city. And I can't imagine what could be more important than that. It took me so long to find it."

They walked on in thoughtful silence for a while, each lost in personal speculation. But by the time their destination came into view, their moods had lightened with the prospect of the party.

The Morales home proved to be all that was promised and then some, Silas discovered when they reached it. Standing atop a hill that was the island's closest claim to a mountain, it overlooked the blue expanse of the Caribbean and a few scattered islands in the distance to the north. With its huge windows and wide verandas, it resembled an old plantation house, but there had never been a plantation of any kind on the island. Instead a grassy meadow swept down the hill behind the house, dotted here and there with clusters of wildflowers before rolling into the awaiting jungle below.

The house itself was constructed of whitewashed stone topped by a dark red roof and dark red eaves fanning out over the veranda. On all four sides, rows of shuttered French doors were thrown open in welcome, the windows of the second floor gazing blankly at the arriving guests. Hester pulled excitedly at Silas's hand, leading him toward the back entrance of the house, through an English-style garden bursting with bright colors and luscious aromas. They picked their way along a brick path and through a latticed gallery, sweet smelling from the abundance of orchids growing all over it. Silas was overcome by the splendid beauty of the place, and stopped suddenly in the gallery to haul Hester up against him.

"What?" she asked when she saw the unidentifiable emotions filling his eyes.

"This place is incredible," he said, losing himself in her amber eyes. "You're incredible. Thank you for everything you've shown me this week."

"Silas, I don't..." she began, but he lifted two fingers to her lips to prevent her from saying anything further. Slowly his head descended to hers and he brushed his mouth tenderly against hers in a whisper of a kiss.

"We'd better get going, or else they're going to come looking for us," he said before she had a chance to voice her confusion. "Come on, which way?"

"This way," Hester indicated, trying to shake the cobwebs from her brain. What had that last little verbal exchange been about, she wondered. Despite everything that had passed between them, Silas still puzzled her sometimes.

When they finally emerged into the yard behind the

house, two large collies came bounding playfully toward them.

"I forgot to tell you about Reynaldo and Susannah." One of the big animals leapt toward Silas in greeting. "That's Reynaldo," she informed him further. "He has no manners whatsoever."

"I can see." Silas smiled as he removed the dog's front feet from his chest and brushed at the damp paw marks left behind. "Now stay," he ordered the big dog firmly. Reynaldo dropped obediently down to his haunches, his tongue lolling stupidly over the side of his mouth. Silas couldn't help but laugh at him. "Good boy," he said and patted the collie affectionately on the head. Reynaldo lapped lovingly at Silas's fingers. "You're a good boy," Silas repeated.

Meanwhile Susannah had affixed herself to Hester's side, knowing she was a generous ear scratcher. As Hester's hand dropped automatically to the soft patch of fur behind the dog's right ear, she said, "They're such con artists. They act like nobody ever pays any attention to them. Actually Teresa spoils them worse than she did her own children."

After a few minutes of petting the big animals, Hester looked up to see the woman in question on the back veranda waving, signaling for them to come inside.

"Hester! Silas!" Teresa greeted them cheerfully. "You are the last ones to arrive. Now we are all here together."

"We had the farthest to come," Hester reminded her.

"Yes, of course you did," Teresa said indulgently. But the older woman's teasing expression suggested maybe they'd taken their time for other reasons.

"Really," Hester assured her.

Teresa just smiled and motioned them inside. Silas was surprised to find that the house had such a European-looking interior. All the rooms were painted in pastel colors with floors of either highly polished wood or mosaic tile. But the furnishings had obviously remained unchanged from generation to generation. Styles went from Spanish to English with touches of the Caribbean thrown in, but the effect as a whole was stunning. Kind of tropical Victorian.

Their hostess had prepared an impressive spread of food, spiced with a local flavor. There was boiled breadfruit, rice and beans yellowed and aromatic from saffron, fried plantains, curried yams, a spicy stew Hester called a pepper pot, and Desmond's favorite, fish and fungi.

"Just what is fungi?" Silas asked warily as Hester spooned a generous portion onto his plate. "And what kind of fish is this?"

Hester laughed at his expression of distaste. "It's probably flying fish, Teresa's specialty."

"Flying fish?"

"Try it, you'll like it. As for fungi, it's a lot like grits. Same texture, same color and pretty much the same taste."

"Oh, great, that tells me a lot," Silas muttered "I don't know what grits are, either."

"Just be thankful she didn't prepare mountain chicken for you."

"I'm afraid to ask, but what is it?"

"It's made from the meat of giant frogs." Hester's eyes danced merrily at Silas's grimace. "But it does taste a lot like chicken."

Silas cautiously sampled a little bit of everything,

liking most of it quite a lot. Especially the papayas and mangoes as they were exotic, but recognizable. He chatted happily with all his new friends, but kept a constant eye on one person in particular. As much as he was enjoying himself, he was anxious to say his farewells and be alone with Hester.

Around dusk, the party began to break up. Everyone thanked the Moraleses and said their goodbyes to Silas, each asking him to return when he could. Out loud, he promised he would be back very soon, but deep down he wondered just how it would be possible to get away from his work for even a short period in the near future. Hester seemed to comprehend his dilemma and remained as quiet and thoughtful as he was when they began their walk back to the hotel.

The moon hung like a bright silver dollar over the Caribbean, spilling a watery sterling tail from the horizon to the shore. The warm ocean swirled around their ankles as they walked through the surf, which twinkled like white Christmas lights.

"Oh, look, Silas!" Hester cried excitedly. "There's phosphorus in the water tonight." She kicked up a stream of water, laughing as it arced and fell to the earth in a starry cascade.

Silas's stomach was clutched in knots as he watched her. He didn't want to leave, but wished he could remain with her forever. Her spontaneity and innocent fascination with life delighted him. Even though he knew he would never be able to live permanently on such an isolated island, he wished there was some way he could merge their worlds into one. There must be some way they could work it out.

"Come back to New York with me, Hester," Silas said suddenly. Only when he heard her quick indrawn breath did he realize he'd spoken aloud. The invitation surprised him as much as it did Hester. Until that moment he hadn't planned on issuing it, but once done, it seemed appropriate. Why shouldn't she come back to New York with him? They were compatible, they had a good time together. It seemed perfectly natural that they should continue their liaison in more socially promising surroundings.

Hester stood ankle deep in water, hopeful and shocked at the same time. Just what was he suggesting? Was this a proposal, or merely an invitation to spend some time with him in the city?

"Under what circumstances?" she asked cautiously.

"What? I don't know," Silas said, somewhat taken aback. He was disappointed that she hadn't gleefully shouted, "Okay!" and hurled herself into his arms. He hesitated uncertainly before venturing, "I just feel like, well, you've had me as a guest for a week. The least I can do is invite you up to spend some time with me."

Hester shook her head and smiled humorlessly. He felt obligated to her, she thought. He'd enjoyed her hospitality, among other things, and now he was inclined to do something similar for her in order to clear the slate and even the score. Then he could be rid of her cleanly and with no loose ends.

"That isn't necessary, Silas," she told him. "Don't feel like you owe me any favors."

"That's not what I meant, Hester," he protested. "I just think that maybe if you came back to New York, you'd see it as a different place than you remember. You could stay with me, at my place."

Just what did he mean by that? she wondered, but said nothing, silently urging him to elaborate.

Silas tried to put his intentions more plainly. "I live

a good life in New York, Hester. I have a big apartment in Manhattan, I go to a lot of parties, I'm well-known in the best restaurants.'' When she still gave no indication of a response, he continued impatiently. ''Look, what I'm trying to say is that I'm rich, dammit. I could show you a life-style that's nothing like you knew in the Bronx.''

Hester took several slow, deliberate strides from the water to stand on the beach a few feet from Silas. ''Go on,'' she said indifferently, her expression bland, her growing anger undetectable.

''I could buy you anything you want—nice clothes, jewelry, a car even. We could go out all the time, wherever you want. I'll spare no expense. I'll even show you how my business works, introduce you to all my associates if you want. It'll be a side of New York you've never known. You won't have to go back to a life of poverty.'' He smiled indulgently, obviously very satisfied with his gesture of goodwill toward the needy. Hester was furiously insulted by his offer.

''Oh, thank you so much, Mr. Duran,'' she spat out at him. ''God knows I'd never make it out of the ghetto on my own, no sir. And you say you'll buy me anything I want? Why, I can't imagine anyone so grand as you taking an interest in little ol' insignificant me. I guess all I'll have to do in return for this great gesture is to speak, heel, lie down and roll over whenever you snap your fingers, right?''

With a fury she never knew existed in her, Hester turned and ran down the beach. She had to get away from Silas, away from his offensive proposition. How could she have been so wrong about him? He was just like all the other powerful corporate executives she'd known, maybe worse. How dare he try to buy her like a kitten in a pet shop? Well he was about to learn the hard way that this time he'd cornered a big cat, one with claws extended and fangs bared.

Why, she had enough of her own money invested and stashed in banks in Miami and New York to see her comfortably through this life and into the next. The sale of her apartment and possessions in New York alone had rendered her a tidy sum. And because of her instinct and savvy in the investment game for which she had once been so well paid, she was probably wealthier than a lot of Silas's ''associates'' he thought she'd find so impressive. She'd crawled from a life of poverty on her own blood, sweat and tears, and become a big success all by herself. She was no one's pet. And if the man she thought she loved considered her so shallow as to accept material gifts and an easy life in exchange for a tumble at his convenience, then they both had a lot to learn.

As she ran into the darkness, her feet pounding the stiff, unyielding sand, she felt the rage surge from her. It was replaced by a feeling of despair that settled into her bones and slowed her pace. Immediately she was tackled from behind by Silas, who seemed to come from nowhere. The two struggling figures catapulted onto the beach, rolling until Hester was flat on her back with Silas straddling her waist, holding her wrists above her head like a drunken starfish. Hester's sundress had ridden up well above her knees, and the straps had fallen down onto her shoulders. As she gasped for air, her breasts and abdomen heaved beneath the softly bunched fabric. Her long hair had come unbound and lay wildly around her on the sand like seaweed, her eyes glittering in the moonlight like the ocean phosphorus.

Silas thought her the most beautiful sight he had ever seen. He, too, panted freely, though from exhaustion or anger he wasn't sure. He was mad, too, perhaps even more so than Hester. He wasn't accustomed to being turned down, whether his proposal be a business deal or a romantic arrangement. Hester had thrown his offer back at him as if it was an insult and he didn't know why. If he'd done the same for any of the other women he knew, they'd have jumped at the chance. Problem was, Silas didn't want any of the other women he knew. He wanted Hester. And her rejection of him hurt.

"Why did you run from me?" he demanded harshly.

Not sure what to say, Hester remained silent, her heavy rasps slowing to shallow breaths.

"Answer me, dammit!" he insisted, gripping her wrists brutally and pressing them painfully into the sand.

"Silas, please," Hester gasped. "I ran because of what you said. I don't care about your money or your life-style. It wouldn't matter to me if you were penniless. For reasons you wouldn't understand, I can't go back to New York, with or without you. Please let me go. You're hurting me."

Silas released her wrists as though he had suffered an electric shock. It alarmed him terribly that he had caused her physical pain as a result of his anger.

"I'm sorry," he muttered, ashamed. "I didn't mean to hurt you, Hester. Please believe me."

"I think we're both a little strung out emotionally right now, and we haven't been getting much sleep recently."

"No, I suppose not," he agreed. "Look, I'm sorry if what I said made you angry. I didn't mean for it to sound the way it did."

"Forget it," she told him and he nodded disconsolately. "It's been rather a bizarre week."

"I feel like I've lived a lifetime since I've come to this island," Silas said. "It seems as though I've known you for years."

Hester gazed sympathetically at him, understanding completely what he meant. It was unbelievable to her, too, that she'd met him only a few days ago. There was something in him that spoke to a part of her that was ageless. She felt as though the two of them had merely picked up on the island where they'd left off somewhere else. In Silas, she felt as though she'd found a missing piece of herself that finally made her whole. How cruel were the fates to show her that she could be complete, only to snatch part of her away again.

Her thoughts dissipated what edge was left to her anger. She realized that despite his brief vacation from the business world, it wasn't in Silas's nature to leave his corporate behavior behind him. He would ultimately view the world in terms of financial gain, and that's why he'd offered her his deal, thinking she would readily accept it. Now that he saw that such a proposition would insult her, he wouldn't bring up the subject again. A typical lack of communication, she told herself. Next time she must remember to keep the lines of discussion open and maintain a fair-minded disposition. Then she remembered that this was their last night together. In a matter of hours Silas would be gone. There wouldn't be a next time.

Maybe for that reason she should tell him exactly who she was and the circumstances surrounding her departure from New York. Maybe then he could understand her reaction to his offer. And if he became angry or disillusioned, if he turned his back on her, at least she would know where she stood. At least she would have the knowledge that she hadn't kept anything from him.

"I think we should go back to the hotel and talk," Hester said. "I think I owe you an explanation."

"What do you mean?"

"I mean I'm not who you think I am. And after all we've been through together this week, I think the least I can do is be honest with you."

"Hester, what are you talking about?"

"I'm saying we need to talk, so please let me up," she urged, indicating the fact that he still knelt astride her.

"Are you going to behave yourself and not go running off into the night?"

"I promise."

"I don't know. I kind of like having you in this position. It's one we haven't tried yet."

"Silas!"

"All right, all right," he consented as he lifted himself off her. "But you'll never know what you're missing."

She stood and brushed off her fanny, mumbling, "Sand in my underwear, that's what I'm missing."

Upon their return to the hotel, Hester made them both a light snack, and they retired with steaming cups of coffee to the veranda.

"Now what about this talk you seem to think is so important?" Silas couldn't hide his curiosity when Hester seemed hesitant to begin the explanation she'd claimed to owe him.

After a fortifying sip of her coffee, she looked out toward the dark ocean and said, "You remember yesterday when you told me I couldn't understand how impossible it was for you to just up and leave your job and stay on the island?''

''Yes.'' Silas nodded.

''Well, maybe I can understand,'' she confessed. ''Maybe I can see even better than you how easy it is to leave all your obligations behind.''

''What do you mean?''

''Do you promise not to get mad?''

''Why would I get mad?''

''Promise not to lecture?''

''Why would I lecture?''

Hester could sense his growing impatience, so she took one deep breath and uttered her admission in a rush of air. ''Because I did exactly what your South American division head did,'' she acknowledged. ''One morning, I just decided I couldn't stand another day of work. Instead I got on a plane that was Caribbean bound.''

''Well, I can't say I'm surprised. Nor can I blame you.''

''What?'' Hester gasped, afraid to believe he might be capable of understanding her predicament after all.

''Hester, tending bar in a strip joint isn't exactly my idea of a good job. You shouldn't have been doing it in the first place. I don't blame you for walking away from it. I'm sure they hired the next person through the door to fill in for you. Big deal.''

''No, Silas, I gave up that job years ago,'' she said frantically. Oh, God, this was going to be tougher than she thought. ''Before I came to the Caribbean, I was a stockbroker and financial consultant for a firm called Thompson-Michaels. On the morning I left New York, I also left my company in the lurch, holding the bag on one of the biggest contracts they'd ever signed.''

"What are you talking about?"

Hester searched her mind wildly for the words to defend her actions to him. She didn't want him to be disappointed in her, but she very much wanted to be honest with him, and that meant explaining everything. In an effort to say several things at once, her words came out sounding hasty, her voice frightened.

"The big boys at Thompson-Michaels sort of considered me a whiz kid. I had a real talent for predicting the market. I could almost always forecast trends before anyone else. Mr. Thompson used to call me their girl wonder. God, I hated that name. Anyway, they paid me a lot of money and gave me a prestigious office. When I was twenty-four, I was making as much as some of the guys who'd been there for fifteen years.

"I worked there for over four years. It was very stressful for me. I wasn't used to the kind of pace necessary to handle that sort of environment. I was working myself to death, and I hadn't even had a chance to live yet. So one morning two years ago, I shucked it all and went in search of something better."

Silas had remained silent throughout her confession, but at this point interrupted her. "I think I'd like a drink before you continue any further," he said calmly, pushing his coffee cup away. "Can I fix one for you?"

Hester swallowed nervously. She knew his peaceful facade probably masked an angry interior. "No," she finally told him, barely able to keep the edge of hopelessness from her voice. "I'm fine. Thanks."

When he returned, he leaned against the veranda railing instead of going back to his seat. His obvious desire to place more distance between them stung Hester deeply and she took a large gulp of her coffee, wondering if maybe a stiff belt of Scotch might have been better. The hot liquid burned her throat and heart on its way to her stomach. She waited for the sensation to pass, then picked up her story where she'd left off.

"Thompson-Michaels got a lot of contracts specifically because of me. In fact, they got the biggest contract they'd ever signed from Baytop Computers because the president of the company was a big fan of mine. He'd read an article about me in *Fortune* magazine about how 'brilliant' I was. Their word, not mine. *He* called Thompson-Michaels himself to arrange the deal. My bosses just sat back and let millions of dollars fall into their laps because of my reputation. But on the morning I was supposed to meet with the president of Baytop, I was on a plane headed fast for St. Croix."

"So you're H. M. Somerset," Silas said blandly. "I read that article, too. They printed another one about your mysterious disappearance after you left Wall Street." He didn't know what else to say. He was shocked and overwhelmed. His earth goddess a successful and celebrated stockbroker? A high-powered businesswoman who'd held a major corporation in the palm of her hand and then shirked her duties on a whim?

"I can't believe you did that," he managed to add. The intensity and scope of his emotions threatened to make him lose control if he said anything further.

"I know it sounds selfish and unreasonable, but I couldn't stand it anymore, Silas," Hester pleaded. "My life had become pointless and worthless. My job consumed my every waking moment; all I ever did was work. I was unhappy, my health was suffering—"

She broke off when she saw the expression on Silas's face. It was one of vast disappointment and disillusionment. Shaking his head in disbelief, he charged,

"You quit your job, ruined any chance of a future career and dumped on the people who'd given you the opportunity to rise above a dead-end life in the ghetto, just because you were in a bad mood one morning?"

"No, Silas, it wasn't like that at all. *They* never gave me a chance to make my life better. I did that all by myself, with *my* brain and *my* sweat. Thompson-Michaels gave me a job, Silas. That's all it was. And it wasn't an important worthwhile job, either. It wasn't like working for the Peace Corps or cancer research or counseling troubled kids. What I did was make rich, powerful people richer and more powerful. When I walked out, the only thing that happened was the president of Baytop Computers threw a temper tantrum, and one of the greedy little bastards I worked with got promoted and moved to an office with a better view. Nobody suffered medical or financial collapse, and the world was not plunged into a global war. But I did something that made *me* feel better."

"You let a lot of people down," Silas accused, enumerating more charges on his fingers as he spoke. "You shirked your duties as a stockbroker to advise your clients, you caused a lot of problems, not to mention embarrassment, for your company. And you never even gave them a hint as to your plans so that they could make preparations for your departure." He made the list of accusations sound like a string of felonies. "Hester, how could you behave so irresponsibly?"

"Ooh, if I hear that word one more time I'll scream!" Hester rose to her feet to face Silas as best she could with the significant height difference. She wanted to grab him by the shoulders and try to shake some sense into him. "Silas," she began again a little more patiently. She knew it was difficult for him to see through her eyes. "Before I left, I was letting *myself* down. I shirked my duties as a *human being* to enjoy the life God gave me. I caused a lot of problems for *myself*. How could I give them notice when I didn't know what was coming myself?"

Silas relented somewhat when she put it like that, but still harbored reservations about her actions. "Do you want to talk about it?" he asked.

"Can you be fair?" She wanted more than anything to talk about her past with him, to clear the air. But not if he'd already made up his mind that she was at fault and had acted negligently.

Silas thought for a moment, then met her eyes. "Yes. I think I can be fair."

"Then yes." She smiled, relieved that he was at least willing to make that concession. "I'd like very much to talk about it."

He gestured toward their vacant chairs and Hester nodded. Once they sat down, she began again, this time feeling less threatened, but still needing badly to make him understand her actions.

"Well, I told you how my life was while I was still living in the Bronx," she said.

"So that part at least was true?" Silas asked caustically. "Did you really have a friend who was killed? Or was that part just meant for embellishment?"

"Silas, I've never lied to you," she vowed, but his suggestion that she had been dishonest hurt. "Any misconceptions you have about me are assumptions you made on your own. Please, you told me you could be fair."

"All right. I'm sorry. Go ahead."

"After Micky was killed, I decided to make some big changes in my life," she began again. "I didn't want it to wind up as meaningless and inconsequential as his had been. That's when I started working at this seedy little diner called Annie's Grill. I lied then—told the owner I was sixteen and gave her a phony name. She really didn't care as long as I showed up and worked my shift.''

"You told me you were only fourteen when Micky was killed,'' Silas interjected.

"That's right.''

"You were working as a waitress in a greasy spoon in the ghetto when you were fourteen?'' He'd thought yesterday by after-school job she'd meant she had a paper route or been a grocery clerk or something equally appropriate for a teenage girl.

"I needed the money,'' she explained philosophically. "I wanted to go to college. Micky was always so determined to get away from the ghetto, to do something worthwhile someplace where it didn't stink and drunks didn't sleep in doorways. In a way, I suppose I wanted to go to college as much for him as I did for myself. So I stashed every nickel I made into a savings account. I never told Lydia about my job. She would have demanded I turn over my money to her. Then after I graduated from high school and got my own place, I had to get a second job. That was when I started at the Satin Dragon.''

As the night grew darker around them, Hester described to Silas the rough times in the old neighborhood, struggling to juggle two jobs and a full-time class schedule. She told him about her quick and mathematically accelerated mind and the professors who told her that she would be a virtual gold mine to the financial community. And she recounted the tremendous change in her life once she was hired by Thompson-Michaels.

"At first I lived in a tiny dump of a studio apartment in Manhattan and socked nearly every bit of my paycheck in the bank." She laughed humorlessly. "I just couldn't believe I was making so much money. I was afraid it was all some elaborate joke and that one morning they were going to shout, 'Surprise! Just kidding!' and take everything back. For months I bought all my clothes at consignment shops and rode the bus. It was so strange having money. I just didn't know what to do with it."

Silas tried to sympathize with what she was telling him, but the truth was he had a hard time doing so. He'd been born with the proverbial silver spoon and gotten everything he'd ever wanted for as long as he could remember. It was tough for him to imagine not knowing what to do with money.

"Eventually I just started buying what other people at work bought," Hester continued with a shrug. "They all had European sports cars, so I bought a Porsche. They had designer suits, so I started shopping in all the chic boutiques. They had posh Central Park addresses, so I got one, too. I guess I just did what I thought was expected of me.

"Because I knew I had finally made it out of the ghetto, I worked to make sure I never went back. I worked like there was no tomorrow, spending nearly every hour of every day in my office or at meetings. When I slept, I dreamt of stock options and growth potentials. When I went to parties or out for drinks, it was with people from work, and all we talked about was business."

"Sounds familiar."

"I'm not surprised," Hester responded quietly. "I imagine my life-style then is pretty similar to what yours is like now.'' She paused for a moment, then feeling a bit more courageous after his statement, braved a question. ''Do you find that you get a lot of migraines lately?''

''As a matter of fact, yes,'' he admitted.

''Backaches and stomachaches, too?''

''Yes,'' he told her reluctantly.

''How about those nagging little chest pains that scare the hell out of you?''

Silas nodded.

''You'd better see a doctor, then,'' she warned. ''I had all those symptoms, too, and my doctor told me I was headed for some serious problems if I didn't take it easy.''

''I have seen a doctor, so quit nagging me about it,'' he replied testily. *And he's told me the same thing,* he added to himself.

''You're short-tempered, too,'' she noted mildly. ''That's a sure sign.''

''Of what?''

''That you're reaching the end of your rope. That you're tapped out. You could wind up just like me.''

''How's that?'' Silas asked impatiently. He didn't like the direction her thoughts were taking.

''Irresponsible,'' Hester ominously voiced the word he so detested. ''You could reach a point where all you want to do is get away from everything that's making you crazy, just like I did.''

''I seriously doubt it,'' he assured her.

''It happens slowly. With me it resulted in drinking and smoking quite heavily. Working too hard made me utterly self-destructive.''

''I'm not self-destructive.'' *Not unless he counted completely disobeying Dr. Norton's orders and consis-*

tently neglecting to take his prescriptions as self-destructive, he reminded himself.

"I was only twenty-seven years old when I quit Thompson-Michaels," Hester told him. "Twenty-seven. A lot of people are just starting their careers then. I was already a corporate executive handling multimillion dollar accounts. Yet I'd never enjoyed some of the most basic of life's pleasures." She groped for the proper way to illustrate to him the way she'd felt that rainy morning two years ago. Finally she resorted to a simple list of things she wished she'd had the opportunity to experience at some point in her life but had never been given the chance.

"Do you know what that means, Silas?" she asked, anguish evident in her voice. "I've never been to a high-school football game. I've never brought a boy home to meet my parents. I've never gone on a shopping spree in a mall with my girlfriends. Never raked leaves in the fall or built a snowman in the winter. Never spent spring break in Florida, or St. Croix for that matter, or taken a family summer vacation. I've never even had a family." Her last statement was choked as she felt her throat constrict with emotion. After a moment, she continued roughly. "Do you understand what that's like? To wake up one morning with thoughts like those, knowing you have nothing in the past, less in the present and nothing much waiting for you in the future, either? Realizing that the only reason anybody wanted you or kept you around was that you were able to make a lot of money for them?

"If I had died then, Silas, no one would have mourned my death. No one. My life, that I thought was so different from the one Micky lost to the streets, would have been as meaningless and without results as his was.''

Tears began to slip quietly from her honey-colored eyes, now bright with emotion. Silas wanted to reach out to her but was afraid she might push him away. He'd had no idea she'd felt the way she described. He was a cold, thoughtless bastard. Hester had been beautiful and vibrant only hours ago, and in a short span of time, he'd managed to make her feel miserable. He really was a contemptible creep.

''I had to get away from that existence,'' she went on, using her hands to wipe the dampness from her face. ''And I'm really sorry, but at the time, I couldn't see any reason for hanging around. My sanity was at stake. So I left. Porsche, condo, career, contract, all of it. None of that was important. Can you understand that, Silas? None of it.''

Silas tried. He really tried to understand that. And maybe deep, deep down, a little part of him did. Yet there was still that other part of him that couldn't quite justify simply throwing away the success she had achieved or letting down the company she worked for. But he couldn't condemn her for her actions. He could see how she had come to the point of no return, even if he couldn't see a reason for going beyond it.

''I'm sorry, Hester,'' he said genuinely, reaching over to her, gingerly brushing the last of her tears from her cheeks with the backs of his fingers. ''I'm sorry you were so unhappy. I wish we'd met then. Maybe...'' He wasn't sure what he had planned to tell her. Something reassuring, perhaps, something hopeful. He wanted to lighten her burden, but he didn't think himself capable of such an act.

''What did you do with all your possessions once

you moved down here?'' he asked after a moment. ''The Porsche, the condo, et cetera?''

''Got rid of them,'' she said flatly.

''How?'' He couldn't believe she'd just rid herself of everything she owned. Surely she had kept some ties to her former life. She couldn't have just removed herself from everything. Could she?

''While I was still on St. Croix, I called one of the lawyers I'd known at Thompson-Michaels. She took care of everything for me. I had Linda give all my clothes and linens and household goods to charities. She sold my car, my condominium and my furniture for me and invested the money the way I told her to. All my financial statements and everything go to her and she relays everything to me through the mail.''

''You don't have anything but investments?'' Silas asked.

''It's a pretty substantial portfolio,'' Hester told him. ''You forget I used to be highly in demand and paid extremely well for my services.'' She hesitated for a moment then grinned at him. ''As you yourself once put it and quite eloquently at that, 'Look, what I'm trying to say is I'm rich, dammit.'''

Silas groaned and looked toward the sky. ''I'm really sorry about that, Hester. If I'd known the circumstances...''

''I know. I'm sorry, too. Sorry I kept the truth from you until now.''

Silas met her eyes and smiled as a realization struck him. ''You know, it's ironic that you worked for Thompson-Michaels.''

''Why?'' Hester asked, her spirits a little higher with the affectionate turn their moods had taken.

"Because Duran Industries just signed a contract with them."

"Really?" She smiled a little. "That is ironic."

"Who knows, we might still have met under different circumstances if you'd stayed with them."

"I'd have been a nervous wreck by now. You would have hated me."

"No," he denied. "Never."

Hester's heartbeat quickened. "Maybe our meeting was destiny," she said whimsically. "Maybe Jah really did drop you here."

Silas grinned at her and lifted her hands to his lips. He nibbled her fingertips and kissed her palms until she laughed lightly and the last traces of sadness left her eyes.

"It's getting late," he finally whispered, reaching out to her and pulling her into his arms. "I think it's about time we turned in, how about you?"

Hester still felt that they had left things unsettled, but knew it would probably be fruitless to continue their conversation tonight. All too soon morning would arrive and with it, Silas's departure. She only had a few more hours left with the man she loved. Did she want to spend them talking or clasped to his heart in his strong arms?

"I think you're right," she said without hesitation. "It's been a long night."

Chapter Eight

Silas was back at work in his office bright and early on Friday morning. After complimenting his nice tan, his secretary told him that Ethan was still in Rio, but from all accounts, everything was going smoothly there. His brother-in-law would probably return before Monday's big meeting with Don Thompson to discuss that major account they'd just opened with his firm.

Silas sat behind his big desk and stared intently at his silent, empty office. There was no ocean breeze here, no softly swaying palms outside the window. Bob Marley did not serenade him with mellow reggae music, nor did the secretarial-pool coffee before him compare in any way to the flavorful Puerto Rican blend Hester had introduced him to. His dark paneled walls and thick gray carpet were a far cry from the whitewash and dhurrie rugs of the hotel, and expensive mahogany furniture took the place of repaired bamboo. The interior decorator who had come so highly recommended to Silas had a lot to learn about warmth, he decided.

One new item in his office, however, did evoke images of his brief sojourn in paradise. On the wall behind his desk, directly above his chair so that all he had to do was turn around to drink in its beauty, was the watercolor painting from his room at the hotel. The pastel blues, greens, pinks, lavenders and yellows in no way complemented the dark Victorian mood of his office, but Silas wanted the picture where he would most often see it. A gift from Hester, it was his only reminder of a week in Eden that even now he was not quite convinced he hadn't dreamed.

He thought of Hester and their last hours together. They had made love one last time as dawn crept over the island. Silas had packed while Hester fixed breakfast, and all too quickly the hum of a plane's engine announced the end of their time together. She had accompanied him to the airstrip, both of them quiet and more than a little stunned. Then with a brief kiss, a touch of her hand and a whispered goodbye, Silas was airborne, looking down at the tiny emerald island as it disappeared from his view. Ford flew him to St. Vincent where he arranged for his plane on the island to be picked up and caught a commercial flight back to New York. No problem. Before he knew it, he was home. But why did home feel so cold and alien to him now? Abruptly an idea formed in Silas's brain, and he quickly began to write.

"Ms. Foster," he buzzed his secretary when he had completed what he thought was a sufficient list of items to enhance his office decor. "Would you come in for a moment, please?"

Ms. Foster was an extremely efficient and business-like executive secretary. She entered his office dressed typically in a gray flannel suit and practical shoes, her short pageboy perfectly arranged, horn-rimmed glasses perched precariously on the bridge of her nose.

"Yes, Mr. Duran?" she asked as she approached Silas's desk.

He looked at her for a moment, comparing her to the woman he'd held in his arms only yesterday morning. A few years ago, the two women probably would have had a lot in common. And yet, Ms. Foster was as far removed from Hester as the earth was from the stars. He had been acquainted with his secretary for nearly five years and knew absolutely nothing about her. After less than one week with Hester, he knew nearly every intimate detail of her life, was attuned to every expression displayed on her face, and knew exactly where to touch her to make her utter that one helpless sound he liked so much to hear.

"Ms. Foster, I'd like you to pick up a few things for me on your lunch hour today if it isn't too much trouble. Take all the extra time you need and put it on my credit card."

Ms. Foster reached for the list Silas extended and quickly scanned it. She was more than a little surprised at her employer, but gave no outward indication of her concern. She often shopped for Mr. Duran on extended lunch hours, using his credit card to buy computer accessories, office supplies, business publications, even electronic equipment. His shopping list today, however, was somewhat out of the ordinary. But Ms. Foster would never be anything but polite and matter-of-fact where her job was concerned. She simply acted as if today's assignment were like any other.

"Were there any specific types of tropical fish you wanted, sir?" she asked pointedly.

"No, not necessarily," Silas said as he leaned back

in his chair and crossed his hands behind his neck in a laid-back position Ms. Foster had never before witnessed. "Just make sure there's a nice assortment of color. Red, blue, orange, that sort of thing."

Ms. Foster made notes on the list in her hand. "And what size aquarium?"

"Oh, I don't know," Silas shrugged. "Something pretty substantial. A hundred gallons, maybe?"

"Fine, sir." Ms. Foster scribbled a few more words on the paper and scanned the list again. "Let's see, I think the rest is pretty self-explanatory. Bob Marley, Ernest Hemingway, Barbados rum…"

"Get a couple of cases of that," Silas interrupted. "And some tonic water."

"Tonic water," his secretary repeated, recording it in her notations. "And Puerto Rican coffee. Um, Mr. Duran, I'm not sure you can get that here."

"This is New York City, Ms. Foster," Silas mumbled absently. "You can get anything you want here." Except for maybe a certain woman he was crazy about and just stupid enough to leave on an island paradise in the Caribbean, he added to himself.

"I'll have these things delivered this afternoon, will that be all right?" Ms. Foster asked.

"Sure," Silas muttered, his mind obviously on other matters. "No problem."

Ms. Foster returned to her desk quietly, wondering all the while whether her boss had perhaps waited too long for his vacation and suffered a mental collapse anyway. She'd never seen him behave this way before. He was like a different person. But then, she reminded herself as she removed the dustcover from her typewriter, her job was not to speculate on what might be transpiring in the CEO's mind. She just followed orders. And if that meant spending an afternoon staring into aquariums picking out colorful fish, then that's what she would do.

When Amanda Duran MacKenzie entered her brother's office without knocking late Friday afternoon, her first thought was that he wasn't in. Then she heard soft strains of some unfamiliar music and a watery sound vaguely resembling that of...an aquarium? She noticed the massive glass box against one wall and its myriad vividly colored and swiftly moving occupants, just before she saw Silas stretched out on his leather sofa, shoes kicked off, reading a paperback.

"Silas?" she uttered tentatively. "Did you make it back from your vacation all right?"

Silas rose slowly from the couch and glared at his sister, taking in her perfectly coiffed dark hair and tailored brown wool suit. "You know, I really had planned to murder both you and Ethan upon my return," he told her.

"But you've changed your mind, right? You realize we had only your best interests at heart, and neither of us wanted the responsibility of CEO when you dropped dead of coronary arrest, as you were bound to if you didn't take a break."

Silas remained silent.

"Admit it, Silas," Amanda insisted. "It did your heart good to take that vacation."

"Amanda, my heart will never be the same again after last week," he said cryptically.

"What are you reading?" she quickly changed the subject. "Lee Iacocca's book or Donald Trump's? You should commission someone to write your story, too."

"It's neither," Silas informed her. "And I have no desire to see my life glued between two pieces of cardboard and priced for the holidays at $19.95. This is a novel by a great American writer that takes place on Key West."

"Since when do you read novels?" Amanda sniffed. Then pointing at the aquarium, she added skeptically, "And why the sudden need for exotic companionship? You've never had a pet in your life. And what happened to the Brandenburg Concertos you usually listen to? This stuff is making me sleepy."

"I don't know what you're getting at, Amanda," he snapped.

"Just what happened to you down there on that island?" she inquired through narrowed eyes. "Did you get sunstroke or eat some bad coconuts?"

"Amanda, what did you want to see me about?" he demanded wearily. "There must have been a reason you came here."

"I wondered if you'd heard from Ethan?"

"No. I understand he's still in Rio and I hear everything is fine." Silas suddenly realized he'd been back at work a full day and hadn't even personally checked up on the status of the business. It must be jet lag that was causing him to feel so tired and uninterested.

"You mean you haven't even got the specifics yet on the state of things in Brazil?" Amanda's shock and disbelief were evident in the panicked tone of her voice.

"I've, uh, I've had other things to see to," Silas explained.

"Yes, I can see how certain things take priority."

"Amanda," he began, trying to maintain a civil tongue, "why don't you have a seat here and tell me everything that's happened in my absence and what the future has in store."

"All right," she consented. "I won't ask any more questions or make any more comments about your unusual diversion from normality if you'll at least fix me a drink. I'm missing happy hour over at Monty's.''

Silas strode across his office to a cabinet by the bookcases that housed a well-stocked bar. ''What would you like?'' he asked his sister.

''I'll have what you're undoubtedly having,'' she told him. ''Scotch. Only put a little more water in mine. You make them so strong.''

''I'm having rum,'' he announced. ''Dark rum and tonic to be precise.''

''Rum and tonic?'' Amanda gaped at him. ''But you never drink anything but...''

''Amanda, remember our agreement,'' Silas reminded her. ''No questions or comments.''

Amanda nodded mutely, wondering if and when she was going to wake up from this crazy dream she was having. Something was phenomenally wrong with her brother, and she was going to have her work cut out for herself discovering what had caused it. In the meantime, however, there were plenty of developments that would need Silas's attention. She only hoped her brother had some left to give.

She began describing the past week's events, everything from the slow-moving progress in Rio replacing their South American division head to the unexpected shutdown of two of their plants in the Midwest. The investigation of their new line of aircraft, like the defective one Silas had piloted, had led to the recall of several thousand models and some bad publicity. Meanwhile there were still some problems to be worked out with the contract they were signing to hire the Thompson-Michaels agency as consultants. As Amanda elaborated on each of the troubles that had arisen with his absence, Silas became more attentive to his corporate duties. With each new setback his sister described, he was further removed from thoughts of the island and memories of Hester.

That became the pattern for the next month. Silas threw himself back into his work with a fierceness that surpassed even his previous workaholic tendencies. His total immersion in his business kept away thoughts of blue skies, turquoise waters, green jungles and a pair of haunting amber eyes. Silas worked twelve-hour days at the office, then took his work home with him, only to return to his office again on the weekends to handle emergencies and tie up loose ends. Within a week, his headaches and chest pains returned, along with the burning sensations in his abdomen. Silas popped pills and ignored his body's warnings, telling himself that it was only something he ate.

At night he lay in bed, too wound up to sleep, and memories of Hester would inevitably assail him. Only in the darkness of his bedroom, on the edge of consciousness would he allow himself to think of her and their time together on the island. He couldn't bring himself to admit that his life had become an empty shell. Long before he'd met Hester he'd ceased to enjoy life. Enjoy life? Hell, he'd ceased to even live it. One week with her was all it took to show him what was possible to experience and take delight in. She had shown him a new way to look at things and new things to see. Yes, he was a powerful businessman who had done many things with his life—created one of the top industrial empires in the country, made many millions of dollars, funded libraries and hospital wings, won the respect of his colleagues, traveled all over the world. But had he done those things for himself or for the business?

Just what had he done for himself? Nothing, until he found himself stranded on a tiny Caribbean island where he'd discovered beauty in simplicity and joy in what he would otherwise have considered the most meaningless of activities. He'd learned to snorkel, shore fish, read for fun and make the perfect piña colada in party quantities. If he'd stayed on the island a little longer, he probably could have graduated to learning crab-trapping techniques, how to play dominoes as well as Ruben and Diego, or any number of things.

He had also discovered an ability within himself to care for someone. Really care. As he lay alone in his bed at night, one realization struck him above all others. He really missed Hester a lot. During the day he could keep thoughts of her at bay. It was easy to lose himself in work when there was nothing else for him. There was no one with whom he cared to spend time or contemplate the mysteries of the universe the way he had with her. But at night, alone, he understood how vacant his life was without her. Maybe when things settled down at work, he could take some time off and go back to the island. Maybe in a couple of weeks, things would be under control and he could slip away. Maybe…

Silas promised himself every night that he would return to the island to see Hester and tell her all the things he thought about. But as the weeks passed and the problems at work increased, his vacation to destinations south slid farther from his grasp. Every time he solved one problem, two more would arise to take its place. So Silas pored over paperwork, attended stressful meetings with board members who raked him over the coals, and consumed little white tablets to dull the physical pains. The spiritual pain remained, however, and Silas was incapable of doing anything to ease it. He needed a strong dose of Hester for that, and the only supply was over two thousand miles away.

* * *

Things on the island were no more pleasant for Hester than they were for Silas in New York. The month following his departure had been the slowest, dullest time she could remember in a long while. She still did the same things she'd always done since coming to the island, but with Silas they had been so much more fun, more fulfilling. Without him, things she'd enjoyed before held very little appeal for her. She missed him everywhere she went. On the beach she was reminded of their many chats and discussions about life and how to live it. In the hotel lobby she remembered his camaraderie with the others at the party he'd attended. In her room memories of their passion assaulted her. Even snorkeling she recalled Silas's boyish enthusiasm when she'd first introduced him to life in the sea, and she was struck with a poignancy she couldn't shake. Instead of fading, her love for Silas grew in his absence.

She missed him terribly. The nights were the worst when she would lie awake in bed feeling again each caress and every embrace. Often her fantasies and memories resulted in bittersweet tears on her pillow as she cried herself to sleep. She wanted and desperately needed to see Silas again.

And as more weeks passed, she discovered there was another reason she had to see him.

"I think I'm going to have a baby," Hester confided to Teresa and Gabriela at their monthly party eights weeks after the one Silas had attended. The three women had removed themselves from the celebration inside to sit on the beach and enjoy the cool evening breeze. Hester dug her toes into the sand as she made her announcement, unable to meet the faces of the other women.

"Are you certain?" Gabriela asked carefully.

"Well, I obviously haven't been to a doctor or anything," she stated. "And it's a little embarrassing to add 'home pregnancy test' to the shopping list I give to Ford every week, but I'm pretty sure, yes." She looked worriedly at Teresa. "All the signs are there."

Teresa smiled at her with reassurance. "How do you feel about it?" she asked.

Hester's bright smile told them all they needed to know before her voice did. "Happy," she acknowledged. "At first I kept berating myself for being so stupid and irresponsible. But I think even when I first started suspecting, it was a happy realization." She shrugged then, looking out over the jungle where the sun hung low and red. "I guess I should have known this would happen after all the times we..." She stopped, blushing when she knew the other women realized what she meant to say. "I mean, I thought I was safe. The timing wasn't right."

"It never is," Gabriela, who'd brought seven children into the world, told her.

"So you are no longer angry with yourself?" Teresa asked.

Hester smiled. "No, I'm not. It feels good, really. Imagine, mine and Silas's baby. Living proof of our feelings for each other." Then, after a pause, "Of my feelings for him, anyway. We're responsible for a new life being brought into this world. A person! Someone I can take care of and teach to be a loving human being. I think it's wonderful. I left New York because I thought my life there was meaningless and unfulfilling. My life here has been terrific, but it took Silas to show me that my life has meaning, and now this baby will give it a purpose."

Hester couldn't verbally do justice to the joy she felt carrying their child. She wanted to describe her constant curiosity about the sex of the baby and who it would resemble. She wanted to tell them her plans for the child, the books and toys she would buy and the way she would guide him or her in becoming an open-minded, intelligent, tranquil individual. She wanted to ask them questions about their own experiences with motherhood. But it was all still a little too new for her to be able to talk about it with others. How could she, when Silas didn't even know about it?

"You'll have to leave the island," Gabriela realized suddenly. "You'll need to see a doctor and deliver in a hospital." She added quietly, "This island is beautiful, but it's no place to raise a child."

"I know," Hester replied soberly. "I've already thought about that."

"Where will you go?" Teresa asked. "I know money is not a problem for you, but I also know you have no family. Are you planning on telling Silas he is to become a father?"

"I don't know," Hester told her honestly. "I've been going back and forth with that question for a week now. I don't think he'll be very happy about it. He's not exactly the paternal type."

"He cares for you, though," Teresa reminded her. "He seems a man of honor. He would probably do the right thing."

"Which is?" But Hester already knew what she was going to say.

"Marry you."

"Teresa, I don't want him to marry me because I'm pregnant. I'd like him to marry me because he loves me and can't live without me."

"How do you know he doesn't?" Gabriela challenged.

"He never told me he did."

"You never told him, either, I'll bet."

"So?" Hester became defensive. "Maybe that's because I don't love him."

Teresa emitted a rude sound of disbelief. "We all know that isn't true, so don't even try to pretend it is. The way the two of you looked at each other while he was here, and the way you've been moping and moody since he left, it can only mean one thing."

"Pregnant women are always moody," Hester muttered. "Love has nothing to do with it."

"Oh, stop," Teresa said. "I'll bet Silas has been as impossible to live with for the past seven weeks as you have. Now cheer up."

Hester smiled a little and said dreamily, "I do love him. I didn't think I'd ever be able to love anyone, but I fell for him so fast. He's just so—so decent and wonderful. He tries to make out like he has no heart, no conscience at all, but it's only a thin facade. He's really very giving and thoughtful. And he makes me laugh. It felt good being with him." Hester let memories of their strolls along the beach and conversations under the palms wash over her like a cleansing wave. Silas Duran was a good man, she thought, and he really did deserve to know he was going to be a father. Even if she just told him and nothing more came of it, at least he'd have the knowledge, to do with as he wished, of his child in the world.

"You should tell him how you feel, Hester," Gabriela counseled her. "How do you know he doesn't feel the same way?"

Hester sighed, rose from the beach and brushed the sand from the seat of her shorts. In deep thought she walked to the water's edge and turned.

"I'm sure Silas cares for me," she told the other two women. "But love doesn't figure into it. It isn't a long-term thing for him. Silas just isn't the type of man to settle down. He'll care for me while I'm there until he gets used to me and someone new and challenging comes along. I think he likes the pursuit. Once he gets what he's gone after he starts to get bored. I just can't believe he's able to devote himself entirely to one person. The only thing he can devote himself to completely is his business. Which he does. He doesn't have a place in his life for a wife. Or a family.'' She waited to see if Teresa or Gabriela would disagree. When they didn't, she added decisively, ''I'll tell him about the baby, though. I can't deny him that. After all, it's his child, too.''

Teresa was a little teary as she said, ''I guess that means you'll be leaving soon.''

''This Thursday,'' Hester informed her, feeling her stomach tighten into a knot of nerves. ''I told Ford the other day that he'd have a passenger. I want to see a doctor in St. Vincent to be sure before I make any definite plans.''

''Where will you go?'' Gabriela asked breathlessly.

Hester released one nervous, humorless laugh. ''New York City,'' she stated without emotion. ''Back where it all began. I once told Silas I'd only return to the city if there was something more important than my own peace of mind at stake. At the time, I couldn't imagine what that could be. I think I can safely say this is.''

The rest of the week passed entirely too quickly for Hester. She barely had time to say her goodbyes and gather her belongings. After stuffing her few clothes into an old army duffel bag donated by Desmond, she dug her credit cards and financial statements from a biscuit tin in the kitchen. She had just under two hundred dollars in cash, so decided to wait until she got to New York to call Linda Griffin, her lawyer. She could charge her plane ticket and hotel rooms in St. Vincent and New York. She hadn't formed any plans beyond that anyway.

When she realized it would still be cool or even cold in New York, Hester elected to send out an appeal to Nicole for some clothes. She seemed to remember the French student having arrived in a sweater and blue jeans last November. Since they were about the same size, she asked Nicole if she might borrow a couple of items to wear on her return to the States, as her collection of shorts, T-shirts and sleeveless tops might be inappropriate for the climate.

"Oh, of course, Hester," Nicole assured her. "Take whatever you want. Lately I've spent so much time in my wet suit that I don't think I'll ever wear anything else again."

"Thanks, Nicole, I appreciate it. I'll return them. Eventually."

"De rien," she replied with a wave of her hand. "They are old things anyway. Do you need shoes, too?"

"Oh, yeah." Hester grinned. "I almost forgot."

Once she had said farewell to Jean-Luc and Fabienne as well, Hester left the campsite with a pair of well-worn Levi's, an oversize olive-drab French army sweater, heavy socks, hiking boots and a very long wine-colored wool scarf. If it was very cold, she could wear a couple of T-shirts underneath the sweater, she decided.

She told Diego and Gabriela she would leave her paintings and art supplies in the hotel for now, until she was certain of her future plans and could make arrangements for them.

"As long as you promise you will return for many visits," Diego said.

"You know I will," Hester promised. "How could I stay away? This island has become more of a home to me than anyplace I've ever known." She felt a warm glow encircle her heart as she added, "And you guys have been the best family a person could hope for."

As she embraced the Santoses one more time amid kisses and tears, Diego told her, "Desmond is going to fill in as manager of the hotel for a while. He said things are too slow at the airstrip. Personally I think he only wants to be closer to the library and kitchen. Not to mention the rum."

"I'm sure you're right." Hester laughed. "But at least you know they'll be well guarded."

On Thursday morning, the Moraleses came to the airstrip to say goodbye. Teresa hugged Hester lovingly for a long time as Ford loaded her duffel bag into the small plane's storage compartment.

"I know everything will work out well for you," Teresa told her. "Just wait and see. You have had much sadness in your life, but now it is your turn to be happy."

"Thank you, Teresa. I hope you're right."

"General Morales," she said as she turned to Ruben and extended her right hand.

"Oh, please, don't be silly," the older man said, pulling her affectionately toward him in a fatherly hug. "Don't you think it's about time you called me Ruben?"

Hester couldn't hide her surprise. "Why, General," she began involuntarily. Ruben held up a finger to check her. "I mean, Ruben. I will. Thank you."

"I'm ready to take off, Hester," Ford called to her from the cockpit of the plane.

"Coming," she said to the sandy-haired man who was donning his radio headpiece over a Cincinnati Reds baseball cap. "I'll miss you both so much," she added with a final smile to the Moraleses and then turned to Desmond.

"Thanks for being my friend, Desmond," she told him as she hugged him in farewell. "Good luck with your new job as manager. I left the fish and fungi recipe where you can find it."

"No problem, mon." He grinned. "Jah go with you, Hestah."

"Thanks, mon." She smiled and climbed into the plane.

Tears blurred her vision as she waved goodbye to her friends, then the plane was rolling down the runway and ascending high into the sky. As they soared out over the blue Caribbean, Hester's tears fell freely. Before they reached St. Vincent, she had completely exhausted Ford's supply of paper tissues.

"Mr. Duran, you have Houston on line one and Philadelphia on line three," Ms. Foster told Silas over the office intercom one week after Hester had left the island.

"Well, they're going to have to wait," he replied tightly. "Because I'm on hold with Detroit at the moment."

"Mr. Davenport in Philadelphia is very insistent, sir. It's about the lawsuit."

Silas gritted his teeth angrily. He wanted to scream. Loud. "Tell him I'll get back to him later. And tell Houston to…" He wished he could say "stuff it," but instead muttered, "call me back in an hour."

What a week he'd had! All hell was breaking loose around him. There was a general workers' strike going on in several of DI's factories across the country, and all efforts at negotiation were going nowhere. The mechanical failure with their line of small aircraft was going to cost the company a bundle of money, not to mention wasted time. A lawsuit had been filed against one of his factories in Philadelphia for alleged illegal dumping, and a bank closure in Houston had frozen a rather large corporate account. Since Monday his phone had been ringing off the hook, at home as well as at the office. Ethan and Amanda tried to take on some of the problems themselves, but Silas insisted on investigating each of the issues on his own. In four days he'd visited both Houston and Philadelphia, along with two other cities where workers were on strike. Living on a diet of coffee and greasy fast food, he'd had almost no sleep. He was tired and cranky, his head had been killing him for days, his stomach was clenched in burning knots and his back and neck felt ready to snap apart. And there was a steady pain in his chest that just wouldn't go away.

Every time he turned around someone was telephoning him with bad news or a big problem, wanting him to bail them out, needing him to settle their differences. What was wrong with these people, he wondered as he slammed the phone into its cradle, not waiting for Detroit to get back to him. Couldn't anybody who worked for him handle his own problems? Why did they always come running to him when something went wrong halfway across the country? Why did he have to do everything by himself?

Because that's the example he'd set all along, he reminded himself. He'd always demanded to know everything that happened at Duran Industries, from its biggest successes to its most minuscule setbacks. If the Louisville office's computers went down, he wanted to know about it. If the Boise factory's sponsored Little-League team won the championship, he flew there to present the trophy. It was because of his own insistence on handling every tiny detail that no one wanted to take responsibility for anything—he'd always done it for them. Face it, he told himself, it's your own fault that you have no life of your own. It's your own fault that you haven't been back to the island to see Hester.

Hester. God, he missed her so much. His life without her had become unbearable. Every morning he opened his bleary eyes to come to work and make himself a nervous wreck. And for what? What was the point? To make a good life for himself? No, he had no life, it was all work. Was it even to allow himself weekends or weeks off for travel or hobbies or relaxation? No, even his weekends were consumed by his job. Was it to make a good life for his family? No. He had no one to come home to at the day's end. No one with whom he could spend an evening and justify the day's travails by her very presence in his home. No, no, no. Strike three. You're out.

But…

He'd had a week once. A week in a tropical paradise with an incredible earth goddess. A week devoted entirely to enjoying life. He'd received more pleasure, learned more about living, seen more beauty in that one week on the island with Hester, than he'd experienced in his entire lifetime otherwise. So why was he beating his brains out here, slowly killing himself for nothing when he could be by the beautiful sea, sipping umbrella drinks and embracing the woman of his dreams?

The realization came into Silas's head as if someone had just opened a door and offered light to the darkness. What an idiot he'd been. What a complete fool. This wasn't living, this daily parade of anxiety and stress. He wasn't performing his job to enhance his own life-style. He was only making it easier for the other guys to enjoy theirs. The regional bosses could take care of most of the problems plaguing DI, but why should they when the president of the corporation would do it for them? This was barely an existence.

The only living he'd done lately had been on a tiny island in the Southern Antilles inhabited by carefree spirits who showed him that life was the enjoyment of simple things. Things like strolls through the surf, fishing on the beach, intimate gatherings of good friends, a hearty Cuban cigar, an evening of romance with a very special woman.

He asked himself again, why in the hell he was sitting here in New York, doing a slow burn while his heart painfully ticked away the moments, when he could be on the island with Hester, absorbed in her company and all the little wonders of life she'd introduced him to. Why wasn't he living his life with her, since she was the one who could make it all worthwhile? He could even do without the beach and the Cuban cigars, as long as he had her. She could make him happy for a lifetime anywhere. He only wondered if he could do the same for her. Because a lifetime with Hester was what he wanted.

The particulars of the arrangement eluded him right now. All he knew was that his life was pointless without her. She gave meaning to everything, and turned simple experiences into bold, new adventures. All he wanted was Hester. The rest of the world, including Duran Industries, could take care of itself. Right now it was his turn. He'd take a chance that she still wanted him, and the future would work itself out somehow. He couldn't worry about that now. He had plans to make.

"Ms. Foster," he said after buzzing his secretary, "you'll need to make some flight arrangements for me."

"To Detroit, Mr. Duran?"

"No, to St. Vincent in the West Indies. Tomorrow morning if possible."

"The West Indies, sir?"

"Yes. And see if you can get in touch with a man named Ford Jones there, will you? I'll be chartering his plane."

"Yes, sir. Right away." It was difficult for Ms. Foster to keep the note of puzzlement from her voice.

"Thanks. Oh, and one more thing," Silas added.

"Sir?"

"I'll be leaving the office early today. You'll have to reroute all my calls to the appropriate departments."

"Whatever you say, Mr. Duran."

"Buzz Mr. MacKenzie and tell him I'll be stopping by to see him on my way out."

"Yes, sir."

He entered his brother-in-law's office unnoticed. Ethan was as harried and disorganized as Silas had been moments before. He sat behind his desk with a telephone receiver caught between his shoulder and ear, riffling through a heap of yellow papers and file folders. A half-eaten sandwich and cooling cup of coffee sat precariously at the edge of the desk.

"No, I know that," Ethan said to the unseen caller. "I know, but we can't just fire everyone, that's ridiculous." He ran a big hand brutally through his blond curls and made a sour face. "Look, I don't care," he continued. "Well, excuse the hell out of me, but that's just not possible." After a moment more of listening to verbal abuse, he stopped searching for whatever he was trying to find in the pile of papers on his desk and took the phone receiver in his hand. "Oh, yeah?" he yelled indignantly. "Same to you, buddy. You can settle your own damn strike, then, it's no skin off my nose!" Ethan crashed the receiver down into its cradle and muttered a few choice obscenities to his now unhearing adversary.

"Bad day?" Silas asked.

Ethan jumped up at the sound of Silas's voice. "Don't sneak up on me like that again."

"Sorry. Who was that on the phone?"

"Stivers in Birmingham. He wanted to talk to you, but your secretary transferred him to me. I had no idea what to tell him. Sorry if I made things worse."

Silas shook his head. "No problem. You told him exactly what I should have told him days ago. To deal with it himself."

"Your secretary said you're leaving early today," Ethan said, his voice laced with concern. "Something wrong?"

"Just the opposite. I'm taking some time off."

Ethan's concern grew. "When and for how long?"

"Now and indefinitely."

"What?" his brother-in-law exclaimed. "You can't leave now. We have too much going on. Silas, this isn't like you."

"Look, there are no problems that won't iron themselves out. Refer the Philadelphia company to the legal department, the Houston crisis can be handled by accounting, and let Design and Public Relations take care of the aircraft recall."

"Oh, right, like it's that simple."

"It is that simple," Silas assured him. "Don't kill yourself over this, Ethan. It's only a job."

Ethan stuck a finger in his ear and shook it vigorously. "I'm sorry, Silas, there must be something wrong with my hearing. I could have sworn you just said this is only a job and not to kill myself over it.''

"I did.''

"Is it just me, or is there some kind of weird role reversal going on here? Have you noticed any strange pods from outer space near your desk lately?''

Silas smiled. "I shouldn't be gone too long. I just need a little time to convince someone that she should spend the rest of her life with me.''

Ethan's expression would have been the same if Silas had hit him or thrown cold water in his face. "I really am worried about my hearing, Silas.''

"Your hearing is fine. I just hope she doesn't find it as inconceivable as you seem to.''

"Does this all go back to that lost, extended weekend you spent down in the Caribbean two months ago?''

Silas nodded.

"You said there were only nine people on that island. How could you have found her there?''

"Don't sell a population of nine short,'' Silas told him. "They were the most fascinating and enjoyable people I've ever met. Present company excluded of course.''

"Thanks,'' Ethan acknowledged dryly. "I suppose one in particular was especially fascinating and enjoyable.''

"You guess right.''

"So what are you going to do? Drag her kicking and screaming out of paradise telling her if she comes to the big city you'll be able to show her all the finer things in life like expensive cars, nice clothes, flashy parties, and oh, yeah, all those interesting people you work with?''

"I've already tried that.''

"And?"

"She didn't fall for it."

"Smart woman," Ethan smiled. "Amanda will like her."

"Besides," Silas continued thoughtfully, "she's already had all those things, but she left them for a simple life on the island. She said she could never return to the sort of life she'd had in New York. Even if she could consider leaving the island, she'd never be able to go back to living in a big city. She said it would be too stifling, too deadening."

"So I ask you again," Ethan said, "what are you going to do?"

Silas looked at his brother-in-law, not sure himself of how to convince Hester she should come back to live with him in a city she feared would destroy her. "I don't know," he said. "I only know that I have to see her and try to make her understand that she needs me as much as I need her, and that I can make her happy here. It will be different for both of us this time. We'll have each other. I hope."

"Good luck, Silas."

"Thanks. Think you can keep the place running while I'm gone?"

"Guess I'll have to."

As the two men shook hands and Silas prepared to leave, the phone on Ethan's desk rang irritably, causing them both to cringe.

"I'll get it," Silas volunteered. "It's probably something for me anyway, and I wouldn't mind one final conflict for the road. It will make the island that much more pleasant."

"I won't argue with you," Ethan said, relieved. "I'll have more than my share of altercations in your absence."

Sure enough, it was Ms. Foster transferring a call from the now even angrier Mr. Stivers in Birmingham. The factory manager didn't appear to be put off by the fact that he was speaking to the CEO and owner of the corporation that claimed his industry as a tiny cog in a big machine. The other man didn't seem to give a second thought to the idea that with two words, Silas could effectively end his career and send him packing to the unemployment office. Instead Mr. Stivers let a week's worth of frustration at a workers' strike bubble over into a fit of rage, and he gave Silas an earful of it. Silas listened calmly and distractedly at first, entertaining instead visions of a white beach and serene blue sea, and a golden-haired houri wrapped in a red sarong. Then as Stivers's attacks became abusive and personal Silas's own anger began to emerge.

"I mean, what do you think you're running up there, Duran?" Stivers shouted furiously at his end of the wire. "Santa's workshop? I could run the corporation better than you do!"

"Is that a fact?" Silas muttered levelly, seemingly unaffected by the factory manager's assault.

"Yeah, that's a fact," Stivers went on. "All you guys in New York ever do is go to parties and delegate responsibilities. Every now and then you might fly to some problem spot for appearance's sake, but you've never done a lick of work in your life."

"That so?"

"Yeah. You all grew up in big houses, got jobs 'cause your daddies got tired of keeping you outta trouble. You come in late, take three-martini lunches and then go home early to snuggle with some rich bimbo who has even less to do during the day than you. You couldn't do an honest day's work if your life depended on it."

"That will be enough, Mr. Stivers," Silas said, quietly enraged. "You have no idea what goes on up here because Birmingham is the closest you've ever come to escaping that backwater dirt farm you grew up on. The only reason I'm not going to fire you for that little outburst is that I know you're speaking out of frustration and sleeplessness." His tension mounted as he tried to keep a civil tongue. His head was pounding unbearably, and a burning sensation in the middle of his chest brought his hand unconsciously up to massage his breastbone. Ethan noted the motion with a worried frown.

"You see, Stivers," Silas continued bitterly, "I know exactly what stress can do to a man because I've been putting up with it from little guys like you for years. And I'm telling you right now that it's going to come to an end." The pulsing ache in his head increased with his anger, and the painful throbbing in his chest became excruciating. His breathing grew difficult and erratic. Ethan took a tentative step toward him, but Silas went on roughly, ignorant of his brother-in-law's concern. "From now on, you handle your own problems. I don't want to hear about them unless they're going to affect Duran Industries as a whole, you got that?

"And one more thing, Stivers," he warned, still pressing his hand to his heart in an attempt to ease the pain. "Don't you ever, *ever*, speculate on what or who my life involves again, do you understand?"

Not waiting for an answer, Silas dropped the receiver into its cradle, closed his eyes and placed the fingertips of his free hand to his temple.

"Silas, are you okay?" Ethan asked cautiously, approaching him slowly. "You don't look so good."

Silas continued to grip his chest and rub his temple.

"No, I'm not all right." A sudden shooting pain in the area of his heart caused him to gasp and collapse into Ethan's chair.

"Silas!" Ethan cried and lurched forward to help him. "What is it? What's wrong?"

As pain after pain shot sharply through his chest and head, Silas began to struggle for breath. "Ethan," he managed to rasp out, "help me. I think I'm having a heart attack."

Chapter Nine

A little after two o'clock on that Thursday afternoon, as the paramedics were rushing a still suffering Silas to the hospital emergency room, Hester lay in her hotel suite, listening to sounds she remembered but hadn't heard for some time—the drone of a furnace, a muted television from the next room, a car alarm in the street below, a distant siren. She was definitely back in New York, and she wasn't any happier to be here now than she'd been when she left it nearly two and a half years ago.

She'd stayed on St. Vincent until Wednesday, enjoying the island's many offerings and gradually becoming accustomed to having more than a handful of people around. Actually her reentry into society hadn't been as bad as she'd thought it would be. Even though St. Vincent was much larger and more highly populated, the people there were warm and friendly and very much like her friends on the island. She had also seen a doctor there, a nice man who had confirmed her suspicions and started her on vitamins and a healthy diet. Once she was certain of her condition, Hester couldn't find an excuse to remain on the island and had caught a commercial flight to New York.

Even making connections in a city like Miami hadn't proved to be much of a culture shock after her two years of self-imposed exile. True, the people there were in a greater hurry than they'd been in St. Vincent's airport, but she'd still seen a lot of vacationers, smiling and casual, and outside the windows of the terminal, it was a beautiful, sunny day. The airport bar where she sipped a glass of pineapple juice while awaiting her flight to New York had been tropical looking, surrounded by plants and furnished with bamboo. It really wasn't *too* much different from St. Vincent or the island. As she sat at the bar, Hester slowly became used to the abundance of people around her. They weren't so bad, she decided. Maybe some were a little too rushed and wrapped up in themselves, but essentially, they seemed harmless. Perhaps she had been wrong to stay away from civilization for so long. She felt pretty good about things. The outside world wasn't nearly as bad as she remembered.

But when her plane had landed in New York, Hester's mood grew steadily more morose. Once she had left the cabin full of friendly flight attendants and returning Disney fans, the full impact of what awaited closed in on her. Walking down the extendable corridor that led from the airplane to the terminal, she felt the cold March air creeping through her sweater, and heard rain tapping discouragingly above her. Outside the terminal window, New York City was gray and damp, just the way she'd left it. The airport itself was big and harshly lit, and people hurried by her as if she weren't there. When she stopped in front of a newsstand to buy a paper, a man in a business suit collided with her, nearly knocking her down. With a contemptuous "Watch what yer doin'" he pushed angrily past her and disappeared into the crowd of others. Sniffing indignantly, Hester set her duffel bag down and inspected the vast assortment of newspapers and magazines.

"Hi," she greeted the tubby vendor who stood stolidly behind the counter chewing an unlit cigar as if it were a piece of bubble gum. He gazed at her indifferently, then looked away. Her smile fell as she picked up a copy of the *Wall Street Journal* and paid for it. Out of unconscious habit, she'd chosen the daily paper she'd read religiously until nearly two and a half years ago. As she tucked the journal under her arm and looked around, her depression grew.

It was impossible to find anything even remotely similar to her home on the island. There was no sunshine or sandy beach, no ocean or palm trees, no soft breeze or warm colors. The people surrounding her were pale and lifeless, dressed in heavy coats of gray and black and brown. They walked quickly and with unseen purpose, never noticing that there was an entire world around them they never bothered to know. None of them wandered aimlessly or took slow, careless strides, nobody stopped to look at something that had caught his eye. Above all, no one took a moment to welcome her. They didn't smile or say hello, and they didn't invite her to have a drink or something to eat.

Hester felt unwanted and more like an outsider than ever before in her life. Clearly there was no way she could fit in with this culture. She'd be better off getting back on a southbound plane and returning to the island. At least there she felt a sense of belonging and being appreciated. Here in New York, she might as well not be alive for the attention it got her. Already she was assailed by feelings of worthlessness and nonidentity. She supposed if people ignored her enough, it was possible she might just disappear.

With that thought, Hester had fled to the women's room where she'd cried for fifteen minutes while other people came and went around her, not noticing or caring that another human being was caught in the grips of despair. When she'd finally let out all the anxiety and depression of the past two months, along with the fears and apprehensions about the future, she could only hiccup in dry breaths. Emerging from the sanctuary of the rest room stall, she washed her face and neck with cold water and stared at her reflection in the full-length mirror. She seemed a little pale beneath her tan, and her braid was looking a little ragged. Dressed in Nicole's old jeans and baggy sweater she looked like a refugee, and she supposed in a way she was. A refugee from paradise, now *that's* funny, she thought with a sad smile. Oh, God, what had she gotten herself into? What was she going to do?

After taking a deep, fortifying breath, she hoisted up her duffel bag and headed for the taxi stand where a skycap directed her to a cab. The driver was young and friendly, and Hester hung on to every syllable of his warm chatter, so grateful was she for that simple gesture of human kindness.

"This your first time in the city?" he asked as they left the airport behind.

"Oh, no," Hester told him. "I grew up in New York."

"Funny," the cabbie said, glancing in his rearview mirror, "you don't look like no native New Yorker."

"Thanks," she acknowledged, meeting his gaze with a smile. "I've been away for a while."

They spoke animatedly as they approached Manhattan, the sky growing darker, the city brighter as they neared the area Hester had requested.

"There it is," the driver told her after they'd traveled to the business district not far from where Hester had worked at Thompson-Michaels. "That's the new Duran Building. She's something, ain't she?"

"Beautiful," she said almost reverently. The big skyscraper towered over the city, magnificent and powerful looking. *It fits him,* she thought. *This is exactly the kind of place where he belongs.*

"There's a nice hotel up the street a block or two, isn't there?" she asked after a moment. "The St. Damian?"

"Yeah. Pretty expensive, though," the cabbie informed her, once again taking in her sad state of dress.

"I used to eat lunch there a lot," Hester reminisced. "I worked just a few blocks from here. I used to be a stockbroker. And financial consultant."

"No kidding?" the driver said noncommittally. She wasn't sure whether he believed her or not, but decided it really didn't matter.

"Just drop me off at the St. Damian," she instructed. "That'll be fine. And thanks for the tour," she added as they pulled up at the luxury hotel.

"Anytime. Listen, you need a cab sometime, here's my card. My name's Nick, my number is on the card. Gimmee a call anytime."

"I will," she promised, paying the fare and adding a generous tip. "Thanks for being so nice, Nick."

Nick winked and waved her off with an "Aw, forget it" as a hotel doorman opened the cab door for her. A white-gloved hand helped her out of the back seat, then reached in behind her to gingerly pick up her duffel bag. The red-coated doorman lifted his brows skeptically as he looked Hester up and down, but remained silent as his gaze followed her into the hotel foyer.

Pink marble, crystal chandeliers, lush ferns and gilt-trimmed walls assailed her as she slowly made her way to the front desk. The St. Damian was definitely a five-star luxury accommodation, a far cry from a wood-and-stucco two-story box by the sea, really much too posh for Hester's tastes. The desk manager seemed to think so, too, as he looked down his nose at her while she signed the hotel registry. Then she flashed her gold credit card, and the world was a better place. The desk manager smiled broadly at her, ringing for the bellboy to get her duffel bag, simpering and ingratiating as he assured her he was at her service. It had occurred to Hester then that as long as she had her credit cards, she definitely had an identity. At least in New York City.

That idea had been reinforced on this morning's shopping excursion, as she'd ventured into some of the exclusive boutiques housed within the hallowed walls of the St. Damian Hotel. Hester had spent a small fortune in two hours on a few choice wardrobe necessities. Yet still she lay on her bed in Nicole's jeans and sweater. She couldn't bear the thought of taking them off to change into one of her new outfits, because they were her very last connection to the island. Once she'd put on her new clothes, she'd be completely removed physically from all she'd known and enjoyed for the past two years, from the only living she'd ever really done.

Silas's office was only two blocks up the street, she told herself crossly. She'd come two thousand miles to see him, so why was she still lying here moping when she could be safe and happy in his arms? But would he be glad to see her? Or would he feel awkward and angry that she was invading his life? After all, he hadn't exactly gone out of his way to contact her since he'd left the island.

Her mind went round in circles as she argued first one point, then another with herself. Finally she covered her eyes with her hands and asked herself a question that was once so much a part of H. M. Somerset's vocabulary: what was the bottom line? The bottom line was that she loved him. She loved him and wanted more than anything to see him again. Even if it was only to hear him say he didn't want her. The bottom line was that she was carrying a child that was a part of him, too. He deserved to know that, even if he ultimately wanted to turn away from that knowledge. And even if he did reject her and their baby, at least she'd know for sure she'd done what she was obligated to do. At least she'd have acted responsibly. Silas should be able to understand that.

Hester showered quickly and changed her clothes three times in frustration. She finally decided on a pair of jungle-green trousers and an oversize coral-colored sweater with matching trim and long sleeves, which she pushed up to her elbows. Her feet resisted the leather oxfords just as they had Nicole's hiking boots, but she managed to get them on anyway. After weaving her hair into its usual braid, she stuffed her wallet into her pants pocket. Then squaring her shoulders and taking a deep breath, Hester left the St. Damian Hotel and entered the streets of New York City for the first time in over two years.

The day was cool and gray, and as she walked among the masses, she could feel claustrophobia creeping into her heart, clutching her throat. Lifting her eyes upward, she saw only buildings and more buildings. The blue sky of the Caribbean had forsaken New York City. How had she ever lived and worked here? There were so many people and they all moved so fast! She hadn't adjusted her inner clock from Island Time to Eastern Standard yet, and her slow, easygoing pace seemed to be a real inconvenience to the pedestrians trying to hurry by her. At one point, her eyes caught sight of a young woman in a business suit, trying to signal a taxi, check her watch and light a cigarette all at the same time. That was me two years ago, Hester realized, stunned, thinking that the young woman's actions looked pretty ridiculous. She wondered if she'd looked that rattled and desperate?

The Duran Building stood proud and intimidating over all the other skyscrapers on the block, causing Hester to hesitate before entering it. For perhaps the hundredth time she questioned whether she was doing the right thing. If Silas had wanted to see her again, he would have contacted her. He'd had two months to do it, to at least let her know how he was. But she hadn't heard a word from him. As soon as he'd returned to New York, he'd no doubt found other things, other people to occupy his mind and time. Obviously he'd forgotten her and all their moments together on the island, so why was she throwing herself headfirst into probable rejection? Because she had to see him one last time. She had to know if there was any chance at all that she could have a future with Silas, and if there was, she had to find some way to make it work. There must be some way they could reach a compromise. She understood that they couldn't return to the island. Silas's job and the baby would prohibit that. But she also knew that she could never live in New York again. Just the short walk from her hotel to Silas's office had depressed and demoralized her, making her feel as if she'd lost her spirit and her identity. There had to be a way they could work something out. There just had to be.

Trying to adopt a positive attitude and lifting her chin, Hester entered the Duran Building looking more confident than she felt. The lobby around her was a massive cavern of chrome and glass rising over a white marble floor. Here and there Boston ferns spilled from brass planters. It was like Silas, Hester concluded— sleek and elegant with just a touch of the jungle. In her casual clothes, with her tanned good looks, she turned more than a few heads as she searched for the building directory. After locating it, she scanned the seemingly endless list of names, finding no mention of Silas Duran. Of course, you idiot, she berated herself. He's the CEO and owner of the entire complex. They're not going to list his office in the general directory for any deadbeat to drop in on. She really had been away from the business world for a long time if she thought she could just drop in on the head of Duran Industries to say, "Hey, mon."

In the lobby was a large desk populated by several frazzled-looking receptionists. Fighting her way through the hurrying throngs, Hester displayed her most brilliant smile and waited patiently for one of the receptionists to finish what sounded like a rather tense telephone conversation. When the woman looked up at her with slumped shoulders and tired eyes, Hester's heart went out to her.

"I'd like to see Silas Duran, please," she said in her most polite tone. "Could you tell me what floor he's on?"

"Do you have an appointment?" the receptionist asked indifferently, reaching for a clipboard full of names and times.

"Well, no, I don't," Hester continued courteously, only somewhat disheartened that the woman didn't return her civil manner. "But if you'll call his secretary and ask her to announce me, I'm sure he'll see me. My name is Hester Somerset."

The woman behind the desk studied Hester with undisguised amusement, eyeing her seeming youth and naïveté. "Honey, if you don't have an appointment, there's nothing I can do about getting you in to see him," she told her dismissively, tossing the clipboard aside. "He's a very busy man. He doesn't make time for just anyone. Come back when he's expecting you."

Hester really was trying to remain polite and sympathetic, but this woman was making it difficult. "But if you'd just make the call to..." she began, but the receptionist rudely cut her off.

"Look, I told you I can't help you if you don't have an appointment," she said belligerently. "Now if you'll excuse me, there are other people waiting who need help." She stared at some point past Hester, making her feel invisible and unimportant. Hester felt she had made a valiant effort to be nice, but this woman simply wouldn't allow it. The time had come to let H.M. Somerset reemerge. She was the one that could get results. The one who wouldn't take any guff from these people. Her future was at stake, after all.

"Now you look, honey," Hester began quietly through gritted teeth in a tone that had at one time made secretaries and receptionists alike scatter in fright. The woman's attention snapped back to her immediately, the fire of combat glittering in her eyes. "I need help, too," Hester continued. "And you're not even trying. Now all you have to do is pick up that telephone, punch a few numbers and, hey, what do you know, you've got Silas Duran's secretary on the line." The receptionist opened her mouth to retaliate, but Hester swiftly pressed on. "And then, you can give her my name, Hester Somerset, and she can give it to Silas. Then once all this is straightened out, if you're lucky, you'll never have to see me again."

Hester really hated being such a bitch, but she should have suspected it would only be a matter of time before her old self would rear her ugly head. It was inevitable that this city would bring out the worst in her. Her stomach was a nervous tangle of knots and a throbbing had begun a steady *bam-bam-bam* in her brain like a jackhammer. Gee, it's good to be back home again, she thought cynically as she watched the receptionist snatch the phone and murderously press a series of numbers. She only half listened to the part of the conversation she could hear, but when the other woman hung up the receiver, her smile was both victorious and vindictive.

"Mr. Duran has left for the day," the receptionist told Hester triumphantly.

"But it's only three-thirty," Hester protested, knowing Silas's workaholic tendencies would never allow him a departure as early as this. "He can't possibly have left yet."

"His secretary mentioned something about him leaving early for an extended weekend out of town."

"He's leaving on a Thursday to go away for the weekend?" Hester asked meekly. He was taking weekend excursions, but he hadn't found any time to come and see her. Or write her. Or even relay a message to her.

"But if you'd like to make an *appointment*," the receptionist said meaningfully, "here's the number you can call next week." She thrust a small card across the desk at Hester and turned her attention to the man behind her. And that's the end of that, Hester thought, feeling dejected. Silas was probably in the company of some beautiful woman at this very moment, on their way to some cozy little hideaway where she'd be smart enough to take precautions against any little accidents happening. So where did that leave her?

As she turned away from the reception desk, looking sadly at the scrap of paper in her hand. Hester was unaware of a pair of cool blue eyes, similar to those of the man she loved, assessing her.

Amanda MacKenzie had received a call from Ethan only fifteen minutes ago regarding Silas's condition at the hospital and had hurriedly left her office to join him there. Silas had been removed from the building via a private entrance and his staff had been instructed not to mention the afternoon's ordeal to anyone outside the main office. Thus unnecessary alarm had been avoided, since it appeared that he was going to be fine. When Amanda had passed the reception desk and heard a gentle female voice requesting to see Silas Duran, she had hesitated. Looking up, she'd seen Hester in her

casual clothes and her dark, tropical tan, and a little
bell went *ding* somewhere at the back of her brain. Her
brother had returned two months ago from an idyll in
paradise that he refused to discuss beyond a superficial
comment here and there, yet which had left him un-
deniably changed. Only moments ago, her husband had
informed her that Silas was now recovering nicely after
experiencing what had at first seemed like a heart attack after announcing his intention to fly south to find
a woman with whom he wanted to spend the rest of
his life. And now, voilà. A beautiful woman with a tan
asking to see Silas, and looking as if she wanted to cry
when she heard that he wasn't in. Curious and delighted, Amanda followed Hester toward the exit and
called out to her.

"Ms. Somerset?"

Hester turned around quickly, her shock at hearing
someone use her name evident on her face.

"It is Somerset, isn't it?" the graceful brunette in
the sapphire-colored suit said as she neared. Hester
tried to place the face, wondering where she could have
possibly met this woman years ago in her work, but
drew a blank.

"I'm sorry," she said vaguely. "Do I know you?
It's been so long since I was in New York, and…"

"I'm Amanda MacKenzie," the woman introduced
herself, extending her right hand. "Silas's sister."

Hester's eyes widened in surprise. "It's nice to meet
you," she rejoined automatically and clasped
Amanda's hand warmly. "Please call me Hester."

"You know my brother," Amanda stated more than
asked.

"Yes, we met several weeks ago."

"On the island," Amanda finished.

"Yes," Hester said slowly, wondering how much Silas had told his sister of his time in the Caribbean.

As if reading her mind, Amanda told her, "I only know your name because I heard you give it to the receptionist. She really is an awful woman," she added parenthetically. "Silas never mentioned you. He never said much of anything about that week."

"Oh, I see." Hester's tone was melancholy.

Amanda's smile broadened.

"Well," Hester began again with forced brightness, "I was just in New York for a visit and thought I'd say hello to Silas, uh, Mr. Duran, while I was here. But he evidently isn't going to be in for a few days. It was nice meeting you, Ms. MacKenzie. Please give your brother my best when you see him." Hester turned abruptly to leave, but not before Amanda had seen clearly the wounded, hopeless look in her eyes.

"I'm on my way to see Silas right now," she said to Hester's retreating form. "Why don't you come with me?"

Hester looked back at Amanda, unsure as to how she should respond. Surely Silas didn't want to see her. He hadn't even considered her significant enough to mention to his sister. She'd be better off leaving now, with the simple knowledge of his not wanting her. To actually see his dismissal in eyes that once looked upon her with desire, and to hear words of indifference from a voice that once whispered erotic promises to her would be unbearable. Best to have memories of Silas wanting her, rather than recurring reminders of him rejecting her.

"No, I'd better not. I have rather a hectic schedule," she said after a moment.

"Look, Hester," Amanda told her softly, "my

brother is a very private person. He never discusses the things, or people, that affect him most deeply. The very fact that he didn't say anything about meeting you, indicates to me that you must be very important to him.''

Hester smiled shyly and Amanda could see why Silas must have been so taken with her. She really was very lovely. And despite her little set-to with the receptionist, Amanda could tell there was a gentleness and sense of humor about her.

''So why don't you come with me,'' she urged Hester. ''I'm sure Silas will be very happy to see you.''

''That's nice of you, Ms. MacKenzie...''

''Call me Amanda.''

''Thanks, Amanda. It's nice of you to say that, but I really think Silas has a lot more on his mind than me. I only knew him for a week. Less than a week, actually,'' she added, still shaken by the depth of her feelings after knowing Silas for only six days. ''If you'll just mention that I was here, I'd appreciate it.''

Amanda had to think quickly. Ethan had told her what Silas had suffered was not a heart attack as he had thought, but a simple, if very painful, response to stress, something the doctor had called a warning sign. However, maybe she could use the episode to convince Hester that she really should see Silas before she left New York. She had the feeling Hester had gotten the wrong impression from the lobby receptionist. It would take more than assurance from a woman she'd just met to convince her that Silas needed her.

''Did you know Silas is in the hospital?'' Amanda asked pointedly.

Hester's face paled despite her tan, and her mouth

dropped open in shock. "What happened to him? Is he all right? Where is he?"

"I'll explain on the ride to the hospital," Amanda told her, satisfied that her plan was working. She'd been wanting her brother to slow down and enjoy life for years. Now it looked as though there might be a few changes made. Permanent ones, if she had anything to say about it, and with the weapon she had at her side right now, Silas didn't stand a chance.

"Silas, how long have I been treating you?" Dr. Norton asked an irritated and bad-tempered Silas in a private hospital suite a few miles away.

Silas remained silent, glaring at the mild-mannered Dr. Norton who stared back at him calmly over ancient-looking horn-rimmed glasses.

"Hmmm?" Dr. Norton prodded, his voice slightly chiding.

"About twenty years," Silas grumbled. The pains in his chest had ceased, but he still had a headache. He'd been relieved to know he hadn't suffered a heart attack, but now he was annoyed because his plans to go south this weekend had been put on hold due to Dr. Norton's insistence that he stay in the hospital for observation until further notice.

"That's right," Dr. Norton nodded, "twenty years. And in that twenty years, have I ever misled you or advised you incorrectly?"

"No," Silas muttered.

"Then why, in God's name, haven't you been taking it easy like I told you? Why do you insist on driving yourself so relentlessly when I warned you that something like this, or worse, could happen?"

"Because there have been a lot of problems at work

lately that needed my attention,'' Silas snapped defensively.

''Oh, really? Problems worth dying for?''

Silas looked away from Dr. Norton's piercing gaze.

''Because I'm not kidding, Silas,'' the older man assured him. ''You're damn lucky what you had today wasn't a bona fide attack. But it was your body's way of telling you that if you don't knock it off, the next one will be. If you don't give it a rest, and I mean more than a couple of weeks at the beach, you might not be around for much longer.''

''Meaning what?'' Silas asked, needing to hear Dr. Norton spell it out for him, unwilling to voluntarily relinquish his duties as CEO at Duran Industries.

The doctor sighed and shook his head. ''Meaning, Silas, that as your physician, and your friend, I'm advising you to retire from your post at DI immediately for health reasons, and take up a less demanding, less stressful line of work. Otherwise, you're risking your life. If you keep up at this pace, you could experience a fatal heart attack before the year is out.''

Silas couldn't imagine stepping down as CEO. He had too many responsibilities and obligations to fulfill.

''And just what kind of living do you suggest I pursue?'' he demanded sarcastically.

''Hell, boy, do anything you want! Go into horse breeding like your old man. Be a sport fisherman, a movie critic, a novelist, an exotic dancer. With your assets and the money you've got invested, it really doesn't matter if you do something enjoyable that doesn't pay much.''

''Are you suggesting I couldn't make money as an exotic dancer?'' Silas joked dryly.

Dr. Norton smiled. It was a good sign. ''All I'm

saying is that you're going to have to change your way of living if you want to keep on living. That's all there is to it. And the sooner, the better.''

"Are those doctor's orders?" Silas asked, feeling defeated.

"You bet those are doctor's orders. Now don't disappoint me by disobeying them. You've done enough of that already, and look what it's got you.''

Silas slumped back onto his pillow feeling drained and confused. Dr. Norton patted him sympathetically on the shoulder and left him in silence.

Silas's mind spun with the implications of his new status. He didn't like the fact but he was going to have to give up his job, even if it was with tremendous reservation. He really didn't have much choice. Good heavens, he'd be unemployed! Just what the hell was he supposed to do with himself? Immediately an answer came to him in the form of an amber-haired water sprite who had commanded much of his attention lately. Hester. In a way, Dr. Norton's orders were a blessing, because now he could spend more time with her. Hell, he could spend all his time with her!

Suddenly his refusal to live anywhere but New York seemed idiotic. Why stay where it was crowded, noisy and lonely, when he could be in Eden with the woman he loved? Because he did love Hester. The realization had struck him like a thunderbolt on the ambulance ride to the hospital. With each painful thump of his heart he'd thought of her, in desperate fear that he'd never see her again. That his life would be over before he'd ever had the chance to live it beyond one week on an island in the Caribbean with Hester. He'd understood then that he'd loved her all along and needed her to complete his life and make it worthwhile. Now all he wanted was to see her again, every day and every night. He wanted to walk with her along the beach, to talk to her in that light, easy way they had of communicating, to dance with her to slow, joyful music, and to make sweet, passionate love night after night. As his thoughts returned to the island and the perfect times he'd had there with her, he didn't notice the door to his room slowly swing open. Instead he closed his eyes and thought of a beautiful creature of nature as she held and caressed him and gently spoke his name.

"Silas?" Hester called quietly from the doorway.

Silas was amazed at the realistic quality his day-dream had adopted. Why, he could actually hear Hester's voice as if she were in the same room with him. Hester, on the other hand, was distressed that Silas hadn't responded to her. Was he unconscious? The doctor had said it was okay for him to receive visitors, and Amanda had insisted she should go in first.

"Silas?" she repeated, taking a few worried steps toward his bed. "Are you awake?"

Slowly and reluctantly Silas opened his eyes. He knew once he did, his waking dream would end and he'd find himself alone in his stark and silent hospital room. And yet he wasn't alone. Hester had emerged from his dream with him and stood at the foot of his bed, her eyes brimming with concern and some other emotion he was afraid to hope was real.

"Hester?" he whispered, afraid she might be a mirage. "My God, what are you doing here? I can't believe it."

"How are you feeling?" she asked, still rooted in place. "The doctor says you'll be fine." He didn't look so great, though, she thought to herself. The light tan he'd acquired on the island had completely faded, and now he looked pale and weak from his experience this afternoon.

"How do I look like I'm feeling?" he inquired with just a hint of a smile. He still couldn't quite believe she was here in New York, in his hospital room, looking gorgeous and worried about him.

"To be honest, you look pretty awful. You could use a week at the beach."

"Is that an invitation?"

Hester shrugged nonchalantly.

"Come here," he ordered quietly.

"Why?"

"Because I want to kiss you," he said. "I need to feel your touch to make sure you're really here and aren't going anywhere."

Hester released her grip on the bed rail, unaware that she'd been holding it so tightly, as if it were a lifeline. She approached Silas and placed her hand gently on his cheek. His blue eyes sparkled at her as he turned his lips to her palm, placing a warm kiss there. Then before she had a chance to protest, he reached up and put his arms around her shoulders, hauling her over him and into his bed. The next thing she knew, she was flat on her back with Silas on his side next to her holding her captive in his arms.

"I missed you," he said and lowered his head to hers, nuzzling her neck to drink in the smell of the sea that still surrounded her. His lips traveled from her shoulder to her chin to her mouth, where he began a thorough exploration of well-remembered territory. As his tongue tasted her lips, his hand eased downward to caress her thigh. Hester moaned with relief and desire. He still wanted her. Seemingly as much as she wanted him. She allowed herself to enjoy his foray until she remembered they were in a hospital bed and he'd just had a near heart attack. Placing her hands softly against his chest, Hester gently ended the kiss and stared up into his eyes. He gazed lovingly back at her and continued to stroke her ribs, his hand stopping just below her breast.

"So I guess this means you're feeling better." Her voice was edged with amusement.

"I do love that perceptive quality about you." Silas grinned.

"Did you really miss me?" she asked, unable to keep the uncertainty out of her question.

He nodded, his smile growing wider. She felt so good to hold again. Better than he'd ever imagined. How had he gone two months without her? No wonder his health had suffered. He'd been without what had become essential to his very life; he'd been without his other half. His life with Hester for one week had been complete and fulfilling. Everything that had gone before or come after was only a shallow facade, a bare existence. Now, as he lay once again with her in his arms, he felt the voids that had opened in her absence fill with warmth and love.

"I love you," he stated simply, the emotion in his eyes as he gazed down at her telling Hester it was true. A little explosion went off in her midsection, the fire from it spreading and warming her throughout her body. She expelled a nervous breath, wondering if he'd change his mind when she revealed her news.

"Oh, Silas, I love you, too," she told him, wanting to burst with happiness. "It feels so good to be with you again. The last two months have been miserable without you."

"I know." He lifted his hand to her face, brushing

her cheek with the back of his knuckles. "I feel the same way. But at least you were still on the island. I had to come back to New York. You know, I never noticed it before, but it is pretty crowded here. What say we go back down to the island together for a little while, say fifty or sixty years?"

"Do you really want to go back to the island, Silas?" Hester asked with some apprehension. "Indefinitely?"

"No, I want to go back to the island definitely—forever."

"Then I can't go with you," she told him sadly.

"Why not?" Silas was really confused now. He'd thought with his imminent retirement, all their problems would be resolved. They'd return to the island and live happily ever after. "Hester, why can't you go back to the island?" he repeated when she didn't answer, his concern punctuating the question.

Hester's eyes shimmered with unshed tears, and she spoke in a near whisper. "Because I'm going to have a baby. Our baby."

Silas stared down at her in awe. Had he heard correctly? A baby? After a moment's thought, he realized he should have expected it. After all, they'd made love how many times... His eyes widened when he mentally totaled the number. A baby. Imagine that. He'd never once in his life considered fatherhood. Except for that day at the tidal pool with Hester when he'd discovered the idea wasn't as frightening or repelling as he'd always thought it before then. As he further weighed the implications of their situation, Silas found that the prospect of impending familyhood delighted him. A baby with Hester. It was all so perfect.

Hester watched the play of emotions on his face go

from surprise to confusion to consideration, and she grew depressed. Before Silas could smile and acknowledge his happiness, she concluded that her suspicions were confirmed. Silas was none too happy about becoming a father.

"I'm sorry, Silas," she stammered, her eyes lowering as tears slipped quietly from them. "I'm sorry I wasn't more careful, I'm sorry I wasn't more responsible, I'm sorry to disappoint you, and I'm sorry we can't go back to the island." Her tears began to fall a little faster, and she turned her head away from him as she added, "But you couldn't stay on the island forever anyway. You have your work to think about."

"I'm retiring from DI," Silas told her, and suddenly his duties and obligations as CEO seemed trivial to him. He had new responsibilities now, more important ones. Now he had a duty as a prospective family man, with a responsibility and obligation to his wife and his child. His new reasons for leaving Duran Industries made Dr. Norton's seem almost insignificant. He wanted to stay alive, yes, but now he knew he had a life to live. Not just some meaningless existence in a daily routine. He had a future now. With Hester. And a baby. How could he have gotten so lucky?

"You're retiring?" Hester's eyes returned to Silas's. Through her tears they seemed more golden than he'd ever seen them.

"Doctor's orders," he confirmed. "And now, CEO's orders."

Hester's brows drew downward puzzlingly.

"Marry me, Hester," he said, his eyes bright, his smile radiant. "Don't you see? This is perfect. Now I really have a reason to retire, and something to look forward to beyond my position at DI. I love you, you love me. We're going to have a baby." With his last statement, Hester thought she felt his chest expand a little in pride. "For the first time I'll have a life. A real life. And so will you. We both have so much to look forward to."

Hester smiled a little nervously through her tears. "Are you sure, Silas? Are you absolutely positive that this is what you want? Because I know it's what I want."

"I've never felt happier or more alive than when I'm with you. And to know that another life will be entering the world as a result of our love is a little mind-boggling. I'd like to be around to see how it all turns out. What do you say? You want to get hitched?"

"What about the island?" Hester asked, still feeling the matter wasn't entirely settled.

"I think we should go for a visit for a couple of weeks every year. Maybe on our anniversary."

"And it will be a great place for a honeymoon. Oh, Silas, I do love you."

"I love you, too. You saved my life, you know." He bent his head to hers in a soul-searing kiss. When it ended, Hester realized he'd performed a similar act of salvation for her.

"It's nice to know we owe each other the same obligation," she told him. "Now let's see if we can't make the lives we saved worth living."

"Oh, sweetheart," Silas murmured, coming in for another kiss. "Have I got plans for you."

Epilogue

The slowly rising sun hung bright and warm above the ocean, clashing with the hint of approaching autumn in the air. Hester and Silas sat peacefully on the back veranda of their new home, sipping their morning coffee and sharing sections of the local Nantucket newspaper.

"Oh, look, Silas," Hester exclaimed, pointing to an ad. "Anderson's Hardware is having a sale. Maybe those glass doorknobs you liked so well will be reduced."

"I've already bought three dozen," he replied, setting down the sports page. "I think that will be more than enough for the rooms on both floors." As he began to clear away their breakfast dishes, he asked, "Did you have enough to eat?"

"Plenty."

"Did you take your vitamins?"

"Yes, Silas," Hester laughed. "Don't worry. We're both perfectly fine."

His gaze fell to her lap, now grown big in her eighth month, and he sighed contentedly. He had been right about one thing. She did look cute in maternity overalls.

"I still can't believe we bought this old house," Hester said when he'd returned with a glass of orange juice that he meaningfully set on the table beside her. "Especially considering all the work that needs to be done on it. Did you ever think you'd see the day when we'd be acting as carpenters, plumbers, electricians and decorators?"

"How about when it's all finished and we're acting as innkeepers?"

Hester rolled her eyes toward the ceiling. "Oh, please, Silas, that's still a long way off."

"Hey, speak for yourself," he responded with mock indignation. "I plan to be open for next summer's tourist season."

"I see. It's going to be a big job, you know," she told him, her eyes twinkling merrily. "I should know. I've been an innkeeper."

"Yeah, sometimes with as many as one guest staying at your establishment."

"That one guest was enough."

Silas smiled, his big hand reaching over and splaying gently across her belly. "Yeah, I'll say," he murmured with smug satisfaction. "I think I like you barefoot and pregnant. But come winter, you're going to have to start wearing shoes. I mean it, Hester."

She smiled happily and covered his hand with hers. "I love you, Silas. I never thought I'd be able to say that to anyone. But I do love you."

"I love you, too," he told her, his blue eyes meeting her amber ones. "You've made my life complete."

"Everything's so perfect here. It's still like living in a postcard. Peaceful and beautiful, even an ocean in our backyard."

"It may not be the Caribbean," Silas said, "but it is a nice island."

"It's more than an island," Hester said softly. "It's home. Our home. And it's truly paradise."

* * * * * *

If you enjoyed what you just read,
then we've got an offer you can't resist!

Take 2 bestselling love stories FREE!
Plus get a FREE surprise gift!